Blessing
in
Disguise

Also by Lauraine Snelling
in Large Print:

A Land to Call Home
The Reapers' Song
An Untamed Land
Hawaiian Sunrise
A New Day Rising

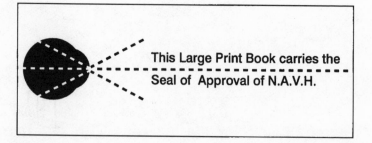

RED RIVER OF THE NORTH
6

Blessing in Disguise

Lauraine Snelling

Thorndike Press • Waterville, Maine

Published in 2003 by arrangement with
Bethany House Publishers.

Thorndike Press® Large Print Christian Fiction Series.

The tree indicium is a trademark of Thorndike Press.

The text of this Large Print edition is unabridged.
Other aspects of the book may vary from the original edition.

Set in 16 pt. Plantin.

Printed in the United States on permanent paper.

Library of Congress Cataloging-in-Publication Data

Snelling, Lauraine.
    Blessing in disguise / Lauraine Snelling.
       p. cm. — (Red River of the north ; 6)
    ISBN 0-7862-4020-2 (lg. print : hc : alk. paper)
    1. Norwegian Americans — Fiction.   2. Red River of the
North — Fiction.   3. Frontier and pioneer life — Fiction.
4. Dakota Territory — Fiction.   5. Large type books.
I. Title.
PS3569.N39 B58 2003
  813'.54—dc21   2002019931

My thanks to the Round Robins:
Sandy Dengler, Pat Rushford,
Ruby MacDonald, Marcia Mitchell,
Elsie Larson, Colleen Reece,
Woodeene Koenig-Bricker, Gail Denham,
Marion Duckworth, and Birdie Etchison
for your wit, your wisdom, your
brainstorming ideas for *Blessing in Disguise*,
and your unfailing friendship and support.
You are all gifts from God to me.

National Association for Visually Handicapped
----------------------- *serving the partially seeing*

As the Founder/CEO of NAVH, the only national health agency solely devoted to those who, although not totally blind, have an eye disease which could lead to serious visual impairment, I am pleased to recognize Thorndike Press* as one of the leading publishers in the large print field.

Founded in 1954 in San Francisco to prepare large print textbooks for partially seeing children, NAVH became the pioneer and standard setting agency in the preparation of large type.

Today, those publishers who meet our standards carry the prestigious "Seal of Approval" indicating high quality large print. We are delighted that Thorndike Press is one of the publishers whose titles meet these standards. We are also pleased to recognize the significant contribution Thorndike Press is making in this important and growing field.

Lorraine H. Marchi, L.H.D.
Founder/CEO
NAVH

* Thorndike Press encompasses the following imprints: Thorndike, Wheeler, Walker and Large Print Press.

Prologue

Oslo, Norway
July 3, 1889

Dear Mr. Moyer,

Thank you for the ship and railroad tickets, as well as the information on your ranch that you sent to me. I am sad to inform you that I will not be able to arrive on the date you specified. I have made arrangements to change my arrival date from September 1 to October 1, due to some difficulties that have arisen with my family. I am sorry for the inconvenience this will cause you, but I was unaware of this situation when I corresponded with you earlier.

I truly hope it will not be too much of an inconvenience and am sending this immediately so that you will know to not meet the train on September 1, 1889. I look forward to our union as

7

our contract specifies. A friend wrote this letter for me in English, like before, since I haven't been able to learn the language yet.

Sincerely, I remain
your future wife,
Asta Borsland

1

"Uff da."

Bridget Bjorklund sank into the rocking chair on the back porch of the Blessing Boarding House and fanned herself with a folded newspaper. Her swollen feet hurt, her back ached, and the thought of rising and doing this all over again in the morning was more than she wanted to think of at the moment.

"Mor, where are you?" Hjelmer called.

"Out here." Her son was the last person she wanted to talk to this evening. If he saw how weary she felt, he'd tell her again to send for Augusta, her eldest daughter and his older sister. Hjelmer thought he knew all the answers, especially since he had become the area's representative to the Constitutional Congress for the soon-to-be state of North Dakota. While they hadn't

9

been formally admitted yet, everyone knew it was just a matter of time at this point. If the representatives and other politicians could come to an agreement, that is.

She plastered a smile on her face and heaved herself out of her chair. After swatting one of the mosquitoes that persistently whined in squadrons around her head, she opened the screen door just in time to almost bump into her son's broad chest.

"Were you sitting down? Are you all right?"

She ignored his questions and only through sheer will kept herself from limping on her way to the stove. "The coffee will be ready in a couple of minutes." She brushed a lock of snowy hair off her forehead with the back of her wrist. After all the wishing for the wind to die down last winter, now she would give an entire day's baking for a breath of breeze.

"Hot, isn't it?"

"That doesn't begin to describe it." She rattled the grate and added a few twigs and bits of kindling to the coals in the stove. "So how was your trip?"

Hjelmer shook his head. "Wrangling, that's what. Those blowhards can find more to argue about than anyone I've ever seen. Every one of them has an opinion on

10

every little issue and thinks his is the only right one. Seems like every time there's something the railroad men don't like, the papers get lost so we can't vote on it. Between the railroad and the flour mills, the owners want to squeeze the life right out of the farmers. I never in all my life have seen such goings-on."

Bridget kept herself from reminding him that he had wanted to serve in the Congress. He was one of only ten Norwegians who'd been elected to represent the counties, and the honor had been good for them all. "Surely losing papers like that can't be legal?"

"No, of course not. But no one can prove anything."

"So when will we be a state, then?"

"Who knows? Even though the territory is officially divided, we have issues to hammer out, and the people must vote to ratify the constitution first, like I told you."

"Seems like Norway's monarchy is easier."

"Mor! There'll be no monarchy in this country. The government is 'of the people, by the people, and for the people.' Remember when I read you the Constitution of the United States of America?"

Bridget didn't bother to tell him how

little she had understood in spite of his efforts to educate the people of Blessing.

He took a chair at the table. "How have things been going here?"

"Busy. Rarely a night that all the beds aren't full. If I had ten more, I could probably keep them busy too."

"You aren't thinking of adding on already?"

She could tell by his tone what he thought of the idea. While the thought had crossed her mind more than once, she wasn't about to tell him that.

"So how is that new girl working out?" he asked.

He would zero in on her weak spot. He had always had a knack for that.

"You want cookies with this?" She gestured to the coffeepot she'd filled with water and coffee grounds.

"Mor? You didn't answer my question."

"All right. She quit. Met a man here in the dining room. He asked her to marry him and go out west to homestead, so she did. Henry helps as much as he can, but the railroad keeps him pretty busy too. Ilse serves and takes care of the rooms, Goodie helps me cook, and Eulah, Sam's wife, does the laundry and helps with the scrubbing up when she's here. Right now she and their daughter Lily Mae are out setting up the cookshack. They'll go along to cook as soon as the crew leaves. We're making do until she gets back. That should be enough."

"But it isn't." Hjelmer tilted his chair back on two legs.

"Stop rocking that chair back. I have enough trouble keeping legs on the chairs. All you men think straight-legged chairs are for tilting back. You want to rock, then go sit in the rocker." She heard the chair legs make contact with the floor but refused to turn and look at her son's face. She'd said too much, she knew that, but somehow the words flew out of her mouth before she could clamp her teeth on them.

Which led to another problem. She'd had a toothache off and on for several weeks, only now it hurt all the time. She'd snapped at Ilse today too, and the poor girl almost broke out in tears. That wasn't fair, and she knew it, but . . . She kept from cradling her jaw only by supreme effort.

"I think you should write to Augusta."

Bridget sighed. "We've been over this before. Augusta is engaged, and unless her young man wants to come to America, she won't leave home."

"But you could write and ask."

"Ja, that I could." So why hadn't she? She knew the reason without asking the question. Augusta had made clear her opinion about her mother's opening a boardinghouse instead of staying with Haakan and Ingeborg, where "she could be cared for." The words still irritated Bridget beyond measure.

Why did they all think she was too old to run a boardinghouse? She'd cooked, cleaned, done the wash, baked, gardened, at every house she'd ever lived in. Ingeborg's and Kaaren's, no less. But here she didn't have little children underfoot. How she missed that.

The coffee began to boil, and she moved it off the hottest part of the stove to let it simmer until strong enough. Going to the cupboard she took out the cookie jar and, setting it on the counter, arranged sour cream cookies on a plate. The jar was nearly empty. Once she'd taken to bagging cookies, the men bought the bags as they left and ate them throughout the afternoon. She could never bake too many cookies. In fact, that's what she should be doing right now.

She thought longingly of her spinning wheel and the new Singer sewing machine at Ingeborg's house. At least doing those things, she could be sitting down. Resisting the desire to knead the aching muscles in the middle of her back, she set the cup in the saucer and poured Hjelmer's coffee first and then a cup for herself. Tipping some of the hot brew into the saucer, she blew on it and sipped from that. Hjelmer followed suit, at the same time reaching for a cookie.

"Um. No one bakes sour cream cookies like you do, Mor." He closed his eyes the better to savor the flavor. He dipped the cookie in his coffee for the next bite, then looked at his mother. "So when are you going to write to Augusta? Anyone can tell by looking at you that this venture is too much without competent help."

Bridget closed her eyes and shook her head. "Is tonight soon enough for you?"

"No, it should have been done weeks ago, but now will do." He loosened his tie and propped his elbows on the oak table.

"Why don't *you* write the letter?" Bridget rubbed her temples with the tips of her fingers. "Isn't that something you have learned to do up there with all those . . . those . . ." She shook her head and got up to find writing paper. She kept a packet somewhere for her guests when they wanted to write a letter home.

Sitting down again at the table, she dipped her pen in the ink and wrote swiftly in Norwegian, since Augusta had either refused or not taken time to learn English. She'd find out what a mistake that was — if she decided to come, that is.

Dear Augusta,

I am writing this at Hjelmer's insistence. Do not feel like you have to come if you don't want to. I know your intended has to make the decision for you both, but if you would consider coming here to Blessing to help me in the boardinghouse, I would be grateful. Every time I get a girl trained to help me, she meets one of my boarders, they get married, and off they go, usually westward where there is still free land. There is plenty of work here for Elmer too, since I assume you will want to marry at home. You will be amazed at the flat country, as all of us have been.

If you decide to come, we will send the tickets immediately. We are well but still missing our dear Katy, who brought so much laughter to all of us.

Your loving Mor

16

"Here, now you add to it." She slid the letter across the table and carefully handed him the pen and ink. "And don't spill any of that on the tablecloth. It doesn't come out."

Hjelmer folded back the tablecloth as she had, then added a few more lines, signed it, and blew on it to dry the ink before folding the paper and inserting it in the envelope. What he didn't want his mother seeing was his description of how tired she looked. If Augusta had any sense of family responsibility, she'd be on the next boat.

"But I didn't tell her all the news." Bridget reached for the envelope.

"You can write more another time." Hjelmer stuck the envelope in his pocket and pushed back his chair. "I'd better be going. Told Penny I'd be here only a few minutes."

"Ja, she doesn't let on, but she misses you terribly when you are gone." *And she wants a baby badly, but she won't get one with you traipsing all over the country and never at home here to tend to business.*

He stood, then leaned forward to peer at her intently. "What is wrong with your face?"

Without volition, her hand flew up to

cover her jaw. "Nothing."

"Mor."

"Ja, so I have the toothache." She glared at him. "It will go away."

"You want I should pull it?"

"Hjelmer Bjorklund, you go on home to your wife." She didn't add *who wants you*, but she thought it.

When he went out the front door, she took her fan and returned to the rocking chair on the back porch, mosquitoes or no mosquitoes. Rocking in the dusk, she watched the evening star appear on the western horizon. The sourdough was set for pancakes in the morning, Sam's boy, Lemuel, had brought up water for the garden, and all the rooms were full. What more could she ask for?

"Screens on this porch, that's what." She smacked another mosquito and, wiping the blood off her arm with the corner of a bit of muslin, went back into the hot kitchen. If it didn't rain soon, the gardens would be a waste in spite of all the watering.

"Uff da. So much to think about." She fetched a whole clove from her spice shelf and pressed it on the offending tooth.

2

Valdres, Norway
July 25, 1889

Augusta Bjorklund read the letter from her mother for about the tenth time. Even so, the plea for help hadn't modified any. But the instructions from her youngest brother made her eyebrows draw a line straight across her forehead, a trait she had inherited from their father, Gustaf, dead now these five years.

If Far hadn't died, Mor would still be here in Norway, where she belongs, not over there. Augusta never had understood this craze to leave for Amerika, when they had a perfectly good country here.

"So why did Elmer have to go and emigrate? And why have I heard nothing from him since he left? Not one word!" She folded the thin sheet of paper and tucked it in her apron pocket.

"Talking to yourself?" Soren, wife of

19

Johann, the eldest Bjorklund son and thus inheritor of the family land, brought a basket of vegetables in from the garden and set it on the oak wash bench.

"Yes, and it's no wonder." Augusta drew the letter from her pocket and handed it to her sister-in-law. "Read this and tell me what you think." Since Augusta hadn't been home for many months, she felt almost like a guest in her brother's house, even though she'd been born and raised here. She wetted her fingertips and smoothed a strand of hair the color of overwintered honey back into the netted bun at the base of her head and resettled the comb that usually held the shorter strands in place. Today nothing felt in place.

"Let me wash my hands first, or I'll get it all dirty." Soren held her hands in the air and turned to the washbasin, pouring water from the pitcher and scrubbing. That done, she dried them on a towel from the towel rack, another of the household furnishings Gustaf had crafted through the years. The tables, chairs, trunks, and other furnishings attested to his skill with wood and lathe.

While Soren read, Augusta glanced around the room. If she went to Amerika, she would have nothing, for there was no money to ship household things. Suddenly all the things she'd taken for granted looked achingly familiar and dear. So many years since she'd lived in this house, so many years she'd wanted a home of her own, complete with husband and children, the good Lord willing. Instead she took care of other people's homes and other people's children.

"It sounds like your mor needs you."

"But what about Elmer? Two years we've been engaged. Six months since he emigrated, and not one word have I heard from him. How will he ever find me in that flat land they call Dakota?" She shook her head. "No, I must stay here until I hear from him."

Soren handed the letter back. "I think you should talk with Johann about this."

The tone of her voice snapped Augusta out of her reverie. "You know something you haven't told me?"

"You must ask Johann." Soren turned back to the dry sink and dipped water from the bucket into her pan to begin scrubbing the vegetables.

Heading out, Augusta closed the screen door without letting it bang. The spring needed fixing again. When Far was alive, things like that had never gone without repair. He always fixed things before they broke. But then Far had sons and daughters to help him work the land, while Johann had none. And though the parcel of land wasn't large enough to support two families, there was too much work for one man. A great-nephew helped Johann in the fields sometimes, but last she heard, he'd been talking of emigrating too.

She kicked a pebble ahead of her as she strolled down the road to the fields. So strange to have time of her own. She drew in a deep breath of brisk mountain air, that, too, far different from the city where she'd been working. If it hadn't been for Elmer Willardson, she could have gone to Amerika with the Larsgaards, the family she'd labored for these last two years.

Elmer, where are you?

If she'd been living at home, she'd be up in the high mountain summer pastures now with the cattle, sheep, and goats like all the other unmarried young women. They'd be caring for the stock, making cheese, and dreaming of the day a strong Viking lad would woo and win their tender hearts. *But young I'm not. Not any longer.*

While Augusta knew she wasn't ugly, she didn't look at her long neck and straight nose as part of beauty either. Nor the full lips that so often got her in trouble for saying more than she should. But she knew how to work hard — all the Bjorklund sons and daughters did. She'd been known as the bossy one, and Katja, dear Katy, as they called her in Amerika, had had the gift of laughter. If she went to that Dakota country, she'd have to admit that Katy really did no longer live on this earth. Living on this side of the ocean, it was easier to pretend that Katy was still alive and making all the family over there laugh as she had here at home.

Augusta would be thirty-one tomorrow and well on her way to spinsterhood.

"Where in heaven's name is Elmer?" For two long years he'd been stealing kisses and promising they'd be married soon. But the cat twining about her ankles said nothing more than a mew, which changed to a rumbling purr when she leaned over to scratch its back. When Augusta straightened, she heard the crinkle of paper from her pocket. Taking all her resolve in hand, she strode down the hill to where she could see her brother with the team. She should have brought a jug of cool water. Now, that he might have appreciated.

She waited at the fence until he stopped

the team in front of her.

"What is it? Have you come to help?" Johann set the brake on the mower and climbed off, checking the doubletree and hooks before he made his way to where she was petting the necks of the horses she used to drive before she had headed to the city for work.

"No, not really. I came out because I need an answer, and from the look on Soren's face, I have a feeling you know more than you are telling."

"Now, if that isn't clear as mud." He lifted his hat and wiped his forehead with the half-rolled-back sleeve of his loose-fitting white shirt. "Did you bring water?" At her headshake, he asked, "Coffee, then?" Again she shook her head and handed him her letter. She pulled and fed the horses bits of clover while she waited for him to read it.

"So Mor needs you. And you have no job right now, so this is a good time for you to go."

"Johann, I have not heard from Elmer since he emigrated six months ago. I promised him I'd come as soon as he sent for me."

Johann looked at the ground as if memorizing every blade of grass.

"Soren says you know something."

He shook his head. "No, she didn't."

"Actually she said to ask you. And that's what I am doing. What do you know about Elmer that you haven't told me?"

"Gussie." He wiped the back of his neck with a handkerchief pulled from a trouser pocket.

"Don't 'Gussie' me. I haven't gone by that name for years, and you know it. Now . . ." She crossed her arms over her chest. *It must be something awful if he won't say. Maybe Elmer is dead, and I didn't even know it.*

"It's only hearsay and you know I don't listen to hearsay."

"Johann!"

"All right, but don't say I didn't warn you. Swen Odegaard wrote to his mor that Elmer took up with a woman on the boat going over and they were married soon as they set foot in Amerika. I always told you he was no good." Johann kicked a rock under the mower, the clank causing the horses to flick their ears.

"Ah." If he had punched her in the middle, she would have felt about the same. When she could breathe, she squeaked out, "Elmer? Are . . . are you sure?"

"Sorry, but that's what I heard. Didn't want to tell you in case it wasn't really so." Johann gathered his reins and climbed back aboard the mower. "You can come down and start draping the hay over the fences anytime."

Augusta straightened her back, her Bjorklund blue eyes sparking off bits of fire. She spun on her heel and stalked back up the lane to the house.

"Where are you going?" Soren asked Augusta as she was leaving the house again after having just arrived back from the field, but this time with her hat pinned firmly in place.

"Down to send a telegram. I'll leave to help Mor as soon as they can get the ticket money to me." Calling Elmer every name she could think of and some she'd just created, she slung her reticule over her arm and stormed down the hill to the village. Thank God for the telegraph. She wouldn't have to wait for a letter to get there, and if she could keep herself angry enough, she wouldn't cry.

Elmer Willardson, that whey-faced womanizer, wasn't worth crying over. Whatever made her think she was in love with him? *Besides,* she comforted herself with the thought, *there are a lot more men than women in Dakota.* She corrected her thought. *North Dakota.* Mor had said so more than once.

26

3

Northwest of Ipswich, South Dakota
Mid-August

Would she like the ranch well enough to stay?

Thomas Elkanah Moyer, known as Kane to his friends, most of whom were Indian of the Mandan tribe, strode twenty paces east of his rambling log cabin home and turned to stare at the structure built by his father just before he had left for the war. He studied the long low porch fronting the house, the stone steps leading to it, and the stone chimney built right up the middle of the shake roof. While his pa had decried the number of windows, his ma had insisted on having them. Right now he was glad she had. Women seemed to like polishing windows and looking out, besides letting the sunshine in.

Since he was so rarely in the house during daylight hours, it didn't much matter to him.

Except now. His mail-order bride from Norway was due to arrive in two weeks. If she thought that he, at thirty-five, was getting up there in years, would she like the house? One thing or another had to make her want to stay.

Not that they wouldn't be married immediately. After all, a real lady didn't ride off in a buckboard with a man barely known to her without either a chaperon or the benefit of that bit of paper with the proper words said over it. Leastways that's what he'd surmised from the few newspapers he bought on his thrice-yearly trips to the general store in Ipswich.

Would she mind being so far from everything?

"Can't help that," he said softly, shaking his head. "I warned her 'bout the distances out here in that first letter." She had agreed to come. That in itself was a miracle of sorts.

Unless she was plain-out desperate. Or had some physical deformity she hadn't told him about.

Those and other thoughts had nagged at him more than once. He knew that a woman needn't be pretty to bear strong children, but how he hoped she was at least passable. He heard horses whinnying and knew Lone Pine, his half-breed friend and foreman, was bringing in a remuda to be broke and trained so they could be sold to the settlers, who were burrowing into the land like prairie dogs. And twice a year the army supply master came by to see what he had. He'd never had horses left over at the end of the season, or livestock either for that matter.

He should have been out on the roundup with them, but getting his house in order took preference.

Morning Dove, Lone Pine's Mandan wife and their cook and housekeeper, had been helping him up until the day before, when she took a short break to have her son. It was the first baby to be born on the ranch since Kane's brother, who hadn't made it past the age of two. Lone Pine's first wife died having his baby.

Now Morning Dove stood straight in the doorway, babe in a sling on her back, and beckoned him with one hand.

"What is it?" He stopped his assessing and headed for the door. "Flowers, that's what's needed. All women want flowers," he said as he leaped up the three steps and entered the house, relishing the drop in temperature. The thick, well-chinked log walls did much to keep out the heat of this South Dakota August. One of the hottest, far as he could remember, and driest.

"Okay, Dove, what is it? Where are you?"

"Here." Her voice came from the bedroom on the north side of the great fireplace.

Kane followed the sound and found her stringing the ropes of the new four-poster bed he'd built from trees cut along the Little John River that bordered his nearly one-thousand-acre ranch. A year-round creek ran a hundred yards behind the house, providing water for both house and livestock, much of which was out on pasture now being herded by one of his ranch hands. One of these days he hoped to fence off the property but so far, there'd never been the extra cash needed to buy that much barbed wire. Besides, fencing would cut off the trail the Mandan followed on their treks to hunt and return to their lodges along the James River.

He'd promised himself and Morning Dove that he'd always welcome her relatives to his home. Several of the tribe had become wranglers for him, and a younger girl helped sometimes with the garden and chickens and such.

"I told you I'd do this." He took hold of the end of the rope and helped her snug the webbing tight so the bed would be well supported. With a corn-shuck mattress covered by a goose-down feather bed, he and his new wife would be very comfortable indeed.

"I know."

He glanced up to see Morning Dove smiling at him, a knowing look in her eye. He'd always slept on a board not much softened by a pallet filled with either corn shucks or fresh hay. "Now, don't you go getting any ideas." He shook his finger at her, only to get a laugh in return.

"Missus like new bed."

"I surely do hope so. I hope she likes everything out here."

"What not to like?" Her dark eyebrows rose in question.

Oh, my friend, you have no idea what a world there is out there beyond our sandy hills. I don't know much about it either, but from what I read . . .

For a man who had never attended school in his life, Kane had learned to look at the world through the eyes of the few books he inherited from his parents and others he purchased when he could. Money was dear, but his mind cried out

31

for knowledge. Before his father went off to fight on the Yankee side of the war, his mother spent hours with him, teaching him his letters and numbers and making sure he became proficient in the three Rs. Beyond that, he'd grown up with the Bible, *Shakespeare's Complete Works*, and *The Farmer's Almanac* by Benjamin Franklin. He devoured newspapers whenever he could get them.

But living forty miles from the nearest town of any size made keeping current with the news next to impossible, so instead he kept a journal, recording life around him, the vagaries of cattle and horse raising, his income and expenses, his thoughts on statehood, his desires for a family, for a wife who would love him as his mother had loved his father. The leather-bound volumes stood beside the other books on the bookshelf next to the fireplace.

No one else knew how to read anyway.

Morning Dove had washed the sheets he'd taken from his mother's trunk earlier, and now Kane watched as she put them on the bed, along with a quilt of the same vintage. He looked around the room one more time. He'd keep sleeping on his hard bunk until he brought her here.

Thoughts of what lay ahead in this room made his throat hot and his ears burn.

"Oh, Lord, do let her be comely. I know that is trivial in thy sight, and I promise to be grateful for the woman you have brought all this way." He stifled the "but" and, after another glance around the room, went out, closing the door behind him.

"I'll be down in the barn," he said to Morning Dove as she headed for the kitchen.

"Dinner in an hour or so," she replied.

"All right. Lone Pine brought in more horses." With the hay cut and the grain not yet ready to harvest, this time was spent breaking and training the horses that were old enough and strong enough. Some of the better fillies he would keep for breeding, and one would be a wedding present for his new wife.

He'd already been working with her. The bright sorrel filly sported a star between her eyes and a tiny diamond between her nostrils. Two white socks flashed in the sun when she trotted. Her canter could eat up the miles at a smooth gait. Morning Dove had been working with the filly too, so she was already accustomed to a woman.

She nickered when she saw him coming and came to the fence, draping her head over the top rail so he would rub her ears. "Ah, little girl, we need to find you a name, but I been thinking that maybe we should let the missus name you after she gets here." He still had a hard time referring to his future wife by her given name. After all, they hadn't even met yet.

The filly rubbed her forehead on his chambray shirt, leaving both red and white hairs on the fabric. She nosed the leather vest he wore and sniffed his pockets. When he didn't respond, she snuffled the hair curling just under his ears and tipped his flat-brimmed hat back, nearly off his head.

"Stop that now." He leaned his chin on his crossed arms on the post. Where could he find a rosebush to plant by the front steps? Surely his wife would appreciate a sweet-smelling rosebush. He rubbed the filly's neck again, then turned and looked toward the sandy hills to the north. Where had he seen roses blooming that spring? The elm tree his father planted at the southwest corner of the house now shaded the porch and half the roof. Several oaks had grown from the acorns tossed out in back, and willows grew along the spring. Off to one side the apple trees that had come across the country in his father's mule pack hung low with a heavy apple crop. The garden lay close to the creek for when they had to carry water to keep it growing. Like this year.

But the rosebush his mother planted by the front steps had died a couple of years after she did. Roses were tender things compared to the native flowers and trees. They took some pruning, fertilizing with manure once in a while, and watering. He remembered his mother always saved the dishwater for her rosebush.

Kane rubbed a callused hand along his jaw and, lifting his hat, brushed walnut-toned hair with a touch of gray back off his forehead and secured his hat again. "I'm going in early to get new duds, a haircut, and a real honest shave before the train pulls in. What do you think of that?" He turned and nudged the filly's nose. She blew in his face, then turned and trotted across the corral, twitching her tail and nickering to the horses in the other pen.

When a rangy sorrel whinnied, she perked up and pranced some more.

Kane figured right away they'd better get the knife out. The young colt giving her the eye wasn't quality enough to keep for stud, but with some added weight, he'd be plenty strong enough to pull some settler's plow. Gelding would settle him too.

Walking on around the filly's corral to the larger one where the newly rounded-up horses were shaking off the dust of the run, some still inspecting the six-rail-high fencing for an escape route, Kane automatically judged the horses inside. They looked to be a good crop. Spring and summer pasture had fattened them right up after the lean winter. Lone Pine had told him they'd lost some due to the terrible blizzards.

"How do the mares and foals look?" Kane asked when Lone Pine joined him at the fence.

"Good. We got some without our brand, some with no brand." He pointed to a heavy dark bay that stood looking over the fence. "Like him."

"He's been broke. Look at the harness scars. Someone didn't take too good care of him." Kane hawked and spat, a direct comment on a man who would abuse his livestock. "Guess we'll have to keep him here till someone comes looking, but" — he shook his head — "I hate to send any animal back to be mistreated."

After the fall work was finished, many of the farmers turned their horses loose to fend for themselves on the prairie. Most rounded them up again in the spring, which was not a hard job, for the released horses tended to band together instinctively. The men sorted them according to brands and took their own horses home for the spring fieldwork. Several in this herd just hadn't been claimed.

"Funny that no one's come looking for them yet."

Lone Pine nodded. Lean as the tree he was named after and as spare of words as fat, he shook out his lasso and climbed over the fence. Within minutes the bay was roped, a loop thrown over his nose and tied snug to the fence. He pulled against the restraint when Kane approached him, his eyes rolling white.

Kane stopped, the low murmur he used on spooked critters making the horse's ears twitch. When the animal snorted and dropped his head a fraction, Kane approached again and laid a hand on the animal's quivering neck. "Easy, boy, easy now. You got nothing to fear here." As if trust were infused through the gentle hand on his neck, the animal dropped his head some more and blew out his fear in a rush. "That's the way." Kane continued stroking the summer-sleek hide, closely inspecting the animal all the while.

The hair had been rubbed off under the

rump pad, on the neck from the collar, and along the shoulders from the harness straps. White scar lines still showed on the horse's lips from where the bit had eaten into them. Kane was sure some of the smaller scars were from the tip of a whip laid on with a heavy hand.

"When someone comes looking, send 'em to talk with me." The tone of his voice matched the smoldering fire of his eyes.

They sorted out several for gelding that they'd left uncut earlier in hopes they would make good breeding stallions, because they got a better price for those, but these didn't measure up to Kane's standards. Three of the fillies they ran into another corral. They'd be trained but kept for broodmares.

The remainder would be broke to both saddle and harness.

"Cut tonight?" Lone Pine slapped his flat-brimmed hat against his thigh to get the dust off. He glanced up to see his wife waving a towel. "Eat now."

"Good. Call the others."

Morning Dove set bowls of potatoes and gravy along with platters of roast beef before the six men around the table, and within minutes the platters and the room were emptied but for Kane, Lone Pine, and Morning Dove. They lapsed back into the easy rhythm of the Mandan language as Kane asked if they knew where any rosebushes grew.

"You know, they have pink flowers, smell sweet, have lots of thorns, and you grind the rose hips in pemmican."

At that, Morning Dove nodded. "I show you."

Lone Pine gave him a puzzled look. "Why you want flowers?"

Kane looked from one to the other. "Women like flowers by the house."

Lone Pine looked at his wife.

She shook her head. "Must be white women."

"All right, so Mandan women would rather plant corn than roses. I just want to bring one here, all right?"

"Can we eat roses?" Lone Pine still looked puzzled.

Kane sighed but caught a look between husband and wife. They were teasing him. "Some things are for beauty's sake alone."

"Beauty? Who is she?" Lone Pine leaned forward, looking more puzzled than ever. His wife nudged his shoulder and scolded him for giving Kane a hard time.

"I'll help you dig roses," she said.

"No, you take care of the baby. Lone Pine can dig roses and maybe get his hands full of stickers." He shoved his chair back. "We'll start on the horses tomorrow. Let's get a wagon and go find those roses. Morning Dove, you and papoose can ride in the back. Bring a water jug and some of that corn bread."

By evening they had two rosebushes planted, even though both husband and wife kept up a banter that let Kane know they thought he was slightly crazy. Kane stood back after pouring a bucket of water around each bush. One shrub on either side of the front steps did look mighty pretty.

"Just remember to dump all the dishwater on them," he said to Morning Dove. "That's what my mother always did." He glanced at Lone Pine still digging thorns from the palm of his hand with his teeth.

"Better to break horses any day."

Kane tried to keep the laughter inside, but it burst forth in spite of his good intentions.

Lone Pine made a rude hand motion and headed for the corrals, leaving Morning Dove and Kane laughing as he went.

"Is good to hear you laugh." Morning Dove patted her baby's back, after having nursed him while the men planted the bushes.

Kane thought about her comment later. She was right. Laughter had been lacking around the ranch for a long time. He wondered about his coming bride. Did she enjoy a chuckle, or would she be serious all the time? Would she fit in here?

"Oh, Lord, what have I gotten myself into?" He sent his prayer heavenward.

4

Blessing
Mid-August

"Why don't we ask Olaf to pull that tooth for you?" Penny said, shaking her head. "You look miserable."

"I s'pose. I've tried about everything. You know if Metiz has anything good for the toothache?" Bridget held a hot wet cloth to her swollen face. Hot as it was outside, it seemed strange that a hot cloth would make it feel better, but she hated to waste the last remaining ice on her face. She had hoped to make ice cream Saturday for the harvesters. They planned a celebration for the beginning of wheat harvest. As usual, the wheat was ready at Baards' first.

"I could ask her if she's back."

"Where did she go?"

"To visit some of her family." Penny studied her mother-in-law's face again. "I think you better ask Olaf."

"Hjelmer said he'd do it."

"Sure, but who do most of the people around here go to with a toothache? You have any whiskey? That would help deaden the pain."

"I don't drink that stuff. Tastes vile."

"No, just to rub it on the gum. Ingeborg taught me that. They use it for the babies sometimes when a tooth won't come in." She rolled her lips together and tried to look innocent. "Of course, we all know that imbibing makes for no pain too."

"Ja, and a hangover like some of those men have had." Bridget shook her head and flinched at the movement. "Go ask Olaf. Maybe he can do it right away before I talk myself out of it."

"All right. Then I need to get back to the store. Do you have any whiskey?"

Bridget responded with the smallest of headshakes and sat with her eyes closed. She knew if she looked as bad as she felt, she'd even scare the grandchildren away. "All this bother over a toothache. Uff da."

"Olaf will bring some."

As soon as Penny left, Goodie arrived with Hans in tow. "Ach, you look terrible. I brought Hans to chop wood for a while. What with the washing, Lemuel can't seem to keep up. I told them if they chop a big stack, they can go fishing this afternoon."

"Maybe we can have fresh fish for supper. That would be a good change." Bridget spoke around the two cloves she now had clamped on her aching tooth. The gum around the offending tooth seemed to have grown twice in size overnight.

"That's what I thought. Eulah has three chickens ready for the oven. We better let a couple of those hens set so we have some more fryers. Unless Kaaren has extra. If Baptiste or Thorliff would bag a deer . . ." As she spoke, Goodie, her stomach now extending with the babe she was carrying, bustled about the kitchen. While Ilse had cleaned up the breakfast things, they had to get going on dinner.

When Olaf knocked at the back door, Bridget waved him in.

"Out here could be a mite cooler," he suggested. "There's a breeze yet."

"You go on and take care of that tooth, then have a bit of a lie-down," Goodie said. "We'll manage things here."

Bridget wanted to argue but no longer had the energy. How could a bad tooth take so much out of one? She took the cup of hot water Goodie handed her, along with some clean cotton for packing, and headed for the back porch.

"I cleaned these pliers up real good." Olaf, still slender in spite of Goodie's fine cooking, held the instrument in the air, as well as a bottle of brown liquid. "This stuff is strong enough to clean pliers. No wonder it deadens pain." He pulled the cork with his teeth and poured a couple of glugs in her cup. "Drink that."

Bridget shuddered as the liquor bit its way down to her belly. Tears pooled in her eyes, and she sniffed, blinking and swallowing again. "Ugh."

"Okay, now put this against that tooth and bite down for a minute or so." He handed her a folded square of cotton he'd soaked with the vile brown stuff.

Bridget closed her eyes and did as he told her, leaning back in her rocker and trying to ignore the fire ignited in her mouth.

"Ready?"

She nodded and opened her mouth wide.

Olaf applied the pliers with a twist of the wrist and a steady pull. The sound of the tooth cracking made him flinch. "Sorry about that." One by one he picked the pieces out and dropped them into the empty cup. "Now rinse your mouth out with this." He handed her a cup of cold water. "And bite down on this. It will help stop the bleeding."

Bridget did as he told her. "Mange takk." She spoke without moving her jaw.

"Maybe I should give up furniture making and the sack house and become a dentist."

Bridget shuddered and shook her head. The world tipped and took her stomach with it. Before she could protest, between Olaf and Goodie, they half carried her into her bedroom off the kitchen and tucked her up in bed with a bit of ice in a wet cloth pressed against her face.

She didn't argue.

"Those clouds look like they might do more than just pass overhead." Reverend John Solberg took off his hat and wiped his beaded forehead with the handkerchief he'd pulled from his back pocket. He swiped the thinning sandy hair back and resettled his fedora. Today he looked more like a farmer than a pastor, wearing overalls like his neighbors and a sweat-darkened long-sleeved shirt with the arms rolled up. His forehead now had the demarcation line of one who spent hours in the sun, hat securely in place.

"How do they look different than the ones we've had almost every day?" His wife, Mary Martha, tipped her sunbonnet-shaded face up to catch the breeze. Together they watched as their niece, Manda MacCallister, worked with one of the young horses she was breaking in the corral.

"Maybe just wishful thinking. We need rain so badly, and yet right now would be a terrible time for a thunderstorm, what with the wheat about ready to cut." He leaned his arms on the top rail of the corral and set one foot on the bottom rail. While he didn't have any wheat planted and his acres of oats weren't ready to harvest, his parishioners all depended on the wheat harvest for most of their income. With the drought, the wheat looked to be stunted already. Beaten to the ground, it would be hard to cut.

Manda snubbed the horse to the solid post in the center of the corral, and after stroking the animal's shoulder and rubbing its ears, she strode over to the fence, where she had a saddle ready.

"I brought some lemonade." Mary Martha picked up the jug at her feet. "Surely you can take a break now."

Manda nodded and set the saddle back

on the rail. "Where's Deborah? She was here a minute ago."

"Gone to pick the eggs. She'll be right back." Mary Martha poured the liquid in the four cups she'd brought along and handed them out. "Let's sit in the barn shade. Got to be cooler there."

Solberg fetched a stool from the barn. "Here, sit on this. It will make getting up easier."

"I'm not an invalid, you know." Mary Martha shook her head, her laugh infectious. "Just because we're having a baby."

Manda sank down against the wall. "Don't hurt to be careful." She took off her well-ventilated fedora. While they'd given her a wide-brimmed straw hat for her birthday, she insisted on the ancient felt, more faded than true brown. It was the last thing she owned of her father's.

"Ma." Seven-year-old Deborah came around the corner of the barn holding the back of her hand to her mouth. "That durn ol' hen pecked me again."

"Don't talk like that!" Manda snapped her order before Mary Martha could open her mouth.

"You said 'that durn horse.' If you can, why can't I?"

Manda picked at a blade of dried grass. "Just 'cause."

Mary Martha exchanged a look with her husband. They both knew it was the "ma" not the "durn" that irritated Manda. She'd just gotten used to calling Katy "Ma" when Katy died in childbirth, just like Manda's real mother had. And while she called Zeb MacCallister "Pa," it hadn't kept him from disappearing after his wife's death. He'd gone back to South Dakota to see to the homestead rights of the girls, but he couldn't bear living on the ranch yet.

Knowing her brother as she did, Mary Martha had a good idea he was back out in Montana searching out that valley he'd dreamed of and filing for homestead rights. She figured any day now he'd ride in with a herd of horses ready to break, then take his girls and head west. But until he returned, she and John had moved from the parsonage soddy by the school to the MacCallister farm, keeping it up and caring for the girls.

"When Pa comes back . . ."

"He ain't comin' back!" Manda whirled on her sister like an attacking badger.

"Manda MacCallister, he ith too." Deborah sometimes had a lisp since she'd lost her two front teeth. Her straw-colored pigtails slapped her chin as she shook her head. "You just . . ."

"All right, girls. That's enough." While John spoke gently, there was no ignoring his command. *Father God, please keep Zeb safe. Heal his grief and bring him back to these two who so dearly need to see prayers answered. To lose two mothers, one father, and now maybe another one, besides the two stillborn babies, is beyond what anyone should bear, let alone those so young. It breaks my heart, and I'm the pastor, not the parent.*

But John knew that if called to be, he would gladly adopt these two. Maybe that would be best if Zeb wrote and asked them to do so. He knew Mary Martha already acted more like a mother than an aunt.

Zeb can't write if he's dead. The thought had plagued him more than once. A man by himself — anything could happen.

"Come on, Deborah, you said you'd ride for me today."

"I will." Both girls handed back their cups and climbed the rails to drop into the corral.

Heat lightning flared against the dark thunderheads. The wind picked up, bending the oat field like waves on the sea.

Mary Martha and John stood and faced the west, grateful for the cooling wind.

50

"It does smell like rain."

"Lightning too." Mary Martha looped her hand around John's elbow and leaned her cheek against his shoulder. "I better get the chickens in."

"I'll go for the cows." John turned and whistled for the cow dog. "Manda, you better put that horse away in case we get lightning strikes." He watched for a moment as Manda led the now docile horse around the corral. She had such a gift with animals, it was a shame she didn't use it with humans too.

"Manda." He raised his voice to be heard above the wind.

"I will."

John whistled again and waved the mottled cow dog out to round up the cows. Again, it was thanks to Manda's training that he didn't have to go out and get the creatures himself.

Even though it was not yet three o'clock, the sky darkened so that it seemed like night. Rain came in sheets across the prairie and struck with a downpour instead of warning drops. John was the last to leap up on the porch without being soaked. The four of them, dog at their feet, watched the ground spring out in puddles as if a heavenly bucket had just been over-

51

turned above them.

Mary Martha stood near the step, her face raised to catch the drifting mist. She spun in a flash, grabbed the girls' hands, circled behind John, and together the three ran out into the deluge.

Drops the size of teacups pounded them and the earth. Within a breath, they were soaked, hair stringing down their faces and into their open, laughing mouths. Manda chased Deborah through a puddle, stamping her foot so the water splashed them both.

The dog yipped at their heels, jumping to catch the splash.

Mary Martha raised her arms above her head and spun in a tight circle, her sodden skirts sticking to her ankles. "I know what." She pulled the pins from her hair and let the mass fall down her back. "Get the soap," she called to John, who watched them from the porch.

"The soap?" John had to shout to be heard.

"Yes, we can wash our hair."

John brought the soap, and they took turns scrubbing one another's hair, then raising their faces to let the rain rinse them clean.

Lightning flared, thunder boomed and

crashed, trees bent over before the wind, and they finally sat down on the benches on the porch. Mary Martha brought out towels so they could dry their hair and the brush and comb to fix it again.

"I ain't never done nothing like that in my whole life." Manda sat shaking her head. She sniffed, and a smile lifted the corners of her mouth. "The air smells so clean again. You think heaven smells pure like this?"

John cleared his throat, stunned at the question and the questioner. Manda had been insisting that God wasn't there, " 'Cause if He *is* there, then why are such terrible things happening?" She'd said such more than once and in several ways. But this glimpse into her heart reassured him. And the smile he'd glimpsed reminded him that in spite of her grown-up ways, Manda Norton MacCallister was still a little girl who needed a father.

"I think it must." He moved closer to her and, with a gentle arm, pulled her to rest against his side. With the four of them crowded on one bench, they watched the storm let up and continue east, leaving the trees and roof dripping.

"Oh, looky." Deborah pointed to the sky. "A rainbow." She looked up at Mary

Martha. "Katy Ma said one time that babies in heaven get to play on the rainbow. You think that's true?"

"I most surely do." Mary Martha kissed the little girl's upturned nose.

"Then our babies are up there, huh? And maybe my two mas are sittin' visitin' and watching them play."

Mary Martha laid a hand on her own belly, where a new baby grew, and hugged the little girl close to her side. "I surely do hope so, Deborah. Such a lovely picture you've given us." She sniffed for a second time and heard John do the same. "I'll never look at a rainbow the same again."

"Me neither."

She turned to see the love shining from her husband's eyes. And to think she'd heard that Norwegian men were cold and unfeeling. Whoever started such a rumor didn't know her husband, that was for certain sure.

"Well, at least it didn't hail." From the shelter of their porch, Haakan and Ingeborg, along with Lars and Kaaren, watched the storm make its way east. The children were all out playing in the puddles, covered with black gumbo and shrieking with laughter. Paws had a bit of brown along his back, but otherwise they now owned a black dog.

"You think it damaged the wheat?" Kaaren asked.

"Some, but most of it will pop back up in a day or so. We'll have to set the binder blade right on the ground to pick it all up." The two men began discussing what adjustments the machinery would need, leaving Kaaren and Ingeborg to laugh at the antics before them. Baptiste and Thorliff took a run and slid through a mud puddle as if they were on ice. Soon all of them, Hamre included for a change, were skating barefooted on tracks slick as an oiled pig. The bigger ones held the littler hands, and when a bunch fell down, giggles erupted as they wiped the mud from their faces.

The ground slurped up the water, and before the sun came fully out, steam began to rise, and the puddles disappeared.

"Okay, everyone, stand by the well and get washed off. We'll have buttermilk and cookies ready when you're clean." Ingeborg nodded to the big boys to take care of the children. "We should have played out in it too," she said to Kaaren.

"I know. Good thing we baked this morning, no matter how hot it was."

Kaaren and Ingeborg made their way into the house and threw open all the windows to let in the fresh air.

Rain. They'd finally had rain. And even if the wheat wasn't dry enough to cut and bind, they'd have the party as they planned. Everyone was in need of a party especially before the really heavy work of harvest began, for once their wheat was threshed, Haakan and Lars would take the steam engine and the threshing machine and travel the country threshing grain.

Ingeborg almost hated to think of the weeks ahead.

5

Nearing St. Paul, Minnesota
End of August

"I never dreamed a country could be so big."

"What's that you say?"

Augusta Bjorklund turned from looking out the train window and glanced at the man in the seat facing her. She hadn't meant to make her comment out loud. It just slipped out. All the letters that described this land hadn't even begun to do it justice. Here she'd been on the train three days, and they still weren't to Blessing. Since the conductor spoke Norwegian, he'd told her that the next big stop where she would change trains — again — was St. Paul, Minnesota. They'd be there by evening.

She shook her head at the other passenger's question, since she didn't understand what he'd said, then turned back to the window. So many fields being harvested.

Wouldn't her brother Johann love to see this — this vast land and all this bounty? Trees and lakes and rivers and farmland the likes of which she couldn't even begin to count.

No wonder the newspapers at home often described this land as flowing with milk and honey. True, the streets of the cities she'd seen weren't paved with gold, but then she'd never believed they were. Otherwise none of the immigrants would have returned to Norway, and some did. They didn't come home wealthy either.

Her stomach rumbled, and she laid a hand over her midsection. Surely she would be able to buy food in St. Paul far cheaper than what she'd seen so far. While Johann had warned her that food would cost dearly, she hadn't dreamed it would be so expensive. Until she found she was running out of money.

She glanced up to catch the eye of the man across from her. The look he gave her didn't need an interpreter. She could feel the heat blossom on her neck and up her face. Had he no manners at all? Why, if she could just speak the language, she'd tell him to mind his own business. That was for sure.

If only she had listened to Johann and

did as the letters from Mor had said. *Learn to speak American.* If she'd heard that once, she'd heard or read it, well . . . She sighed and returned to the window.

When his foot nudged hers, she shot him a look that could have scorched corn.

He tipped his hat and winked at her.

Of all the colossal nerve. Was this the way of American men? If so, give her a good solid Norwegian any day.

That of course brought her back to thoughts of Elmer. That no good, lying . . .

The conductor made his way down the aisle, swaying along with the rocking train. He stopped beside Augusta's seat. "Two more stops and you'll be getting off, miss."

Oh, how good to hear her beautiful Norwegian language. "Mange takk." She gave him her best smile. "And how do I know what train to go to there in St. Paul?"

"The ticket agent will direct you. Just go up to the window and ask."

"But . . . but what if he doesn't speak Norwegian?"

"Oh, most of them do, a bit anyway. We get lots of immigrants from Norway out here. Swedes too and other Scandinavians, Germans, Russians. There's lots of people going west for free land. Not as many as a few years ago, but still a lot. You got family waiting for you?"

Augusta nodded. "My brother Hjelmer and Mor. Others too."

"I'll be by to make sure you get off at the right place." He touched a finger to the bill on his uniform cap and continued down the aisle.

Augusta wanted to summon him back and ask more questions about the changing of trains. But he had a job to do, so she sank back against the seat. With great care she kept her gaze from meeting that of the man on the other seat. Then he nudged her foot again. Tucking her booted feet as far under the seat as she could, she glared at the man and locked the metal in her spine so that she sat ramrod straight. She gathered her travel-stained skirt closer to her legs and turned slightly toward the window. Short of stabbing his foot with a hairpin, she had no weapon. Obviously withering looks didn't count.

She knew he was watching her, could feel it with every nerve in her body. Should she tell the conductor? But what could she say? This man is bothering me?

If there were other seats available, she could just get up and move, but the car was full except for the seat next to her and the seat next to *him*. If he was cramped for foot room, why didn't he move over?

The nudge again.

The conductor made his way back down the aisle calling out the next stop as the train whistle cried and the train began slowing down.

Dear God, please make this man get off here.

But he didn't. Instead he lit a cigar and waved it at her whenever she made the mistake of looking up.

If the window wasn't so important to her, she'd have moved over. After all, she did have her knitting along. She could hear her mor admonishing her to not waste a moment of precious time. But she wanted to see this new country.

Augusta tightened her jaw. There he was again, this time touching her ankle. *That's it!* She rose, regal as a Viking princess, and deliberately planted her heel on the top of his foot. Then turning to give it a good mash, she headed for the necessary. The grunt she heard as she left more than made up for the discomfort of deliberately hurting another. She started to think *person* and changed her mind. But she couldn't call him an animal either. Animals weren't obnoxious like that, so she guessed he was a man. She shook her head. At least God had spared her meeting men like that in her past.

Dirty rude man.

When she returned, he took the cigar out of his mouth, nodded to her, and moved his feet out of the way so she could resume her seat. The leer was gone, his expression now showing a measure of respect.

If only she could get her heart to return to its normal place and pace.

When they finally arrived in St. Paul, he was right behind her as she stepped off the train.

The conductor pointed her in the direction of the information window and the huge board that showed train arrivals and departures. A man on a ladder was erasing some lines and writing in others. Wheels screeching, steam hissing, vendors hawking their wares, babies crying, children running and laughing, men shouting — the tumult made her want to clap her hands over her ears.

The man stayed right behind her. Even above the cacophony, she sensed his presence.

Heart thundering in her ears, she waited in line to ask her questions. The line moved slowly. She could hear him humming under his breath.

Shivers chased each other up and down her spine. *Why, oh why won't he go away?*

She stepped up to the window and, keeping her voice low, asked, "Which is the train to . . . to . . ." She had to check her carefully written-out itinerary. "G-Grand Forks." Would the man with the green visor above his eyes understand her Norwegian?

"Right over there, number. . . ." A voice over a loudspeaker drowned out his words.

The man behind her cleared his throat.

"Mange takk." She clutched her tickets tightly in hand and nearly ran across the marble-tiled floor. Surely there would be only one train in that spot right now. If not, she'd have to ask again. She glanced back over her shoulder.

Here he came! Would he never leave her alone?

She went down the stairs and followed the crowd. But there were three trains, all lined up with only a walkway between them. Which one? She studied the numbers on the front of the engine. *What did he say? Oh, Lord above, what number did he say?*

The man was drawing nearer. Two others came down the stairs together, singing some song at the top of their lungs. She recognized the signs. At one of the homes she'd worked in, the master frequently came home inebriated like that. A black man dressed in the uniform of a conductor stood at a step stool leading to an open door on the middle train. Her hands shaking so badly she could hardly hang on to her carpetbag, she let him help her up the steps.

There was only one other woman on the car, the smoke from the cigars of the men giving the room a silvery haze. Wishing for the fresh air of home, she sank down in a vacant seat and leaned against the back. This time there was no seat across from her, only the backs of the ones in front. She set her carpetbag in the seat by the window and prayed the man wouldn't get on this train.

"All a-b-o-a-r-d," the familiar words came, and the train inched backward. She'd only have one more change to make, in Grand Forks. Relief made her almost dizzy. The rude man hadn't gotten on this train. She stood to place her coat in the rack above and glanced around the half-full car. No, he wasn't there.

But at the other end near the cast-iron stove, the two drunks were tippling their bottles and laughing as if they'd heard the best joke ever.

At least they were at the other end of the car.

The train stopped, the wheels and brakes screeching, then at a shout from someone outside, it began to pull forward. Within minutes they were passing between brick buildings and the backyards of houses with wash hanging on lines and children playing under the shade trees. Soon they were out in open farmland.

The noise from the inebriated men grew, the laughter taking an uglier tone.

"Tickets, tickets, everyone." The dark-skinned conductor came through the door between the cars and made his way down the aisle.

Just as Augusta handed him her ticket, a shout came from the rear. A shot rang out. A woman screamed.

"Oh!" The conductor headed for the fracas. "Stop that! Now you . . ."

Augusta glanced down at the floor to find her ticket lying there. Breathing a prayer of thanks, she scooped it up and put it back in her reticule.

Drunken fights on the train, a man who accosted her, what was this world coming to? Another man in uniform bustled down the aisle, and the fray settled down again. *Ah, the stories I have about my trip to North Dakota. At least there wasn't a storm at sea like Carl and Roald had endured.* The ocean part of her journey though long, seemed almost commonplace compared to this portion.

Her stomach made hungry noises again. She sighed and shook her head. She hadn't even taken time to find something to eat. Surely there would be a stop soon where she could buy some bread or something.

At least she wouldn't die of hunger in the next twelve hours, and there was water in a jug by the necessary. Mor would have a good meal ready when she got to Blessing. It was over two years since she'd seen her mother. And Hjelmer, her baby brother — was it really six years since she'd seen him? He'd be a man now, not that he hadn't thought he was when he left home.

Thoughts of her family took over her mind. Memories of her two brothers, Roald and Carl, who died the second winter in Dakota Territory, and her baby sister, Katy, last winter. So many gone now, Far included. Home had seemed desolate without him and Mor there. That had made the leaving easier. She retrieved her coat from the rack and folded it to use as a pillow against the window. Warm as it was, she didn't need it as a blanket. In the morning she would be in Grand Forks, and then it was only an hour or two to Blessing. Almost there. She glanced out the window again, but the moon hadn't come up. A light shone once in a great while. Otherwise complete darkness hid the land.

So huge a country. One could surely get lost easily.

6

Ipswich
September 1

Kane studied the black clouds mounding on the western horizon. They looked like rain, but then so had many others, and right now with harvest in full swing, the farmers didn't want any rain. Wasn't that just the way of it?

He should have been at home helping to cut and bind the oats. Instead, in another hour or two he'd be in Ipswich, and a couple hours after that, if the train was on time, he'd meet up with his soon-to-be bride. He'd left the ranch before daybreak the day before and had camped at a spring off the road, the same place he camped every time he came to town.

His stomach knotted. Would she be happy here? Well, she surely wouldn't if mountains were important to her. While he'd heard of sky-piercing mountains out to the west, mountains that carried snow all year, he'd never been farther than Pierre, and that only once. He clucked his team into a trot. Be good if he could beat the rain to town. No sense appearing like a drowned rat.

But like the blackbirds flitting and singing from the brown cattails in the dried-up swamp, his mind took wing and dreamed ahead to the woman arriving on the train. How would he recognize her?

You're a sorry sort, he scolded himself. *Borrowin' trouble like that. Just how many women traveling alone are going to get off that train looking around for someone to meet them?* When the team lagged, he clucked them up again, this time flicking the reins so they knew he meant business. Dust bloomed from under their feet and added another layer to his boots propped against the footboard. He'd better give them a rubdown too, or his new clothes wouldn't look quite so good.

Again he shook his head. "Why in tarnation am I buying new? These are all still hanging together." He studied the patch on one knee and the about-to-need-one state of the other.

The horses swiveled their ears to listen and kept up their steady pace. One snorted and tossed his head, adding to the jingle and squeak of the harness. One wheel groaned, reminding Kane that they needed greasing. Always something to fix. And if he weren't home harvesting, he should be home repairing machinery and fixing fences.

"Instead, I'm about to get married." He sent a glance heavenward. "I sure do hope you know what you're doing here. Why did I let myself get talked into this?"

But he knew why. The letter that he found of his mother's, written years earlier, had laid a load of guilt bigger than any hay load he could haul. Then Lone Pine and Morning Dove had started in. It seemed that everybody who ever had a wife and baby wished them off on everyone else. Even in his Bible reading it seemed that everyone had children, lots of children if the lists were accurate. The patriarchs needed sons to pass on their land to, and so did he. He reminded himself that though the Bible didn't list all the daughters born, he could have those too. Girls were good for helping their ma about the house and all. At least, so he'd heard, never having had a sister of his own. Being an only son, an only child, had never seemed a hardship to him, but he knew his mother had wished for more children.

A meadowlark trilled and another answered. Were they a pair? The Bible said God made mates for his creatures; otherwise everything would have died out long before. And now it was his turn.

He swallowed again. Must be the dust that was making his throat so dry.

Heat lightning slashed the approaching black clouds, but there didn't look to be any rain falling. A breeze kicked up, bending the black-eyed Susans that frilled the roadside. Sunflowers shuddered and grasses bowed. A crow's black shadow crossed the road ahead of them, his raucous cry grating on nerves already stretched with apprehension. It almost sounded as if the bird was laughing — or warning him.

"Good a reason to laugh as any. A man marrying a woman he ain't never seen." Maybe he should have taken his mother's advice and traveled back to Pennsylvania, where his folks came from, and looked up some of his relatives. They might have had friends and neighbors who knew of a comely young woman wanting to go west.

"Yes, they might have. But this is what you did, and this is what you live with." The horses snorted again, their ears twitching to pick up all the sounds, including his voice.

What will it be like to have someone to talk with in the evening? Someone to wake up to in the morning? He rubbed his hand over his face. Better leave that part of thinking alone.

A rider on horseback nodded and tipped his hat as they met. Off to the east, he could see a dust cloud. Must be another wagon on the way to town. Dogs barked from a farm alongside the road, a two-lane track where wheels had worn off the grass, showing the way to the boxlike house and white hipped-roof barn. Like most places, the available money was spent on the barn, not the house.

Sweat darkened the hides of his team as he trotted them into town and halted them in front of the livery. He wrapped the reins around the brake handle and stepped down to the dirt street, grunting as his legs warned him they'd been in one position far too long.

"Can I help you, mister?" A towheaded boy with one overall suspender hooked and the other missing a button greeted him.

"You work here?" Kane stretched, trying to get the kinks out. He'd rather ride a horse than a wagon seat any day.

"Yep. Pa's shoeing a team right now. I can unharness yours for you, brush 'em down, and water and grain them, all for two bits. How long till you need 'em again?"

"Oh, couple hours. Got some things coming in on the train." Kane dug in his pocket and flipped a quarter in the air. "You make sure they don't get too much water till they're cooled down."

"Right, mister." The boy caught the quarter and shot Kane a cheeky grin. "And if'n you feel like tippin' me 'cause I did such a good job, I wouldn't be one to turn it down."

Kane shook his head and smiled back. "We'll see about that." The picture of the boy stayed with him as he headed for the hotel, if you could call it that. If and when he had a boy, he hoped his son would be sharp like that. Taking the three steps in one, he pushed open the double doors and strode up to the desk.

"How can I help you?" The clerk looked up with a smile.

"I need a bath, a shave, a haircut, and new clothes." He almost added *because I'm getting married this afternoon* but clipped that off in time.

"All right. You go two doors down for

the shave and haircut, across the street for the clothes, and we can have a bath ready in between the two."

Kane nodded. "You get it hot, and I'll be back." He started out, then turned to ask, "Is there a pastor in town?"

"Sorry, no. Not regular. Itinerant preachers come by, though."

"Thanks." Kane continued on out the door.

Some time later, clipped, scrubbed, and sporting everything new but hat and boots, he turned in his long list at the general store, checked with the stationmaster to make sure his windmill was on board, and headed for the livery to get his team and wagon. He also inquired to make sure the justice of the peace was in town. Since the judge was itinerant but based in Ipswich, the chance was good he'd be available. There was no way he could head out across the rolling prairie with an unmarried female in tow.

Contrary thoughts kept stabbing at him as he helped the boy harness his team. What if the justice wasn't there? What if his Norwegian bride changed her mind and didn't want to marry him, at least not right away? What if she wasn't on the train?

He ignored his wayward thoughts the best he could, handed the boy a dime extra, and touched the brim of his hat at the exuberant "Thankee, sir."

At least he'd made one person happy today. The train whistle wept from a distance. He took in a deep breath and stepped up into his wagon, then clucked the horses forward. The station was only a short block away.

He stopped the horses in the shade of an elm tree and, snapping a tie rope to one bridle, knotted it to the hitching post. Was it really this hot or . . . ? He lifted his hat to wipe his forehead with a new red kerchief. He walked on over and stood in the shade of the wide-roofed station house, which looked about as tired as the rest of the town.

The train eased into the station, steam billowing and wheels screeching. A uniformed man stepped out of the first passenger car and set a metal stool on the platform for the passengers to step down.

Kane's breath caught in his throat.

A man in a black suit swung down with a portmanteau in his right hand.

Kane took a step forward.

A woman with a small boy came next. She hadn't said anything about having a child, so that left them out.

Two more men, both in the uniform of the United States Army.

He saw another dress in the shadows of the car. He gulped. A woman, round as she was tall and with hair the color of clean sheep wool, beamed at a young couple who rushed forward and hugged her.

Kane breathed a sigh of relief.

The conductor waited. Kane waited.

A woman's face remained in the shadow for a brief second, and then the conductor reached up a hand to help her down. A dark skirt topped by a dark jacket and a bit of white at the neck appeared. She was slender but with a strength about her, straight shoulders, long neck, and a face that . . . *Oh, thank you, Lord. She is more than comely. She is beautiful!*

He glanced around the platform. Maybe there was someone else to greet her. But the look on her face said that wasn't the case. He strode forward, hat in his hands.

"Miss Borsland?" He had to clear his throat and say her name again. He hoped he was pronouncing it right.

She turned and looked at him with eyes the blue of a summer sky, only more so, if that were possible.

"Ja, Miss Bjorklund." Augusta looked

76

around. Now what should she do? The conductor had never said Blessing or Grand Forks or anything she recognized. And since he hadn't spoken Norwegian, she couldn't make her questions clear.

Who was this man? Had Mor sent him to fetch her? How far away was Blessing? The letters on the front of the station didn't look anything like the ones on the letter in her reticule. She looked up again. *I-p* surely didn't look like a *B*.

The man stepped forward and, smiling, reached for her carpetbag. "I'll carry that for you."

He seemed to expect her. "Mange takk." She let him take the bag, grateful for the courtesy. Her legs felt as though she still rode the swaying train, and the platform took on life beneath her feet. Oh, what she would give for a bath or at least a chance to wash up. She'd done her best in the tiny bathroom on the train, but a dipper of water didn't go very far.

"Right this way." The man motioned toward a team and wagon off under a tree.

If only she could understand what he was saying. "Will you be taking me to Blessing, then?"

"Ah yes, indeed. Your being here is surely a blessing." He wished he had been able to learn some Norwegian. How in the world were they going to talk with each other? And those eyes, never had he seen such color. She was tall — tall enough to fit just under his chin, a Nordic princess, for certain sure. It was all he could do to keep his feet from dancing.

He led her to the wagon and, after helping her up, motioned for her to stay there. When she started to stand again, he shook his head and smiled.

She smiled back and sat down. *He must be in a hurry to get going. How long until I see my family? What a joy that will be. Thank you, heavenly Father, for a safe journey, even though this looks nothing like Mor's descriptions of the flat prairie. I thought sure from what she said that the train stopped right in front of Penny's store and Hjelmer's blacksmith shop. But then, I never saw Grand Forks either.* She shook her head and drew a handkerchief from her sleeve to wipe the sides of her face and neck. Perhaps those black clouds would bring cooler air with the rain they must be carrying. Would they arrive in Blessing before the storm hit?

She watched as the man who'd come for her strode back from the station house.

A cool wind blew at her skirts and rustled the leaves above. The horses flicked

78

their tails at the flies. She turned her face to the breeze, wishing she could take off her jacket and raise her arms. But that wasn't seemly in the least, not in this place where she knew no one, grateful as she was that someone seemed to know her and to expect her.

He smiled at her again as he untied the horses and climbed up in the wagon. He turned them in a tight circle and headed back for the station.

Surely he was going for her trunk.

Thank God the crates came in, Kane thought. He glanced at the clouds again. They seemed to be staying south of the town. Maybe they'd clear by the time they were ready to head out. He backed the wagon up to the loading dock and wrapped the reins around the brake handle. Motioning her to stay seated, he gave her a smile that evoked one in response.

At least they could smile at each other. Augusta wondered if anyone in town spoke Norwegian. If only she had taken her brother's advice and learned American. Some of it, a bit, anything. She felt as if her face might crack from smiling. She buried the nigglings of fear under an avalanche of smiles. She watched as they loaded wooden crates into the bed of the wagon, all the time wondering what it was. The two men shook hands, and her stranger returned to the seat of the wagon.

"We are going to Blessing now?" she asked. If only he could understand her.

"I agree. Such a blessing." *Why is she so locked on blessing?* Kane wondered. "As soon as we pick up the supplies from the general store here, we'll go to the justice of the peace." He accompanied his words with a broad smile, grateful for the one in return. Her eyes crinkled at the edges, her dark lashes accenting the blue. Oh, the blue of her eyes.

He drew his gaze away with an effort.

More things were loaded into the wagon, filling up the spaces in and around the machinery.

"My trunk. Where will my trunk go?" She looked from the wagon back to the station platform. Even though her trunk was small, she'd not seen it unloaded from the train. Had it gotten lost? Would it come later? What would she do for clothing in the meantime?

Kane shrugged. If only he could understand her. Something sure had gotten under her smile. Her eyes darkened like the sky before a storm. He followed her pointing finger back to the train platform and then tried to decipher her hand motions. Something long and deep and square.

"A box?" He mimicked her motions.

She nodded, and lo and behold the sun returned. "Ja, my trunk."

"Ah." He nodded, motioned her to wait, and headed back to the depot.

"Sorry, nothing came in with that name on it," the stationmaster said. "In fact, your windmill and some things for the store and the hotel were all the freight this time. Real low what with harvest starting. All I can say is check back with us tomorrow."

"Tomorrow I'll be halfway home, and the lady will be without her things." Kane shook his head. It wasn't like he could run into town anytime he pleased. Should they stay over? He kept on shaking his head.

"I could have someone going out your way bring it to you when it comes. Sometimes these things happen, you know."

"Guess that will have to do. I got to get on home. That binder breaks down again, and no one else there can fix it." If only he had taught Lone Pine the intricacies of the limping binder.

When he got back to the wagon, he made the box motions again, shrugged, and shook his head. "It'll come later."

The look in her eyes said clearly she didn't understand. So he said it louder.

Why is he yelling at me? Where is my trunk? Augusta chewed on her lip. So she would just have to make do. Obviously her trunk would come on a later train, and they would just have to . . . just have to what? She had no idea at the moment. Her stomach grumbled, and she blinked at a wave of dizziness. It had been more than two days since she'd eaten. Right now that seemed more important than her trunk.

Kane studied her through narrowed eyes. He heard the sound of her insides. Hadn't she eaten on the train? Surely he'd sent enough money so she didn't starve. But at the pale look taking over her face, he had a good idea she hadn't eaten for some time.

Well, as soon as they stood up for the ceremony, he would take her to the hotel for a meal. Or he could ask them to fix a basket.

He nodded and smiled again. That's what he'd do. They could eat on the way. If they didn't put some miles under those wheels by dark, it would be another day before he got home. And by then both Morning Dove and Lone Pine would be sending out scouts. He bid her stay again and trotted across the street to the hotel.

"Now where is he going?" Augusta whispered into the fingers she'd used to rub her temples. *Oh, Lord above, I have said I will trust you, but let me tell you, right now that isn't very easy. Who is this man, and when are we going to Blessing so that Hjelmer can make everything clear?*

After picking up his supplies at the general store, they drove down the street, and he stopped the wagon again. This time he motioned her to step down and held up a hand to assist her. She laid her hand in his, feeling she had no strength left, only to discover a power running from his hand and directly up her arm. She paused in the act of stepping down to the step and looked into his eyes — amber in color with flecks of gold like promises of riches to come. She could see no guile, only concern and a hint of joy, as if the curving of his well-formed lips weren't enough and he was trying his best to reassure her.

Taking a deep breath, she placed her foot on the step and swung to the ground, his hand now cupping her elbow. Again came that sensation of a transference of strength. Who was this man anyway? Might he become a friend, or even more? After all, she was single, thanks to that no-good Elmer. But perhaps this man wasn't.

She felt like sighing again but refrained. Sighing was not in her nature, and she promised herself she wasn't about to develop the habit.

He guided her up the steps and held open a door to an office of some sort. At his direction, she went on in and looked around. Surely a business office. What had they come here for?

Another man, a book in his hand, entered the room and stood before them. He nodded at her, and she nodded back. Her companion smiled and said a few words to which the older man responded.

She tried to think of the cool lakes and mountain streams of home, but instead, all that came to mind was a plate of roast beef, potatoes, rutabagas, and pickled beets on the side. There would be a plate of lefse, a cup of steaming coffee, and her mor's smiling face. Her stomach rumbled again. She could feel the heat of embarrassment color her face even brighter than she knew the oppressive heat already did.

What would they think of her?

"Do you, Miss Borsland, take this man as your wedded husband?"

The man with the book looked at her as

if waiting for an answer. *What is he saying?*

She looked to the man beside her, and at his nod, she nodded to the man who, now that she thought about it, looked official. Maybe this was something to do with coming into the new land. Hjelmer had talked about how important it was to become an American citizen.

If only she could understand what they were saying. Now the gentleman asked a question to the man beside her. He also nodded and smiled.

"I now pronounce you man and wife."

Kane felt his heart leap. He'd actually done it. Gone and gotten himself a wife. A beautiful wife. All he had to do was teach her English so they could talk to each other. And he would learn some Norwegian too. Make it easier for her. How, he wasn't sure, but then he'd learned to speak Mandan, and that was no easy language either.

The man with the book said a few more things, then smiled and reached out his hand. First the man beside her shook the official's hand, then motioned for her to do the same.

After shaking their hands, he turned to a book open on the desk and wrote a few things in it before handing the pen to

Kane. He wrote something and handed the pen to her.

She studied the lines. They must want her to sign her name. Ah, that she could do.

"So am I a citizen now?" she asked with as bright a smile as she could muster. When she leaned over like that, she had to fight against the dizziness again.

When they both nodded, she let out the breath she'd not realized she was holding. Becoming an American certainly was simple. Why had Hjelmer made such a big thing of it?

Kane took her arm, said good-bye to Justice Rhinehart, and took his new bride out the door. From the look on her face, he'd better feed her before she fainted on him.

He was counting his blessings for sure. Not only was she lovely as the sunrise, she was agreeable too.

"We're going to Blessing now?"

He nodded. "You bet. Blessings in abundance. I'll pick up our lunch basket, and we'll be on our way."

7

Blessing
September 1

"Where is she?"

"Mor, I don't know." Hjelmer watched the train pull away from the plank platform in front of the sack house.

"But Augusta was supposed to be on this train." In her consternation, Bridget Bjorklund abandoned her newly learned English and reverted to Norwegian.

"I know she was, but she must have missed a connection somewhere. She'll be on the train tomorrow for sure."

In the small town of Blessing, North Dakota, the St. Paul and Pacific Railroad ran west in the early morning, again around noon, and a third ran east in the late afternoon. And since this train had been late, the group on the platform had been waiting for some time.

"Will Tante Augusta sleep in a station?"

Thorliff, Bridget's oldest grandson, asked.

Standing behind Bridget, his mother, Ingeborg, caught his eye and gave a minuscule shake of her head. No sense in making Bridget's worries any worse.

"Now, Mor, don't you go worrying. Augusta is a grown woman, and she's been out in the world for almost fifteen years, taking the train to Oslo to work with that family and all. She'll know how to take care of herself." Hjelmer wiped the sweat off his brow with a kerchief. Here it was September and still hot as August.

"Ja, well, I better get back to the boardinghouse, then." Bridget shook her head. *Uff da!* She'd had a feeling when she woke up that the day wasn't going to go too well. But she'd never thought of something this bad. *Father God, please take care of that daughter of mine. I know she is your child, but sometimes a mother worries more than a father.* She thought of reminding Him how she felt about His care of her youngest daughter, but one didn't talk to God that way, leastways she didn't. Katy and her babe were in heaven, where at least they were safe, not like Augusta, who was only God knew where.

Bridget scratched a mosquito bite, set to itching by the trickle of perspiration that meandered down her neck.

"I'll go check with Gunnar and make sure there hasn't been any trouble on the line," Hjelmer said.

Just that summer they'd gotten a real telegraph office in Blessing. The operator, Gunnar Erickson, took over a corner part of the sack house. Surely Augusta would have sent them a telegraph if there was a problem. If she thought of it. If she had enough money. The ifs were as irritating as the black flies. He brushed one away and blinked in the dimness of the building after the brilliance of the morning sun.

"Hey, Erickson," he called as he drew closer to the telegraph office.

"Ja, vat you vant?" Pushing his green visor up on his shiny bald head, the man turned from his machine.

Hjelmer leaned on the window ledge. "You heard anything about problems on the lines from New York? My sister was supposed to be on this train, and she wasn't."

"None. Leastways nothing come through here. Anyting of any importance vould be passed on."

"Just thought I'd check." Hjelmer rubbed his chin, all the while shaking his head. "She'll probably be here tomorrow with a wild tale of mix-ups. Sure wish she'd listened to me and all the others and learned some English."

"Anyone traveling wit her?" Gunnar asked.

Again Hjelmer shook his head. *Leave it to Augusta.* As the eldest daughter, she'd always been extra sure of herself, as if she knew more than the younger ones. And since he'd been one of the two youngest, he, as well as Katy, had learned to stay out of her way when she got on a tear.

But he'd never wished anything bad on her. And right now all the traveling tales he'd heard, some of which he'd experienced himself, were coming home to roost. "Takk." Hjelmer started to leave, then turned back. "Let me know if you hear anything, okay?"

"Ja, sure." Gunnar went back to his machines, and Hjelmer headed for the boardinghouse. Dinner would be in full swing right about now, but he knew his mother needed every bit of good news he could dredge up.

"Thank the Lord for that," Bridget said as soon as he finished telling her.

"We'll see her on the train in the morning, you just watch." Hjelmer hoped he sounded more confident than he felt. If she didn't show and didn't wire, he could be sure he would be the one sent to find her. Talk about a wild-goose chase.

"You want to eat?" Bridget gestured to the table set up in the kitchen for family and help to eat at after the guests were served.

"No thanks. Penny will be waiting for me. Don't worry, Mor, all right?"

Bridget leveled a gaze at him that reminded him of when he was young. "Hjelmer, I don't worry. I let God do that. After all, He never sleeps anyway."

The twinkle in her faded blue eyes cheered him up again. So many times he had heard her say those very words. Surely she must believe them or she'd not say them. Surely.

Now, if only he could adopt her strong faith. The thought of what losing another daughter, this so soon after Katy, might do to his mother was more than he cared to contemplate. Or what it would do to all the rest of them either.

He waved to Goodie and Ilse as he left through the dining room and crossed back to the general store, which was owned by his wife, Penny, not by him, as so many people thought at first. The blacksmith shop next door was his, and he also managed the First Bank of Blessing, which occupied a room off the store. Sam Lincoln, a Negro he had met working the railroad, now did most of the blacksmithing, and Anner Valders most of the bank work, since Hjelmer had been elected to the Constitutional Congress for North Dakota. Lately he'd been gone much more than he'd been home.

"Dinner's ready, soon as you wash up," Penny said as he entered the back door. She turned from stirring something on the stove and gave him a smile that chased away his worries. He crossed the room to drop a kiss on the back of her neck on the way to the washbasin.

"While it smells mighty good in here, you smell even better." He inhaled and kissed her again.

"Hjelmer, someone might come in."

"Let them." He ran a tender finger down the slight groove in the back of her slender neck.

"That tickles."

He could hear that slightly breathless tenor of her voice, the one that made him feel as though he could conquer the world. She leaned back against him and turned her face up to meet his lips, her long lashes sweeping down over eyes of gray or blue, depending on her mood. Today they sparkled azure as high mountain lakes in the spring.

"You taste even better than you smell." He whispered the words against lips that had gone soft beneath his. While she came barely up to his chin, her slender body housed a character strong enough to run her own store and a heart big enough to help make sure no one in the Blessing area went without the necessities. She could charm the quilting women of the church into fighting for women's rights and cause her husband to dream dreams that brought him home again as soon as he could possibly manage.

Like now. Her fragrance teased his senses as his lips teased hers.

"Aren't you hungry?" She kissed him again.

"Um."

"Anybody here?" The call came from the store. Neither had heard the bell over the door jingle.

Penny shook her head. "Just when this was getting interesting. Where do you suppose Ephraim has gone? He said he'd mind the store."

"I'll take care of the store while you put the dinner on the table." Hjelmer patted her behind as he stepped back. "We'll have to pick this up again — later?"

Penny could feel the flame up her neck, and she knew it wasn't the stove. Perhaps this would be the time. She'd been praying for a baby ever since they were married, but more than three years had passed, and God still hadn't seen fit to open her womb. The thought of being barren gave her nightmares more times than she cared to count.

As soon as Hjelmer returned, she set a platter of fried chicken on the table next to the bowl of potatoes and went back for the gravy. "So what did you find out from Erickson?"

"Nothing." Hjelmer took his seat and tucked the napkin into the neck of his shirt to protect it from grease splatters. He really should have changed first. "He said he hasn't heard a thing about problems on the rail lines. Mor says she isn't worrying, but she's —"

"Letting God do that." Penny finished his sentence for him.

"That's fine for her. I'm worrying enough for both of us."

"Hjelmer, so Augusta missed a train. That can happen to anyone. If one was late somewhere —"

"I know. I've given myself all the rational arguments, but something about this really bothers me."

Penny took her chair and laid her hand on his. "Would you say the grace?"

They bowed their heads, and after asking the blessing on the food, Hjelmer added, "And please, heavenly Father, bring Augusta here on tomorrow's train." Penny joined him in the "amen" and passed him the chicken.

School had let out for the day, and the mail had been sorted into the named slots on the wall, so things were quieting down again when Olaf Wold, Kaaren's uncle and manager of the sack house, came in the store. Penny looked up from her order pad. "Onkel Olaf, good to see you."

"Not so good, I think, Penny. Is Hjelmer around?"

"Back helping Sam with something, I believe. I'll call him." Before the man could answer she darted to the back door and called her husband. When he didn't answer right away, she stepped down to the stoop. "Hjelmer!"

"What?"

She could tell he was in the smithy, so she raised her voice and called him again.

"I'm coming."

As soon as he stepped outside, she beckoned him with a flurry of her hand. "Hurry."

Hjelmer broke into a trot. "What is it?"

"Olaf is here, and I got a feeling something is bad wrong."

Hjelmer followed her into the store to find Olaf studying the Grand Forks *Herald* that Penny had taken to pinning to the wall.

"What is it?" Hjelmer got right to the point after the greeting.

"Well, you know that when the train comes in, the baggage handlers cart everything into the sack house and people pick up their belongings there?"

"Ja." Hjelmer wished Olaf would talk faster but knew that wasn't the way of the man.

"Well, we were all kind of busy about then, what with waiting for your sister and all . . ." Olaf shook his head. "I just now got to checking on what was left, and I found a small trunk." He paused.

"A small trunk." Hjelmer leaned forward. "And?"

"And, well, the trunk has your sister's name on it. Augusta Bjorklund, clear as you please."

Hjelmer closed his eyes, but when he opened them again, the look on Olaf's face hadn't changed. Neither had his pronouncement. Augusta's trunk sat in the sack house. So where in thunderation was Augusta?

"You want I should go tell Bridget?"

Hjelmer thought quickly. "No, I think not. No need to get her all worried tonight. Surely Augusta will be here on the first train in the morning, and then Mor would have worried for nothing."

"If you think so." But the look on Olaf's face shouted his disagreement louder than any words.

"Ja, I think that is best." Hjelmer wasn't sure if he was trying to convince Olaf or himself.

"I don't know," Penny said after Olaf left the store. "I think Bridget would want to know right off. At least I would."

"Ja, well, she's not your mother, and . . ." He stopped at the wounded look in her eyes. Taking a deep breath, he spoke more softly. "I'm sorry, Penny, I just think this is best." He shook his head again. "I don't know what to do."

"Well, your mor would start to pray and ask everyone else to pray too. She would remind God that He promises to take care of his chicks and lambs and that He needs to get right on this one."

Hjelmer halfway turned his head and watched her from the corner of his eye, a smile making his eyes crinkle around the edges. "You sound so much like her, I swear I would have thought she walked right into this room. I know Mor says she doesn't worry, that she lets God handle that, but this is her only remaining daughter, and" — he rubbed his temples with the forefinger of each hand — "I don't want to be the one who tells her, that is for certain sure."

"Let's go do it now together."

Hjelmer shook his head. "Let me finish that poker out in the smithy, and I'll take her that at the same time. After supper would be a better time, I think."

The bell over the door tinkled, and Penny put a smile on her face for the customer. "Why, Pastor Solberg, what brings you in?"

"Good afternoon, Penny. I need the mail, and Mary Martha needs a packet of needles." He glanced over at the half wheel of cheese under a glass cover. "I'll take a wedge of that too." He spread his fingers about three inches apart. "About this big."

"So how is school going?" Penny handed

him the mail from his slot on the back wall and took out a knife to cut the cheese.

"Good. Seems strange to have started so early this year, but now that we're almost a state, we have to abide by more rules. The big boys are still out helping with harvest, so I have extra time for the little ones. I think that Andrew is going to be as smart as his big brother. My, the things he comes up with."

"Those two sure are different, though." Penny set the wedge of cheese on a piece of brown paper. "Anything else?"

Solberg leaned closer, lowering his voice. He nodded toward the sewing center in the west end of the store. "I want to buy Mary Martha one of the machines for Christmas. What do you think?"

"I think she'll throw her arms around you and kiss you silly."

"Penny Bjorklund!" John Solberg stepped back and stared at her, his eyes wide and red creeping up his neck.

"Oh, pshaw, as my tante Agnes says." Penny chuckled. "You're married now. You got to get used to a bit of teasing."

"I know, but . . ." He fanned his face with the two letters in his hand. "You caught me by surprise, that's all." He looked back at the Singer sewing machine atop its cabinet. "You think she'll like it, then?"

"Yes, I *know* she'll like it. And then she won't need to come and use mine." Penny nearly bit her tongue. *Please, God, don't let him ask why she's using my machine.* Mary Martha had special-ordered some fine black wool and was sewing her husband a new suit for Christmas. Even with the sewing machine, the garment was only slowly taking shape.

The bell tinkled, and Solberg turned to see who had arrived.

Penny breathed a sigh of relief and sent her thanks heavenward.

"Ah, there you are, Pastor. I went by your house first, and Mrs. Solberg said you were here." Mrs. Valders wiped the back of her hand across her forehead. "Sure is warm for September, don't you think?"

"That it is. Is there something I can do for you?" Pastor Solberg picked up his brown-wrapped packet of cheese.

"Yes. It's about the letter you sent home with the boys." She shook her head. "Those two." But her smile had the hesitancy one wore at the prospect of bad news.

But at the same time Penny could see a slight glint of pride in the woman's eyes.

She and her husband, Anner Valders, who helped Hjelmer with the banking, had adopted two boys who had hitched rides on trains clear from New York City. They had slipped off the train in Blessing to steal something to eat and got caught in the store. Toby and Jerry White Valders had a well-earned reputation for causing trouble.

"Well, I warned them about chasing the little girls with a garter snake, and instead of administering the paddle, I said I would write you a letter."

"I know what the letter said. Did anyone get hurt?" Hildegunn Valders rolled her eyes and straightened her shoulders.

"No, but the boys need to learn more kindness for others, so I wanted to talk with you and Mr. Valders about what we could do to help them learn that." When she started to say something, he raised a hand. "I know they have had a hard life until now, and that is why I believe we both need to pray for them and think of ways to help them become the fine young men God meant for them to be."

Penny wanted to ask how the snake had fared, but she kept her thoughts to herself. She remembered the times she'd been the one chased and had her pigtails pulled by an older boy.

"So if you and Mr. Valders would bring the boys by my home one of these evenings, I think we should all sit down and have a talk. Don't you agree?"

"I . . . I guess." Mrs. Valders turned to Penny. "Could I please have our mail?"

"Here you go." Penny fetched the envelope and handed it across the counter. "Sure seems strange without Anner here."

"I know. At home too, but he should be back tomorrow or the next day. That meeting had better have been a good one. Land sakes, going clear to Bismarck to help with the banking laws." She nodded to both Penny and the pastor, then sailed out the door.

"So where was Andrew during all this?" Penny asked Pastor Solberg as soon as Hildegunn was out the door.

"Locked in Thorliff's arms. He was going to take a stick, a big stick, to both of those boys for scaring Ellie and Deborah."

"I can just imagine." Penny had no trouble picturing Andrew on the warpath. "What did you do?"

"Toby and Jerry spent the afternoon splitting and stacking wood. And I sent the letter home. I almost took out the paddle, but I've never believed that is necessary for a good education. Might have to change my opinion, though, with those two." He sighed and shook his head. "I'll be back to fill out the paper work on that sewing machine."

"Good. We'll be ready."

Solberg turned back. "Any word on Miss Bjorklund?"

Penny shook her head. "But her trunk is here."

"Oh dear. How is Bridget?"

"We're going to talk with her again after supper."

"If it isn't one thing, it's another. I'll be praying for that young woman's safety."

Penny walked with him to the door and turned the sign to "Closed" as he left. Now to get some supper on the table.

Lamps were lit by the time she and Hjelmer had made their way to the boardinghouse. They found Bridget sitting in her rocking chair on the back porch while the others were finishing the cleanup in the kitchen.

"Are you all right, Mor?" Hjelmer asked after closing the screen door behind him.

"Ja, just needed a few breaths of cooler air." Bridget put her knitting back in the basket at her feet and looked up at her son. "Why is it you are here?"

Hjelmer sighed. "I have something to tell you."

"I figured that. What is it?"

"Olaf found Augusta's trunk in the sack house several hours after the train left. The baggage carriers left it there."

"So . . . so how could that be? Where . . . where is Augusta?"

"I wish I knew. I only wish I knew."

Bridget rocked for a few minutes, then looked up at her son. "You must go and find her."

"Mor . . . I . . . ah . . . we . . ." He looked to Penny for assistance, but she shrugged and shook her head.

"Perhaps she'll be here in the morning."

"If she's not, you will have to go look."

Penny felt her stomach lurch. How were they ever going to have a baby if Hjelmer was never home? Where in the whole country of America was Augusta?

8

Between Ipswich and Kane's Ranch
September 1

Augusta had never seen such hail.

"Come on!" Only Kane's hand on her arm pulling her with him told her what he wanted. They clambered over the side of the wagon, and she followed him under the long wooden bed. Then motioning her to stay, he crawled out to unhook the traces from the singletrees, and then with icy fingers he unhooked the wagon tongue and brought the horses around to tie them to the wheels.

The hail had beaten his wide-brimmed felt hat down around his ears. Several hailstones the size of walnuts rested in the crown of his hat.

Augusta stared at him, her eyes wide and her mouth trembling. The ground lay white around them, and hail bounced like popcorn on a hot stove. Mor had written of hail like this, but Augusta had really thought her mother was exaggerating a bit.

She hadn't been.

With her arms clenched tightly around her raised knees to keep her skirts covering her modestly, she turned to look at the man who rejoined her under the protection of the wagon bed.

"It will be all right. The hail doesn't usually last long."

The sound of his voice and the smile he gave her did bring a modicum of comfort. If only she could understand what he said. When he smiled, kindness radiated from his face, his crinkled eyes warmed, and the cleft in his strong chin deepened. She allowed herself to study the man sitting cross-legged beside her. His dark hair with warm glints reminded her of the mink pelt one of her brothers had trapped once. Instantly, the full memory returned — the silky warmth of the fur and intricacies upon intricacies of color, just like this man's hair. Would it feel the same? She almost flinched with such an unseemly thought threading her mind. What could she call him? Surely not "that man" or "hey, you." She had an idea he had given her his name back at the station, but with all the worry about where she was and where her trunk had gone, his words had flown past her like birds before a hawk.

She returned to her study. His shoulders were broad enough to match those of her Bjorklund male relatives, and he was tall enough to make her look up to him. Since she'd been given extra height for a woman, at five foot nine she'd been called a giant when she was growing up. But the teasing had stopped when she could jump farther and run faster than most of her schoolmates. If her mor had known of her unladylike behavior, she'd have been scolded for sure. But then that wouldn't have been unusual either.

When he stared back at her, she felt heat blooming up her neck, so she rested her cheek on her dark skirt. Right now she was grateful for the wool of her skirt and her fitted jacket. How could it have gotten so cold, so fast? What a strange country this was.

Where was Blessing?

She hesitated to ask him again, since every time she mentioned it, he only nodded and said something that included the word "blessing." *Oh, Lord, never did I think to be in such confusing circumstances. Now, I know you see all, and this country is yours just like my homeland is. And I know you know where I am and what is going to happen, but could you please, in your mercy, share a bit of this information with me?*

She stared out at the hail-covered ground, anywhere to keep her gaze from wandering back to the man beside her. Was it getting lighter? Surely it must be. Surely if one of those balls of ice touched her cheek, it would melt in a flash.

Kane's thoughts turned to prayer as he in turn watched her. *Oh, Lord above, she, this wife of mine, is so lovely, far beyond what I dreamed of or deserve. Your mercy is indeed higher and wider than I can comprehend. Now, if you could, please give me a hint as to how to talk with her. See, she looks at me and then away. She is not only lovely, but modest too. And I have a feeling that while she is dressed so fashionably now, she isn't afraid of hard work, and on the ranch there will be plenty of that. See how she takes this hailstorm in her stride? She is not cowering or crying. She followed my swift instructions without a qualm, even though she didn't understand what I said. Oh, God, my God, how gracious thou art to me a sinner, albeit right now a very happy one.*

He followed her gaze at the world beyond the wagon wheels and smiled reassuringly when she glanced at him. "Yes, the storm is passing. We'll be on our way soon." He hoped they would get another hour or two of travel in before it grew too dark.

Within a few minutes he began to hitch the team back up, then turned around to see her striding off to the west, kicking up drifts of hail as she strode so purposefully. He started to call her back and then stopped. Of course. Why hadn't he thought? And there weren't even very many bushes for her to hide behind. He finished hooking the traces back to the hooks on the ends of the singletrees and, whistling under his breath, scraped hailstones out of the back of the wagon so they wouldn't melt and ruin the supplies.

When she returned he touched a finger to the brim of his hat and helped her back up on the wagon seat. *When I was learning Mandan, how did we do it?* He thought back. *One word at a time, that's what, so I guess we start now. That'll be one way to pass the hours.*

He turned to her and pointed to his chest. "I am Kane."

She smiled back at him.

He pointed to her. "Now say your name."

Her eyes clouded like the sky bowl above

when the wind blew up from the west. She shrugged.

"I am Kane." He spoke more slowly and louder.

Her brows straightened into a flat line, then she nodded and pointed to him. "I am Kane."

He resisted the urge to laugh and pointed to his chest again. "Kane."

She nodded. "Kane." *So what did the other words mean? Oh, of course.* She pointed to herself. "I am Augusta."

"Augusta?" Now it was his turn to look confused. *But I thought your name was Asta. At least that's the way I read your signature on the letter. Perhaps she is like me and not using her given name but just a part of it. After all, Thomas was my father's name also, and who wants to be called Elkanah when my Mandan friends couldn't pronounce it anyway?*

Much to her relief, he smiled again and repeated their names, pointing to each as he said them. So she did the same. When she looked back at him, his smile had warmed by twenty degrees, just like the sun that was peeking out to turn the hail into slush and trickling water.

She quickly looked out over the horses' broad rumps, then down to her hands

110

clenched in her lap. Why did the sight of his warm, gold-flecked eyes make her want to fan her face?

"Augusta?"

She turned back to look at him.

He lifted his hat. "Hat."

Ah, he was trying to teach her his language. "Hat." She pointed to her own, the soft velvet somewhat worse for having been pummeled by the hail.

The cloud flitted over his face this time before he smiled and nodded. "Hat." He touched his and then hers.

Now it was her turn to smile and repeat both words. He continued with more words — shirt, boots, wagon, horses. He decided to stay away from pants and skirt. Some things were better off left alone.

When a crow flew over, he pointed to that, again naming it and wishing he could figure a way to tell her that the word she was learning didn't apply to all birds. The sun setting behind the sandhills made him twitch the horses to a trot. He'd better be looking for a place to camp.

Augusta turned the words over in her mind, mentally pointing to each of the things they'd named and reviewing. Wait until they got to Blessing. Such stories she would have to tell her family. Getting to

Blessing reminded her that she hadn't a stitch of clean clothes with her. They were all packed in her trunk, wherever in all this vast country her trunk had gone. What she wouldn't give for one of her cotton dresses instead of her wool traveling outfit. At least she had her hairbrush and a comb in her carpetbag.

When the man beside her pulled on the right rein and turned the horse off onto what could somewhat be called a road, she looked at him, wishing she could ask what he was doing.

"Whoa."

The team stopped, and as soon as the harness ceased jingling, she could hear what sounded like water running. She looked at Kane and raised her eyebrow.

He nodded. "You heard right — water. Over there." He pointed to some rocks and trees dead ahead. He stepped down from the wagon and went about unhitching the horses, talking to them while he freed them from their traces. He stopped between the two at their heads and raised his voice to say her name.

"Augusta."

"Ja?"

He beckoned with one hand and held the horses with the other. "Come."

With a shrug she climbed down from the wagon seat and walked with him between the rocks to see a cattail-rimmed pond fed by a small creek that gurgled around the rocks and clumps of grasses.

"Oh." She clasped her hands to her breast. Water. Finally more than a dipperful at a time. Perhaps he would let her wash, and she could brush her hair and make herself presentable for when she finally got to Blessing. Surely it couldn't be much farther.

She refused to let herself think of her mother's description of land so flat you could see for miles in any direction. That surely wasn't what she was seeing. But they would get there soon. Most assuredly they would get to the wide flat land soon.

Kane stuck his hands in his back pockets as he let the horses drink. He'd let them graze while he started a fire and got their supper going. He had plenty of food, having picked up supplies in Ipswich, and there was still bread, cheese, and part of the cake left from their basket dinner. Maybe if he set a snare, they would have fresh rabbit for breakfast. He pulled the horses' heads up before they drank their fill, since they were a bit warm from the trotting, but he had wanted to get to this spot where he knew there was water and grass and dead-wood for a fire.

"You want to wash?" He pantomimed scrubbing his face and hands, pointing to the water at the same time.

Her smile kicked him in the gut.

"Ja."

Her nod made him wish he could offer more, like a privy and a bathtub and a real bed. And himself. At that thought, he hustled the horses back to the wagon and divested them of their harness before hobbling them in a nearby patch of grass.

Augusta returned to the wagon and reached in the back for her bag. Taking the bar of soap and a washcloth and towel, she made her way back to the creek. While the water felt chilly, it wasn't cold, and after laying her jacket across a rock, she knelt and dipped in the cloth. She closed her eyes in bliss and held the dripping cloth up to her face.

Later, washed at least partly, her hair combed and rebound in the bun at the base of her neck, and her jacket tossed over a bush to air, she sat across the fire from the man she only knew as Kane and watched as he turned ham steaks in the pan and stirred some potatoes he'd sliced for frying. *If*, she decided, *there is a man for me in this new land, I would like him to be like this man here.* While Elmer had been good-looking in an icy Nordic way, this man radiated kindness, like the fire radiated heat. Here he was taking her all the way to Blessing and cooking her supper besides.

She sighed in contentment. The thought made her smile. It had been a long time since she felt this elusive feeling, how long she didn't dare contemplate. Out here in the middle of who knew where, far from anything she'd ever known, with a man she couldn't even talk with, she felt contented. How Mor would chuckle at that.

"This is ready."

She looked up and met the smile that danced in his eyes like the golden flames before him. A tingle ran down her spine and up again, even making its way to her fingertips. She nodded, and when he came around the fire with a plate for her in his hand, her hand shook taking it.

What in the world was going on with her? She studied her hand like some strange specimen that surely belonged to another.

"Mmm." She inhaled the smoky fragrance of the meat and, as usual, nodded and smiled to show her appreciation. "Mange takk."

"I have a feeling that means thank you." Kane returned for his own plate and came around the fire again to sit beside her. "You are more than welcome." That smile of hers could turn a man inside out. How in all the mercies of heaven had she lived this long without being married? What was the matter with those Norwegian men?

He continued the lesson in language as they ate, identifying plate, fork, ham, potatoes, and coffee, along with the cup that contained it. When he poured her a cup of hot coffee, she smiled as though he'd just given her a priceless gift. Blowing on the hot liquid, she studied him across the rim.

As Kane caught her looking at him and watched the light dancing in her eyes, he forgot what he was doing until the sizzle of overflowing coffee caught his attention. At the same moment, his finger registered that hot coffee had splattered on it.

He set the cup down with a clatter and stuck his finger in his mouth to cool it. "Ow!" When that didn't help a whole lot, he splashed his hand in the water bucket.

He could tell by the way she had averted her eyes and was now being careful not to look at him that she was fighting back laughter.

"That was hot!"

A tiny giggle escaped her clenched lips. Actually it was almost a little snort but decidedly ladylike.

"Go ahead. Laugh if you want." He tried to look wounded but failed utterly. When he saw her shoulders shaking, he started to laugh himself.

He shook the water off his hand and stuck his finger back in his mouth. That did it.

Her laugh played like dust motes dancing in a shaft of sunlight, airy and phosphorescent and with perfect aim. His heart constricted, and it was all he could do to breathe.

Yes, he had a wife, and yes, he had hoped and prayed he would love her easily, but so soon? He took a seat beside her on the blanket he had spread on the ground, and they both sipped their coffee, listening to the night sounds and the crackle of the fire. While his arm ached to circle her waist, his mind screamed, *Too soon. Don't rush!*

Obeying his mind took great self-control — and a walk around the fire to put the supper things away. With a long spoon he tucked some coals in the cast-iron spider to start the fire with in the morning, then unfolded two quilts and two elk hides. He spread the quilts over the hides to keep the moisture in the ground from seeping up and under the wagon in case it rained.

He wanted to put them together in one bed. He knew he had the right, for after all, they were married, but something told him not to. The same something that had said "Don't rush" a bit earlier. He'd waited thirty-five years for a wife, and a few more hours or days wouldn't hurt.

"I'm going to water the horses again and give them some oats, so if you want to . . . ah . . . well, the bed's ready. Take either one." Without waiting for an answer, he strode away as if a pack of starving coyotes were yipping after him.

Augusta sat by the dying coals and watched him get all flustered. She figured from his actions that one bed was hers, her only concern being the proximity of the two bedrolls under the wagon. But then the wagon bed was not big enough for them to be too far apart.

Should she ask him to sleep under the stars instead? And maybe get hailed on? She decided against that. After all, there was space between them.

After heading the opposite direction and wishing for an outhouse with an actual seat, she returned before he did and took off her shoes, tucking them under the quilt farthest from the fire. Then, with her legs bent underneath her, she undid the net that confined her hair and finger-combed it over her shoulder so she could begin braiding it. The wagon bed above didn't give her enough room to brush the waist-length waves well, but even so, the nightly ritual added to the sense of peace.

She had the quilt well tucked around her shoulders as she faced the other way when he came to bed.

Even so, every nerve end she owned stood at attention and saluted as he tugged off his boots and, with a deep sigh, settled into the other bed.

"Good night, Augusta."

"Ja, god natt."

Long after he'd settled into the even breathing of sleep, she lay wide awake, hearing every rustle and sigh, listening to the horses graze, and finally, tucking her head under the covers to get away from the pesky mosquitoes.

The fragrance of boiling coffee brought her awake when the sun was just cracking the eastern horizon. She turned on her side and watched the man squatting beside the fire. He was turning something in a pan that smelled delicious. *Someday,* she thought, half praying, *I'd like a man like Kane to be my husband. That is, if marriage is what you have in mind for me, Lord. After all, you've taken two almost-husbands from me already. Someday, ah yes, someday.*

Throwing back the covers, she adjusted her skirts around herself before crawling out from under the wagon. How had he gotten up, started the fire, fetched the water that she could see steaming at the side of the crackling blaze, and cooked breakfast all without her hearing a thing?

She smoothed her hair back, fearing she looked like one of the trolls in Norway emerging fresh from a life under the bridge. Come to think of it, the bed of the wagon did look something like a bridge.

"Good morning."

"Good morning." She repeated his words back, they being so similar to the Norwegian she was sure she knew what he meant.

"Breakfast is almost ready."

She smiled and nodded in return. Oh, to know what he said. He lifted the pan and motioned her to sit. Ah, so that was it. She smoothed her hair, tucking strands into the braid again, and stooped back under the wagon for her jacket that she had rolled carefully and placed under her head for a pillow. The air felt like fall had sneaked in overnight. After shaking out the wrinkles as best she could, she slid her arms into the sleeves and took her seat.

"Coffee?" He raised the pot.

"Ja, please." *Now if he would just teach her the words for please and thank you.*

This time his fingers touched hers when he handed her the full mug of coffee. Like a flash, her arm was warm clear to her shoulder. "Mange takk."

"You are indeed welcome." He smiled at the question that crossed her face.

When she nodded, he continued. "Mange takk." He pointed to her. "Thank you." He pointed to himself.

"Thank you." She nodded with another smile, this one wider than the last. Now if he would just tell her the word for "please." How did one ask for words like this? She blew on her steaming coffee, grateful for something in her hands to keep busy.

By the time they'd finished breakfast, put out the fire, and harnessed the horses, the sky had filled with long Vs of honking and quacking waterfowl on their migration south. The wild song made her stop brushing her hair and watch in wonder.

121

Never had she seen such numbers of flying birds at one time.

Kane stopped in the act of setting the collar on the off horse to watch the wonder on her face. Her high cheekbones were pink from the early-morning chill, and her hair rippled liquid gold down over her shoulders as she paused in her brushing to stare at the sky. When she looked toward him, he could have sworn bits of summer sky came down and smiled from her eyes.

His breath caught in his throat. He started to say something but smiled instead to give his heart time to flutter back to where it belonged. When he could speak, he hooked the last trace and motioned toward the seat. "We'd best be on the road. Home is still a long way off." He watched as she deftly worked her hair into a bun at the back of her neck. *What a beauty she is. Thank you, Father.*

Language lessons continued sporadically as the trotting horses ate up the miles up and down rolling hills and past flat valleys where sod houses told of other settlers. Herds of cattle could be seen once in a while and farmers either finishing harvest or plowing fields.

One thing Augusta realized early on was that the farms were few and far between.

Shouldn't they be getting close to Blessing sometime soon? Every time they crested a hill, she hoped to see the town ahead or the flat land she read about in the letters back home. And each time she kept in a sigh of disappointment.

Kane watched her, wondering at the sadness he sensed more than once. Was she not happy with the land they were crossing? If not, the ranch wouldn't appeal to her either. His land looked much like this.

Black clouds piled on the horizon again, and the wind kicked up, bringing with it a chill that seemed even colder after the heat of the day. Dusk fell early as the clouds drew nearer and lower. Kane reached behind the seat and pulled up the elk hides he had rolled and set there. He handed one to Augusta and motioned for her to put it over her head while he did the same with the other.

The rain hit with drops the size of the hail the day before and almost as cold. Knowing they had only about five miles to go, Kane kept the team at a trot, all the while fighting with his other hand to keep the hide from blowing away. Rain poured down the hair side and soaked every bit of them not covered by the hides. Mud splashed up from the horses' hooves and splattered the hem of her skirt and his pants.

But when he motioned for Augusta to climb over the seat back and huddle down in the wagon bed, she shook her head and clamped the hide covering more tightly.

If the horses hadn't known where to turn off, he might have missed the track to the ranch in the rainy dark. The dog barking brought Morning Dove to the door, and the golden opening looked good as heaven's gates to the weary and drenched travelers. Together Morning Dove and Lone Pine helped Augusta from the wagon seat and into the house.

Augusta's teeth were chattering so hard, she couldn't talk, and the shaking consumed the remainder of her body as well. It wasn't until she saw their faces by the lamplight that she realized they must be of another race. Perhaps these were the Indians she'd heard so much about. But it didn't matter. All she cared about was the heat that emanated from the fire in a stone fireplace big enough to roast an ox whole.

Kane and the two were talking together, but since she didn't understand a word they said, she just turned to face the fire, warming her hands and face. If only she had dry clothes to change into. Even a blanket to put around her while her clothing dried. She heard the other woman leave the room, and Kane came to stand beside her.

He nodded to the man with mahogany skin and black hair that was braided much like she did hers at night. "Lone Pine." Kane bobbed his head just a mite, so Augusta repeated the name. When the woman returned, he nodded at her and said, "Morning Dove."

Morning Dove brought blankets with her and a garment over one arm. "You men, go now." She waved for them to leave, and when they did, she turned with a smile to Augusta. Motioning for her to take off her wet things, she held out a blanket to warm by the fire and then wrapped it around the still-shivering woman when she had stripped to her underthings. "Now take off rest."

Augusta shook her head when she realized the meaning of the gestures and clamped the blanket more tightly around her.

"Nei, I will be fine."

But Morning Dove ignored the pleading and gestured again. "You take them off." Her words carried a warning that made Augusta fear the woman would follow through if she didn't do as asked. While Morning Dove held the blanket, Augusta stripped to her skin, letting her wet garments pool at her feet.

The Indian woman guided her to a hide-covered chair she had pulled nearer the fire and gently pushed her into it, then she proceeded to remove Augusta's boots and stockings. Her dark eyes radiated nothing but friendship, and by this time Augusta was too tired to care.

She ate the food they put before her, each bite taking an act of will, for she only wanted to go to sleep. Even the steaming coffee did nothing more than lull her into the twilight of near sleep. When Morning Dove took her to the bedroom and handed her the nightgown she'd found in the carpetbag and dried at the fire, Augusta murmured a thank-you and, after slipping it over her head, crawled beneath the covers of the bed.

Thank you, Father . . . was all she managed before falling into the depths of sleep.

Sometime in the night she almost surfaced enough to feel heat coming from near her. She turned to the source and slipped back under the waves of rest.

A rooster crowed and another answered. Augusta smiled at the comforting sound and stretched as she yawned herself awake. Her hand thumped into a decidedly warm and solid body beside her. She looked to her right, directly into warm golden eyes.

With a shriek Augusta flung herself from the bed and stared at the smiling man in openmouthed horror. "What do you think you are doing in my bed?"

9

Blessing
September 2

Augusta was not on the next morning's train. Nor the next.

"You don't really mean for me to go try and find her?" Hjelmer stared at his mother, not doubting for a moment that was what she really meant.

Bridget shook her head, a wisp of snowy hair waving on one side of her heat-reddened face.

He breathed a sigh of relief.

"No, you will not just try. You *will* find her!" Bridget clapped her hands on her roundly padded hips and glared at her recalcitrant son. "She is the only sister you have left, after all, and she might be in terrible trouble. How would you know?"

She had him there. Never would he share with her some of the horror stories he'd heard of lost immigrants, women especially "But, Mor . . ."

"No 'but, Mor.' " She even imitated his voice. "Which train will you be leaving on?"

"Look." Hjelmer held out his hands palms up in a peace offering. "I never said I wouldn't go, but it seems foolish to me to run off on a wild-goose chase when she could be coming tomorrow."

"Then why hasn't she sent a telegram?" Bridget had visited the sad man behind the green eyeshade, Gunnar Erickson, at the sack house both morning and afternoon since her daughter failed to arrive.

"Maybe she has run out of money." He recognized his mistake before the words finished passing his lips.

"Oh, well, that makes your staying here in your comfortable home all right, doesn't it? What if she is starving to death?"

Wisely he refrained from answering *that* question. "All right." He raised his hands in the air and let them fall in surrender. "I will wait today, and if she doesn't come, then I will go to St. Paul tomorrow to see if there is any knowledge of her there." Since the trunk got here, that means it was transferred to the St. Paul and Pacific. Going to Chicago didn't bear thinking of. How in the world was he supposed to find her anyway? While the flood of Norwegians to the new land had slowed the last year or two, still, one young woman — or rather not so young, he thought a bit spitefully — who didn't speak a word of English and had foolishly started out on her own rather than waiting for a group, well . . . It certainly wasn't going to be easy to find her.

Leave it to Augusta! He conveniently forgot the many times she had bailed him out of trouble in his growing-up years and only remembered her tendency to order her baby brother and the others around. Augusta had always thought she knew best.

Bridget stared down at hands clenched in her apron. "Mange takk, and go with God."

It might just take one of God's miracles to find my sister. Hjelmer shook his head. "I'll try to stop in to see you in the morning before I leave. Better get back on over home and get things caught up before I go." He thought of the stack of letters he needed to answer and the area people he needed to talk with to determine how people wanted him to vote on upcoming issues of the Congress. He should have already been back in Bismarck, but between the bank, the smithy, and his machinery sales, he had more than enough to occupy three men, and now he had to head east on what he hoped was not, but feared was, a wild-goose chase.

Should he contact the police in Grand Forks and St. Paul? How did one go about searching for a missing relative? Or a missing anyone for that matter. Hjelmer left the boardinghouse and strode up the newly installed boardwalk, walked past the general store, and turned in at the shed he'd built to house the smithy and what machinery he had in stock. With harvest about done and fall fieldwork starting, he had purchased several plows, discs, and harrows. If anyone wanted something else, he could order it for them.

"What's up, boss man?" Sam looked up from the piece of steel he was working in the forge.

Hjelmer rolled his eyes and shook his head. "Boss man, eh? I wish."

"You goin' then, huh?"

"You ever tried arguing with *my* mother?"

Sam shook his grizzled head. "No, an' ah don't plan to. She a woman with a mind of her own, but she got a heart big as this plain round about heah." His soft voice still bore traces of his southern upbringing.

"Somewhere ah heah tell that Norwegians be a hardheaded folk." The twinkle in his dark eyes brought a smile to Hjelmer's face. "But then you don' likely know 'bout that."

Hjelmer shook his head again and hooked his thumbs in his pockets. "Other than my mother and missing sister, how have things been going?"

"Ah keeps busy."

"I *know* that. I take it Eulah left with Haakan and Lars' threshing crew?"

"Yes, suh. She and Lily Mae took the little ones along too, and they's driving the cook wagon all over the countryside. Miz Bjorklund say they won't be home for a month or so, depending on the harvest."

"If it isn't any better than here, it'll be less than a month."

"Ah figured that. Us coming to Blessing be a right good thing." Sam gave the bellows a pump to keep his fire hot. "You got time to help rim a couple wheels this afternoon? Lemuel's goin' to help get the fire goin'. We chopped wood half the night. Keepin' wood to heat the rim is the hardest part."

"I know. Your idea to keep a couple of extra wheels handy has paid off well."

Sam ducked his head at the compliment,

then flashed a smile at the man beside him. "You ready to put off your go-to-meeting clothes and come do some *real* work?"

Hjelmer laughed and clapped his friend on the shoulder. "Let me go talk with Anner, and then I'll be back. Let's get those wheels fit as soon as possible. I saw a few more wobbly ones on wagons in line over at the sack house." A good part of the blacksmith business was shrinking the metal rims to fit on the wooden wheels of the area wagons, and while some farmers looked ahead and got this done before harvest, others didn't. Heating the rims and putting them back on the wheels, then shrinking them was a two-man job, along with a boy to keep the fires burning hot enough.

"Sorry I haven't been here much."

"Got to get that constitution done too." Sam pushed the metal bar back in the white-hot coals. "I been reading the paper 'bout all the arguin' goin' on. Give me a hot fire and iron to work any day. Guess I'll be helpin' milk cows for t'other Miz Bjorklund too."

"You wouldn't believe the fighting that goes on. Bunch a crooks, those railroad people. If they had their way they'd be running the whole West, and we'd all be working for them instead of the other way around."

Sam took a hammer and, laying the now white bar on the anvil, began the shaping that would make a heavy chain.

"See you later." Hjelmer tapped his shoulder and raised one hand in a salute.

Sam nodded and kept on with his labors.

Having just returned the night before from his meeting, Anner Valders nevertheless had the account books spread on the table in front of him and ready for Hjelmer's inspection. With one sleeve tucked in where his arm — lost in a threshing accident several years earlier — had been, he flipped pages and wrote in entries with the other hand as if he'd been one-handed all his life.

"Harvest is down, no thanks to the dry summer and that thunderstorm, and the shipping charges are up. Won't be as much capital to work with as in the past." Anner never had been one to look on the bright side.

"I know. Anyone having trouble keeping up with their loan payments?" Shifting gears from blacksmith to banker had never been a problem for Hjelmer.

"Not so far, but I hear talk that could be coming. If so, this would be the first fall we have defaults." He ran his finger down the page and pointed out a couple of names. "Here and here, maybe."

Hjelmer nodded.

"Your mother paid her entire loan back already."

"She did?"

"Talking about building on."

Hjelmer nodded. "Not surprised. There most likely will be some new regulations coming through after the constitution is ratified. I'll keep you up-to-date."

"If they let us alone, we could do business better."

"I know." Hjelmer looked around the room off the back of the store, noting the heavy safe, the ledgers lined up on the shelves alongside the books they'd accumulated on banking. Since both of them learned banking because the community decided to organize a bank, thanks to the women, they had collected as much as they could to help them do it right. So far, the First Bank of Blessing was a profitable concern, with all the investors having a say in who received loans and where the money was invested.

"You heard anything about the possibility of building one of those grain elevators here?" Anner closed the book they'd been looking at and put it back on the shelf.

"Ah, that rumor's been going on for years."

Anner shook his balding head. "No, but I heard from Henry over at the boarding-house that a company is seriously thinking of building one here."

Hjelmer narrowed his eyes and, nodding slightly, worried his bottom lip. "Not if we build one first. They aren't going to control us here in Blessing like they do in other places. I better check with the Farmers' Alliance board, see if they've heard anything. Is the amount of grain going through here getting to be too much for the sack house?"

"I don't hear Olaf complaining. 'Sides, there was more last year, and he did all right." Olaf Wold managed the sack house, where farmers brought their sacked grain to be weighed and stored until it could be shipped. They had never had a graft problem like in so many other areas of the state.

All this to be done, and I have to go looking for Augusta. Hjelmer kept his face blank. No sense letting the whole world know his family business.

"So you going to look for your sister?"

Hjelmer stifled a groan. Of course the women had been discussing things again. How they got any quilting done when they spent so much time solving the world's problems, or at least the problems around Blessing, he never knew.

"Ja, not because I want to, though." He studied the noncommittal look on the face of his friend and employee. "All right, I can tell you have something you want to say, so just say it."

"I'm not one to intrude."

"I know, I know, but the women . . ."

A twitch of the corner of Anner's narrow lips said the comment made them totally in agreement.

"It'll be worse'n finding a needle in a haystack." Anner shook his head, giving Hjelmer a pitying look. "Glad it's you, not me."

"Thank you so very much. You come up with any ideas on how I should accomplish this, don't stand on ceremony — tell me."

"Ja, I will. You thought about putting an ad in the papers?"

"No. She can't read English."

"No, but if someone is helping her, they could."

"True." Hjelmer fingered his chin. "Anything else?"

"When you are asking, you might mention the color of her eyes. Not too many people got the Bjorklund eyes. If your sister is like the men in your family her eyes will stand out."

"Good point." Hjelmer thought again. "And she is tall — for a woman, that is." He knew that her bossiness wouldn't be something that others would notice, but that's what he remembered most about her. But then he hadn't seen her for over five years. "Thanks, if you think of anything else, let me know. If she doesn't arrive, or we don't hear from her today, I'll be leaving on the early train tomorrow."

Hjelmer greeted several people shopping and visiting while waiting their turn for Penny in the store and made his way upstairs to their bedroom to change into work clothes. If only he had a picture of Augusta, that would be a big help. But he'd asked and Mor said no. And she had no idea what Augusta might have been wearing. She was given clothes often by the people she worked for and so was able to dress more fashionably than many others.

Setting wheel rims was preferable to setting legislators straight any day. Though his shoulders ached by suppertime and the burn on one hand reminded him that he needed to be more careful, when he sat down at the table, he knew he had accomplished something that would stay fixed for a while at least.

"What?" At Hjelmer's groan, Penny stopped ladling up the stew.

"Just trying to stretch these tired muscles of mine." He tilted his head to the side and flinched.

She set the plate in front of him and one at her place. "You say the grace."

They bowed their heads, and in the Norwegian they both learned at their mothers' knees, he said, "I Jesu navn, går vi til bords . . ."

At the amen Penny looked up. "You want I should give you a back rub tonight?"

"Do you have to wait until night?" Hjelmer looked outside. "Seems to me it is getting dark enough now."

"Hjelmer, you can wait that long." She passed him the plate of freshly sliced bread. "Besides, I made apple pie for dessert."

He made no comment and continued to stare out the window.

"Ephraim won't be able to run the store

tomorrow, so I've asked Anner to take care of it."

Hjelmer gave her a puzzled look.

"We have quilting tomorrow."

"Ah."

"And I have a new idea to propose."

"Ah."

"Hjelmer, you are not listening to me."

"Sure I am." He took another bite of stew.

"The house is on fire."

"Ah." He nodded.

"I'm in the family way."

"Good." Another nod.

Penny slammed her fork down on the table. "Hjelmer Bjorklund, where in the world are you?"

"Huh?" Hjelmer blinked and looked at the furious face of his wife. "What's wrong?"

"I'll tell you what's wrong. You have no idea what I've been saying, and here you are going off again tomorrow, and you might just as well have left tonight."

Hjelmer had the grace to look embarrassed. He reached a hand across the short space between them. "I'm sorry Penny, this trip to find Augusta has me flying in all directions. I have so much to do here, and I need to be in Bismarck. Instead, I'm

140

taking the train to Minneapolis on a wild-goose chase."

"What a thing to say! Your own sister is lost, and you think all that other . . . other . . ." She threw both hands in the air and shook her head so hard a pin fell out of the roll she wore around the base of her head. "Your mor is right."

Hjelmer half squinted his eyes, certain he wouldn't like to hear what his mor was right about. He kept his mouth shut, but his wife had the bit between her teeth, and like a runaway horse, she kept on going.

"Ever since you got elected to the Constitutional Congress, your work and your family have taken bottom place."

"Now, Penny . . ."

"Don't 'now Penny' me. You know I want to have a baby more than anything in this whole wide world, but how can we ever hope to have children if you aren't around to father them?"

"So how is my going to look for Augusta going to help that, unless you want to come with me?"

"Oh, sure. I come with you, and who will mind the store? And if we don't have the store, how will we have money to buy the train tickets so you can run all over the country?" Penny threw her napkin down and pushed back her chair. She surged to her feet so quickly that the chair tipped, making the red spots on her cheeks ever brighter. "Oh . . . oh, you . . . you . . ." She spun away and headed for the stairs to their bedroom, stomping so hard on the risers that he thought they might break.

"Well, I'll be . . ." Hjelmer slowly shook his head and watched the door curtain swirl in the wind from her passing. "Whatever did I do to deserve this?" He put the bread back in the bread keeper, scraped the dishes into the cat's bowl on the back stoop, and set them in the enameled pan Penny had ready with soap curls and water on the back of the stove. After brushing the crumbs off the tablecloth, he washed and rinsed the dishes and dumped the water on the rosebushes by the back door.

The kitchen seemed twice as big without Penny beside him and dreadfully silent. Even the chiming of the clock and the cat scratching at the back door couldn't penetrate the silence. Did she feel this silence when he was gone? On one hand he figured maybe he should go apologize, but on the other he couldn't see where he had done anything wrong. Other than miss a few words his wife said, but then . . . he thought back to the scene at the table. Had she said something about the house on fire? Surely not.

He banked the fire so that couldn't happen, and instead of moving the lamp over to the table by his chair so he could read the Grand Forks paper, he lit a candle and blew out the lamp. An early night wouldn't hurt; that was for sure.

"Penny?" He paused in the doorway to their bedroom.

The moonlight silvered the hair that now hung down over her shoulders as she sat by the window looking out at the moon-bathed fields. With her elbows propped on the windowsill and her back toward him, he could still tell she wasn't happy with something or someone, him in particular. Otherwise she'd have answered.

He set the candle in its holder on the dresser and crossed to stand behind his wife. Putting his hands on her shoulders, he began to work on the tense muscles of her neck and shoulders, then moved his thumbs up, massaging the base of her head. Leaning forward he inhaled her scent, fresh like she'd been bathing in the dew of the rose petals and hollyhocks.

Her head dropped forward so he could reach the sore places more easily. "I'm still angry at you, you know."

"I know." His hands made their way forward up her shoulders to the base of her slender neck. "I'm sorry, my love." He brushed her hair aside and kissed the tender skin at the back of her neck. "You smell so good."

"Keep rubbing, there." She tipped her head to the left, and a giggle escaped when he nibbled her neck rather than using his fingers.

"Aren't you getting chilly here in front of the open window?"

Penny sighed and let her head fall backward, revealing her throat for his questing lips. "It won't be long until we can't have the windows open anymore."

"I know." When she started to rise, he scooped her up in his arms and deposited her gently in the middle of their bed.

Perhaps a baby will come tonight, Penny thought as she surrendered to her husband's kisses.

Hjelmer woke to a rooster's crow and the sound of weeping. He threw back the covers and shivered in the brisk air. "Penny?" He followed the sound down the stairs to where his wife, tears streaming down her face, was starting the kitchen fire. "What is wrong?"

"Oh, Hjelmer, I want a baby so bad, and now I know God must hate me."

"Penny, dear one, shush such talk." He hugged her close and rubbed her back with both hands.

"B-but I've started my monthlies again, and now you are going away, and I . . ." She gripped the lapels of his robe with shaking fingers. "It's not fair. Other women get babies, lots of babies. What is wrong with me?"

10

Blessing
September 3

"This meeting is called to order. Ladies?"
Penny raised her voice. "Ladies."

The group of women gathered at
Blessing Lutheran Church settled into
their seats around the quilting frames and
the cutting tables. Someone hushed the
small child at her side, another picked up
her sewing kit that had fallen to the floor,
and finally silence reigned.

Penny looked over the group, wishing
she were anywhere but here. After the
crying bout in the early-morning hours,
she felt as though everyone could see
through her as if she were a wavy glass,
and all they felt was pity. Tante Agnes
Baard had already asked her what was
wrong, and Ingeborg and Kaaren both
looked at her with concern in their eyes.
She knew they'd have asked what was

wrong if she'd stood still long enough to let them.

Why can't someone else lead this group for a change? She kept the smile on her face with difficulty but she managed.

"Hildegunn, would you please lead us in prayer?" Penny glanced at Kaaren to see if it bothered her to not be asked, since she usually did this, but the serene smile that greeted her glance quieted that concern. Besides, Mrs. Valders had asked if she might do the devotions today. And since she asked, what else could Penny do?

Hildegunn Valders rose and, with her finger marking the place in her Bible, walked to the front of the room. Today they would hear the Scriptures in Norwegian, no matter that several of the newer people didn't speak Norwegian, including the pastor's wife, Mary Martha Solberg.

Penny tried to rub her head without anyone noticing. She, who never got headaches, had one now — a pounding one right behind her eyes. She knew it was from crying. Inside she still wept. She started to turn to Mary Martha to translate, but Kaaren was already doing that.

A bustling could be heard at the door, and Bridget entered, her cheeks red from her hurry. "Sorry I'm late."

Hildegunn nodded. "I'll wait."

Penny motioned for Bridget to sit beside her and patted her hand when she settled in.

"Hjelmer got off all right?" Bridget whispered. "He was supposed to see me before he left."

Penny nodded and looked up to catch Hildegunn's disapproving eye. That woman could make one feel like a recalcitrant child faster than anyone she knew. If she treated the two boys with that look all the time, no wonder they caused so much mischief. *They'd have been better off if they'd come to us.* Penny almost clapped her hand over her mouth in case she'd said the words aloud. How awful, how unchristian to even think such a thing. The Valderses were giving Toby and Jerry a good home, and it wasn't the adoptive parents' fault that the boys had lived on the streets most of their life.

Penny forced her eyes and her mind forward to concentrate on the Bible reading. Hildegunn did read well and had chosen a passage that reminded her how much God loved each of them.

She'd sure expressed her doubts of that this morning.

"I chose this passage because I needed

to be reminded not to worry. God loves me, and I love Him, and that is all that matters. All will be well."

Were those tears in Hildegunn's eyes?

Penny felt shame roll over her like a cloud of smoke. It made her eyes smart and her throat burn. All she'd been thinking about was her own disappointment, her own resentment. She heard a sniff from someone behind her.

"Shall we pray?" Again the wait for silence. "Father in heaven, we come before thee with painful hearts, with joyful hearts, with pleading hearts. Thou hast promised to be all that we need if your kingdom be first in our hearts and minds. Thou sayest that if we seek first thy kingdom and thy righteousness, all these things shall be added unto us. All will be well, Father, we seek thy precious face and look to do thy will. Today and forever, amen."

All the women echoed the amen and waited for Penny to take over the meeting again.

Penny hesitated to disturb the silence, for it seemed alive and pulsing with promise. The urge to kneel at her chair made her knees itch.

A voice started from another part of the room. "My Jesus, I love thee, I know thou art mine." Others joined. "For thee all the follies of sin I resign."

Penny could hardly force the words past the lump in her throat. "My gracious Redeemer, my Savior art thou. If ever I loved thee, my Jesus, 'tis now."

The melody rose, and she was sure she could see it curling around the altar and up above them, a sweet incense before the Lord.

When she got to her feet and stood in front again, she could see many eyes being wiped and noses being blown. And to think she'd wanted to stay home.

"I have a feeling we've met the Holy Ghost, the Comforter, here and now. Thank you, Hildegunn, and all the rest of you." Penny sniffed again and took out her handkerchief to wipe her nose. "The only old business I know of is the matter of the Morton girls' homestead, and I know that Zeb went down there this summer and took care of that. Does anyone else have any old business?"

She waited a minute and then asked, "Any new business?"

Agnes Baard raised her hand. At Penny's nod, she stood and faced the others. "Don't know if you all know about that new family who took over that crumbling soddy just north of us — the Rasmussens. Well, they lost just about everything but their lives in a train wreck on the move west, and I thought maybe we could tie off a couple of quilts and collect household things to help tide them over, you know? They got the mister and missus and three little ones, not even school age yet. I don't know how they are going to make it through the winter."

Mary Martha stood with Agnes. "Mr. Carl Rasmussen came to call on my husband, asking if there was anything he could do to work for food. We gave them what we could, and then Pastor sent him out to the Bjorklunds." Her soft southern accent sounded strange amongst all the Norwegian.

"He's going to be doing fall fieldwork for us while the men are gone with the threshing machine. They'll be staying in our soddy until they decide what they're going to do," Ingeborg said with a nod. "I invited Elvira — that's Mrs. Rasmussen — to come today but she said she just wasn't up to meeting so many people yet. I've hardly seen her myself since they got there."

"They're Swedish, you know, so maybe that is part of the reason," Kaaren added.

"How old are the children? Are they boys or girls? Where did they come from? How did they happen to come here?" The questions flew, and Penny finally raised both hands and her voice.

"I take it we are in agreement that we will do all we can to help them?"

No one voiced any disagreement, and after a moment of pause, Dyrfinna Odell raised her hand. "I volunteer to keep track of what is gathered in." Her voice squeaked on the words. Dyrfinna had never volunteered for anything before.

"Thank you." Penny smiled at the timid woman, who reminded her so much of a skittish mouse. "Why don't we all tell Dyrfinna what we can offer while we are quilting? The wedding ring quilt will be needed soon if Petar Baard has his way, and since I brought my machine, we ought to be able to stitch up a couple of quilt tops today. So, ladies, let us get right to work." She turned to Mary Martha. "Petar is Joseph's nephew, and he is sweet on a girl in Grafton. He's talking marriage, but she's not sure yet."

"Are you going to tell me what made you look so sad?" Agnes leaned closer to Penny so that she could ask without letting everyone hear.

Penny pulled her thread through the stitches and sighed. "Just more of the same. I got my monthlies this morning, and since I was a day or two late, I thought just maybe I could be . . ."

Agnes patted her niece's knee. "In God's good time, my dear. I know He has heard your prayer and those of some of the others of us. I have to believe He knows best, but sometimes the waiting is terrible hard." No one loved babies more than Agnes, and ever since a little girl was stillborn to her several years earlier, Agnes had not quickened again, much to her sorrow.

Penny nodded. "I know you understand how I feel, but at least you have children already. What if I never have any?" Voicing the fear that, like some mythical monster, had crept to the surface in the dark of night helped relieve the burden, which had grown far too heavy for Penny's slender shoulders to bear.

"Abraham's Sarah waited ninety years."

"Ja, well I don't think God plans on starting a whole new people with me like He did with them."

Agnes tried to look stern but chortled instead. "Ah, Penny, you are such a treasure to me. Be that as it may, I do hope and pray that He intends children for you, but if not, I know He has something else in mind. And it will be good."

"All will be well?"

"Ja, indeed all will be well."

"Well, I think having Hjelmer home more would be a good step forward. God did design life to come from two people after all." She whispered that so Bridget, sitting on the other side of the quilting frame, wouldn't hear. No need to hurt her mother-in-law's feelings for sending her son out to look for his sister.

"What are you two whispering about over here?" Ingeborg laid a hand on each of their shoulders and leaned down to hug them both.

"Same old." Agnes raised one eyebrow.

"Ah, we three should form a club of our own."

"What? The barren sisters?"

Ingeborg chuckled. "Well, as long as we can laugh about it, we're all right."

"And cry."

"Ja, well, that too." She hugged her two friends again and took a vacant chair at the other frame where they were tying off a nine-patch quilt rather than quilting it.

"Whew, with that sewing machine going like that, it takes three people cutting to keep up." Kaaren stopped next to Agnes.

"We could very well bring ours over next month too. You should see the crazy quilt I did on it."

"Did you bring it?"

"No, but I took pieces of muslin and started out with a piece of Lars' old coat in one corner and stitched it on one side, then kept laying the other pieces of quilt with cut ends even to the one before, and so all are stitched down to the muslin. It's like laying building blocks. It goes so fast you can't believe it. I'll bring it next month to tie off. Have to card more batting first."

All the while she talked, she used a couple of pieces of cotton to show what she meant.

"Are you going to do decorating stitches like other crazy quilts?" Agnes tied off her thread and clipped the end.

"I don't think so, because I've used all sizes of pieces. Less seams that way and I could get done fast. No waste that way either. The wool ravelings I've added to the batting."

Agnes nodded. "My mor used to do that. Said wool was wool whether carded or spun." She looked up at Kaaren. "How are the sign language classes coming?"

Kaaren's face brightened. "Oh, you

wouldn't believe it. Besides what I teach at the schoolhouse on Tuesday and Thursday afternoons, Grace and Sophie are teaching other little children, and by the time they all get to school, Pastor Solberg will have to tell them to keep their hands still, no talking."

"Ja, I saw those two little ones of yours saying something in church last Sunday all by sign, mind you, and both of them giggling afterward. Made me want to know what they'd said."

"Isn't it strange how God is taking what I, well, so many of us, thought was a tragedy of Grace not being able to hear and making it something beautiful. Well, strange isn't the right word, but you know what I mean."

"Amazing is more like it."

"I've started teaching Grace to say some words too. Her tongue and mouth work even though her ears don't." Kaaren reached behind and pulled up a chair. "I should be cutting rather than just visiting like this, but I have an interesting letter I want to read to you."

"Really?" Agnes squinted to get her thread in the needle. "Pshaw, this fool needle, the thread just won't go in."

"Here, let me." Penny took the thread

and needle and, after one try, handed it back threaded. "It's your eye's, not the needle's, fault."

"Don't need to tell me that. Why do you suppose I sit in front of the window to sew nowadays?" She shook her head, shuddering at the same time. "Go on, Kaaren, read your letter."

Kaaren took the envelope from her apron pocket and extracted the thin paper.

"Dear Mrs. Knutson,

It has come to my attention that you have learned of a way to help a deaf person communicate with those who can hear. My daughter was born deaf, and she is a handful, let me tell you. I feel so sorry for her and thought that we must prepare ourselves to take care of her all of her life. I am not complaining, mind you, just stating things as we see them. Would it be possible for you to teach us what you have learned? Sincerely . . ."

Kaaren looked up from her reading.
"My land." Agnes paused in her stitching.
"God is giving you a school." Penny

breathed the words, awe rounding her eyes.

"A what?" Kaaren looked up from refolding the paper.

"A school." Penny's voice grew more animated. "I can just see it — a school for deaf people to learn how to sign, adults too, not just children. Why, they would live right here in your school for a year, and then when they've learned it all, they'd go back home and teach others. Can't you see it?"

Kaaren sank down on a chair. "Oh, Lord, is this really what you have in mind?"

"You always wanted to teach, and when Olaf took over the school, you were heartbroken. Remember?"

"How could I forget?" Kaaren shook her head. "But that was a long time ago now. And I have all the children and Lars and the farm and teaching two afternoons as it is, and the . . ." Her eyes shone like fifty candles were lit behind them. "Oh, Penny, what if —" She choked on the words and started again. "What if this is really God?"

Ingeborg and Agnes exchanged glances. "Who else would it be?"

"But I don't know anything about starting a school."

"Moses didn't know anything about leading people either. He herded sheep." Agnes took several more stitches in the quilt. "But we all know that if God is calling you to start a school, then you better keep your ears open and get your feet walking on the path so He can lead you. After all, if Bridget could get a boardinghouse, no reason why we can't build you a school."

"That's right," Penny agreed. "It doesn't have to be huge to start. And the students could help on the farm and with the cooking and all. That could be part of their training, just like in a real home. Say you started with only a couple of students. Right now the girls could teach them."

"Penny, you forget," Kaaren objected. "Grace and Sophie are not even five yet."

"So, you been over to the parsonage to watch the little ones? Half of them can sign words already."

"And you have the schoolchildren learning to sign," Ingeborg said. "God gave you a chance to practice. See, He's been training you up, just like He promised.

"What if . . ." Ingeborg paused, her eyes distant as she marshaled her thoughts. The others waited. "What if your school-age students could go to the regular school here, since the children will know how to sign?"

"And the teacher will learn," Penny said. "Pastor Solberg has already been learning with the children."

"Pastor Solberg will learn what?" Mary Martha joined their group.

"To sign and to teach with signing." Penny glanced up from her stitching.

"Of course he will. Why?" Mary asked.

"Because Kaaren is going to start a school to teach deaf people how to sign," Penny said, as if all the plans were in place and everyone already knew all about it.

"I think I may have to faint." Kaaren leaned her head back against the chair. "Oh, Lord, what are you getting me into now?"

By the time the quilters broke for dinner, all the discussion centered around the school.

"We got a sack house to ship grain, a community bank, a school, a church, a boardinghouse, and an elected member of the Constitutional Congress. Now God is giving us a new direction." Hildegunn Valders looked around at the seated women. "We women can do anything He sets us out to do. Now just to get the men to agree."

"Oh, they'll agree all right, just might take some talkin'." Mary Martha smiled and raised one eyebrow. "And ah know who to start with." Chuckles rippled around the room.

"Whoever would have thought God brought us all together for something like this?" Mrs. Magron's voice held the awe to be seen on the others' faces.

"And I thought it was all because of the good farmland." Ingeborg raised her hands shoulder high and shrugged.

Kaaren leaned forward. "I know one thing for sure. We all better do a heap of praying about this . . . this vision we've been given. I mean, just think of it. Three hours ago all we wanted to do was make quilts, and now we're thinking of starting a school for the deaf. Have you thought about where we are going to get the money and everything else we would need?"

"God says He owns the cattle on a thousand hills. Maybe we should ask Him to donate some."

"Better make it a whole herd, then."

"Or at least a prime breeding bull or two." Ingeborg arched one eyebrow, her smile gathering a flock of chuckles from around the room.

11

The Ranch
September 3

And I thought I was safe with this man!
Augusta fled to the farthest wall.

Kane pulled his pants on and turned to
face the woman across the room. "Look, I
know this must be sudden for you, but
after all, we *are* married. What did you
think would happen?" He stared at the face
before him, the eyes round with horror, the
mouth gaping like a fish trying to breathe
out of water.

Augusta tried to stifle a sneeze but
failed. The second was worse than the
first. And the third . . . *If only I could under-*
stand what he is saying. Why isn't he leaving
the room? Oh, God, my God, what kind of
trouble have I gotten into? You said you pro-
tect the lost, and right now I feel so far lost I
don't know if I'll ever be found. When she
sneezed this time, it felt as though the top

of her head had blown right off. Her eyes ran, her nose ran faster, and she realized she had a headache that reached clear to her toes. Where in the world would she find a handkerchief? She took her gaze off the man to search for her carpetbag. And her trunk — where was her trunk?

The sight of her open carpetbag by the side of the bed almost brought her to tears, if there were any way to differentiate between tears of sorrow and fear from the drops raining from her eyes and making her sneeze again.

"Look, I'm going to leave now, but somehow we will find a way to talk with each other. In the meantime, I'm going to let you have this room, and I'll sleep in the other if that will make you feel any better."

Augusta looked at him as through a veil of running water. What in the world was he saying? What difference did it make? She darted to her bag and dug in the side for a handkerchief. The fine cotton square she pulled out had her initials embroidered in the corner, worked so carefully and with so much love by her mother. She choked back a sob and blew her nose. When would she ever see her mother again?

The questions came as fast as the tears running down her face. No matter how hard she fought, they continued. When she heard the door close, she crawled back into the bed and sobbed into the pillow.

A gentle hand smoothed her hair back and handed her a cup of water. The gesture to drink made perfect sense, and she did as told, gazing through bleary eyes into the dark depths of those of the Indian woman. Augusta drained the cup. "Mange takk." She laid her hands together under her cheek and fell into a vortex that sucked her down into oblivion.

"I don't know what to do," Kane said to Morning Dove out in the kitchen. "You'd think I attacked her the way she shrieked."

"I heard."

Yes, I imagine you did. They probably heard in the ranch ten miles south too. Kane sipped his morning cup of coffee and shook his head. "If I could only talk with her. Somehow I guess I just figured she'd speak English. After all, her letter was written in English. And look at her. I know she's coming down with something, not surprising considering all she's been through."

"She sleeping now."

"Good. Maybe when she wakes up, she'll feel more like talking." He snorted at his own words. "Sure, she'll talk Norwegian, I'll talk English, you can throw in some Mandan, and Lone Pine can add Kiowa. Then no one will make any sense whatsoever."

"She come around." Morning Dove set a plateful of steak, eggs, and fried potatoes on the table. She went to the door and called her husband, then carried two more plates to the table, added a stack of toasted bread, and sat down. "You eat."

"Maybe I should take a plate in to Augusta."

"She sleep, you eat."

At Morning Dove's insistence, Kane followed Lone Pine out the door after eating, and within minutes they were involved down at the corrals, where the man had been breaking the younger horses since finishing with the oat harvest.

"Did you get a hailstorm here?"

Lone Pine shook his head. "Rain, but grain is shocked, so not so bad."

"I asked Wilson to bring his thresher by when he can." Kane studied the horses in the corral. "Let's team that sorrel up with Queenie and get her going good under harness. Most of the rest I think the army will pick up. How many more to saddle break?"

"Three. Not more'n green broke, though."

"I know, but Major Grunswold wants them before winter. Let him feed them instead of us."

"When's he coming?"

Kane shrugged. "Usually makes it around the first of October." Kane studied the herd some more. "That makes three teams, four if we can get that sorrel ready, fifteen head for saddle —"

"Sixteen. The paint is broke too."

"Okay. Then we can send the rest out to range. Anyone come by for that bay mare?"

Lone Pine shook his head. "You want to winter her over? Might make a good broodmare."

"I guess." Kane turned his back on the horses and looked toward the house. *Is she still sleeping? Is she getting any sicker?* "Think I'll go work with the filly. Call me if you need me."

Kane spent an hour or more brushing the filly down, picking and trimming her hooves, and riding her out in the field beyond the barns where he could let her run, stop, turn, and lope again. By the time he finished with her, she wore dark patches of sweat on shoulder and flank, but she seemed to enjoy the work as much as he did, her ears flicking back and forth listening to his commands.

When Morning Dove rang the triangle for dinner, he stripped off the saddle and hung it on the corral bar. The filly trotted around the enclosure, head up, neck arched, seeming to float above the dust. "Yeah, you're the perfect lady's horse, you know. I wonder if Augusta knows how to ride?" With that thought in mind, he headed for the house. If she didn't know how to ride, he would find great pleasure in teaching her. Perhaps this afternoon he'd bring her down and introduce woman and horse.

"She running fever," Morning Dove announced when he raised an eyebrow in question.

"Bad?"

"Bad enough. I give her willow bark tea. She coughing."

"I got some whiskey in the medicine box. That with honey and hot water might help."

Morning Dove nodded. "You eat. I care for her."

"In a minute." Kane quietly opened the door to the bedroom where Augusta lay sleeping. Sweat had curled her hair around her face, a face flushed with fever. While she'd thrown back the covers, now she lay shivering, so Kane pulled the sheet and quilt up over her shoulders. Sitting down on the edge of the bed, he laid the back of his hand against her cheek. Hot, all right.

Augusta moaned and jerked in the spasm of a cough.

Kane picked up the water glass from the stand by the bed and, burrowing his arm around her shoulders, lifted her upright. "Drink this. It will help."

She opened her mouth when he touched the glass to her lips and obediently swallowed, all without opening her eyes. He found himself wishing to see the blue of her eyes, see again the laughter he'd caught several times on the trip home. Why hadn't he just holed up and not let her get so soaked in the rain? He snorted and laid her back down. Hindsight. How often had he wished foresight was as wise.

Back at the table he joined his two friends and the three hands. "We need to bring the cattle in from the hills so the major can take the steers too." He chewed without paying attention to what he ate.

"Tomorrow we go?"

He thought about the sick woman in the bedroom. How he hated to leave her. A sigh worked its way up, only to be drowned in a sip of coffee. He'd never been a sighing man — until now. She had traveled clear across the ocean, then across the United States, only to be felled by illness once she arrived, thanks to his carelessness. Maybe she was sickly and had kept that a secret.

He shook his head. No, she was the picture of health, tired but blooming when she stepped off that train. The hail and rain and pushing hard, that's what done her in.

By nighttime she was worse instead of better, thrashing about and mumbling in her sleep. Together he and Morning Dove bathed her, changed the sheets, and bathed her again, anything to cool the heated flesh. They forced liquids down her throat, laid cool wet towels across her body and made her drink again.

"I'll take the first watch." Kane moved the chair closer to the bed.

"Call me."

"I will." Kane stayed beside her, changing the cloths when they heated up, spooning liquid into her mouth whenever he could get her to take it.

Sometime later Morning Dove appeared at his side. "My turn. You sleep."

"I don't know. . . ."

"Go."

When he woke in the early hours of the still-dark morning, she was no better, but then she was no worse either. She slept on. At Morning Dove's insistence that she could handle the sick woman and Lone Pine's admonition that they needed to bring in the cattle, Kane rode out with his hands and spent the day in the saddle rounding up strays.

Roundup was something he'd hoped Augusta would enjoy too. The filly would have carried her mistress over the hills and down into the washes and valleys with a surefootedness born of growing up half wild. As usual, some of the cattle carried either no brand or a brand of one of the neighboring ranches. They brought them all in anyway, finishing the last miles in the wash of moonlight that gilded the ranch and tipped the horns of the cattle with silver.

"She 'bout the same." Morning Dove answered Kane's question before he could ask.

He washed up, then took over the chair by the bed. Augusta seemed to be wasting away before his very eyes. Her cheeks and eyes were sunken, leaving bones white

170

against alabaster skin. When he took her hand, the fingers clenched his, hot and burning. He disengaged his hands and dipped the heated cloths in cool water to lay them across her body again.

Like this he had cared for his mother those long years ago. He felt the years slip away and he was again fourteen, too old to be a boy and not yet a man. And his mother lay dying. His father had never returned from the war.

Morning Dove broke his reverie. "You go eat. I care for her." She gave him a gentle push toward the door. "Then you sleep, and I watch."

Good thing he could eat without thinking because his mind refused to stay in the present. While it had taken months for his mother to cough her life away, the final days went swiftly. Was this to be his reward for seeking a wife? Watching another woman die? What kind of God would allow that to happen?

"Father God." He buried his face in his hands, his knees planted on the rug beside the bed. "I believed you brought her to me, and now she is so sick. Please, I beg of you, come with your healing power and burn out the disease." He could hear her coughing. All those days, weeks, and hours he had heard his mother coughing as she lay dying. The memory matched the sound from the other room. "Please, Jesus, be merciful to me, to her. I beg of you, be merciful." He pulled his Bible from the shelf above the bed and began reading, searching for the promises that spoke of God's healing power. *And with his stripes we are healed,* "*Ask, and it shall be given you,*" and "*Lo, I am with you alway.*"

He fell back on his knees. "I believe, Lord. Help thou my unbelief." He listened to the coughing, hearing Morning Dove murmur as she cared for the sick woman. Fear tasted like the most bitter of dregs. "Lord, you said 'fear not,' yet I am consumed by fear. Please forgive me."

He knew he slept when he awoke with a cramp in his thigh from kneeling so long. With a groan he pushed himself to his feet, glancing out the window as he tiptoed back into the other room. Must be the dark before the dawn, it was so pitch black outside. Not even starlight to brighten the darkness.

"How is she?" He stared at the pale face of the woman in the bed, no longer flushed with the fever. Was that good or bad?

"Better, for now anyway. You go back to sleep."

"I'd rather be here. You go on." He took the chair that Morning Dove vacated and, leaning his arms on the bed, watched Augusta breathe. Yes, she was better. He could both see and hear it. Maybe it hadn't gone into pneumonia after all. Or the influenza that took so many lives, or the wasting disease of his mother. But then, maybe God had just worked another miracle.

He smoothed her hair back from the broad forehead and laid his fingers against her cheek. How could he possibly care so much so quickly? The thought of burying her up on the hill with his mother and father ripped his heart like the sharpest of knives. Was joy to come with the morning?

12

St. Paul
September 4

Where in the world could Augusta have gone?

Hjelmer stared around the bustling train station in St. Paul wishing he were anywhere but here. The high-domed ceiling and marble floors and walls echoed with the cries of babies, boarding announcements, and hawkers calling their wares. The constant screech of unoiled train wheels made his ears hurt, even though he was used to the ring of the blacksmith's hammer.

He wanted to clap his hands over his ears. Instead, he walked over to the wall that posted the train schedules and looked to see when the trains arrived from Chicago. After jotting down arrival times, he checked the date his sister should have arrived in St. Paul and headed for the ticket booths.

"Where to?" the man asked, barely looking up.

"I have some questions."

The man behind Hjelmer cleared his throat.

"Make it quick. These people need to catch their trains."

"Who would I ask about a missing passenger?"

The agent nodded to the right. "That office right over there."

"The one marked private?"

"That's the one. Next?"

Hjelmer frowned at the man's abruptness, and when the man behind him stepped forward, bumping him in the passing, Hjelmer shot him an indignant look. "Excuse me." He dragged the words out to show his disgust and made his way to the door indicated.

"How can I help you?" asked an older woman with wire-rimmed glasses perched on the end of her nose.

"I hope you can. You see, my sister is missing."

"Oh, my goodness. Please sit right down there, and I'll see if Mr. Franklin can see you. How long has she been missing?"

"Four days." It felt like forever.

Within minutes Hjelmer was ushered

into the next office and began answering a barrage of questions. When he'd finished telling his story, the lodge-pole man with piercing eyes clasped his hands on his desk and leaned slightly forward.

"You're sure she got as far as here?"

"Ja, her trunk came to Blessing, and it had been stamped through here."

"Good. We know that much at least."

"Here are the arrival times from Chicago." Hjelmer laid his notes on the desk.

Franklin nodded and, pulling out a drawer, extracted some papers. "Here are the full schedules. We can see when she came in and what other trains were leaving about the same time as the St. Paul and Pacific left for Grand Forks. Somehow she must have gotten on the wrong train. Or . . ."

Hjelmer didn't want to think about the possibilities of the *or*.

"We can check with the guards to see if any of them saw anything suspicious, though they would usually report that to me."

Hjelmer looked at the grids on the paper, knowing that Franklin could decipher them much faster than he. "What I don't see is how she could have gotten on the wrong train. Every time I've ridden one, and that's been plenty lately, the conductor checks my ticket as to the destination. If she was on the wrong train, wouldn't he put her off at the next station and send her back here?"

"You'd think so, but sometimes crazy things happen. And when one can't speak English . . ." Franklin stopped and shook his head. "You wouldn't believe the stories I could tell you. Shame the immigrants aren't required to learn English before they come here. You should have told her."

At that point Hjelmer could have cheerfully strangled his sister. "Oh, I told her, and so did the others, but you don't know my sister."

"Ah." Franklin bent to studying his schedules. The silence lengthened, but Hjelmer kept himself from shifting on the chair so as not to distract this first man who'd offered to help. "All right. Far as I can figure, if she asked for the train to Blessing or Grand Forks, the two other trains waiting in the same area would have been one going south, ending in Ipswich, South Dakota, or the Northern Pacific heading for Fargo and parts west. End of the line there is Seattle in Washington Territory. She could have gotten on either one of those and gotten off at any stop along the way. If she lost her ticket or ran out of money or . . ." He paused, then leaned forward again. "I surely do hope you are a praying man, Mr. Bjorklund, because if the good Lord ain't watching out for her, you got a mighty big heap of trouble."

"Please, don't remind me." Hjelmer rubbed the end of his chin with one forefinger. "Any suggestion on how I should proceed?"

"Well, you could notify the police and turn in a missing persons report. You got a picture of her, by any chance?" When Hjelmer shook his head, Franklin continued. "Stick around here a couple of days, and you should be able to ask all the conductors, ticket agents, and baggage handlers if any of them might have seen her. Anything distinctive about her other than her speaking only Norwegian?"

"She is tall — five nine or ten — and she has blue eyes the color of mine. A family trait."

"Heavy? Slender? Hair color?"

"Blond hair usually worn in a bun. Not really slender but not fat either, you know." How did one describe a sister he hadn't seen for so long? What if she had cut her hair?

Franklin was writing as fast as Hjelmer

was talking. "Okay. Tell you what I'll do. I'll post this description in the sign-in area to see if we can trigger any memories, and I'll give you a list of the men working that day. Then, if you want, you can wait down there by those trains and ask your questions when the trains arrive and leave." He stood and extended his hand. "You're not the first person to come looking for a lost person, and I'm sure you won't be the last. Good luck, Mr. Bjorklund. And please, let me know what you find out."

That evening after hours of questioning, Hjelmer sent a telegram to his mother.

No luck yet Stop Keep praying Stop Hjelmer

13

"I've written an answer to their letter. You know, the one about teaching the little deaf girl." Kaaren crossed the cucumber patch with swift strides.

"And?" Ingeborg dropped another handful of cucumbers in her basket and stood, stretching the kinks out with her fists rubbing the small of her back.

"Hi, Tante Kaaren." Astrid plunked her pickings in the pail beside her, her sunbonnet hanging down her back by its strings. With nimble fingers she searched the leaves for more of the right size. "Sammy's sleeping." She nodded to the blanket lying in the shade, a toddler sprawled in the middle.

"Thank you, Astrid, for watching him for me." Kaaren handed the letter to Ingeborg. "See for yourself."

180

Ingeborg took the letter from the envelope and pushed her sunbonnet off with the back of her grimy hand. "I'll get it dirty."

"No matter." Kaaren looked around. "Where are the girls and Trygve?"

"Scrubbing cucumbers with Mrs. Rasmussen. I sent them to the well house where it was cooler." Ingeborg read between comments. When finished, she smiled at her sister-in-law. "My land, your soddy is going to start a new life. Have you thought of a name for your school yet?" She reread a portion of the letter. " 'I will inform you as to when we will be taking students, and you can bring Margaret Louise to us.' "

"I'm thinking that we should call it the Blessing School for the Deaf. This will indeed be a blessing for those who come. As you can see, Margaret Louise is ten years old. She'll fit right into the regular school after some intensive help." Kaaren nibbled her bottom lip. "But how can I call it a school when I have only one pupil?"

"Oh, I have me a feeling that God will send all you can handle to your door." Ingeborg tapped the envelope on her forefinger. "You thought of sending a copy of the book you used to this girl's folks?"

"That's a good idea." Kaaren took the letter back and put it in her bag. "Let me get an apron on, and I'll set the vinegar water to boiling. You have the crocks all washed out?"

"And lined up in the cellar. We can fill them there."

"Good. Penny sure was grateful for the butter and eggs and cheese. She asked if the boys had been hunting lately, hoping we would smoke geese again like last year. She says she can sell all we can supply."

"Have they heard anything about Augusta?"

Kaaren shook her head. "Not a word. It's like she disappeared in the smoke. I just wish there was more we could do to find her." She shook her head again. "Poor Bridget." A sigh accompanied the head-shake. "Oh, she wondered if you had cheese for her too. I left her eggs and butter."

"Soft but not cured." Ingeborg bent back to her picking as Kaaren headed for the house. If only she could wear pants again. These skirts were always in the way. And what she wouldn't give to go hunting herself. While the deer were nowhere near as plentiful as they used to be, the ducks and geese still half darkened the sky as they migrated south. They should be able to hang twenty or thirty at a time in the smokehouse. Good thing they would have extra down for more feather beds now with the new family here and Kaaren's coming boarders.

"All done, Ma." Astrid could barely hoist her bucket, she'd filled it so full.

"Good girl." Ingeborg dropped the last of the cukes in her full basket and, picking up both basket and bucket, headed for the well house. "Thank you for picking so many." She glanced at the rows of bending dill, heads heavy with seeds. What they didn't need for the crocks, she'd hang to dry, both to use in the winter and to save for seed next year. The carrots she had kept over the winter and replanted for seed looked about ready to pick too.

She glanced up. Sure enough, the sun was straight up. Time for dinner, and it wasn't on the table yet. With the men gone, she seemed to get a bit lax. "Let's get these in to the others, and you can set the table for me."

With Astrid helping with the bucket, they opened the door to the well house and set the bucket and basket inside. "Dinner in a few minutes," she said to the group cleaning cucumbers and shook her head with a smile. "Look at how many you got done." Scrubbed cucumbers filled a washtub.

"I done the most." Trygve sloshed his hands in the water.

"Uh-uh." The oldest Rasmussen boy, Thomas, shook his head. "My ma done the most."

"Boys." Slender to the point of emaciation, Elvira Rasmussen laid a hand on her son's shoulder. "You both did good."

"Me too, huh, Ma?" While Thomas was five, Sarah, at four, refused to be left behind.

Ingeborg wiped her brow with the corner of her apron. "Let me tell you, I'd rather be in here scrubbing than out there picking. Elvira, would you please bring in that jug of buttermilk when you come?" Ingeborg fetched the butter crock, which she handed to Astrid, and another of sour cream. "Think I'll slice some of these cucumbers, and we'll have them in sour cream. How does that sound?"

"Sounds heavenly." Elvira laid a hand on her youngest — Baby, they called him — who had decided that splashing the wash water would make the time pass more quickly. "I can't remember when we had so much good food to eat. Things were hard back in New York. That's why we come west. Mr. Rasmussen says we will find a homestead out west. Can you believe free land?"

"Ja, well, you will work mighty hard for your free land." She smiled at the woman on the stool. "But it's worth every drop of sweat and aching muscle." She reached up on a shelf for the soft cheese. "Four years since we proved up this piece. Blessing has come a long way since we homesteaded the first sections."

Ingeborg held the door open for Astrid, and they headed for the house. In the days since the Rasmussens had arrived, she'd never heard that woman say more than three words at a time. What had gotten into her?

Good smells greeted them and the clang of a stove lid being set back in place.

Kaaren turned with a smile from checking the oven. "Good, I was about to call you. Astrid, you want to go ring the triangle so Mr. Rasmussen knows dinner is ready?"

Astrid set her crock on the table and dashed back out the door. While the ringing went on longer than usual, Kaaren and Ingeborg only exchanged smiles. Astrid did everything with a boisterous enthusiasm that frequently had to be shushed. If Mr. Rasmussen didn't hear *that* summons, he was hard of hearing for sure.

As soon as everyone was seated, Ingeborg nodded to Trygve to say the blessing. He led the Norwegian prayer in a clear voice, and while some of the smaller ones stumbled over the words, the amen rang loud and clear.

When everyone's plates were filled, they felt as if it had been days, instead of hours, since they ate.

A few minutes later Mr. Rasmussen mopped his gravy with a slice of bread and accepted a refill of coffee. "I was thinking that if maybe my family could stay here, I would go on out west and see if I can locate land for a homestead. Elvira here would help you around the place in exchange for their food."

Ingeborg looked up to see a terrified-rabbit look in Elvira's eyes before she looked down at her plate. "I guess I was hoping you would decide to stay on for a while. There's plenty of work for you here, and it would give you a chance to get back on your feet a bit."

The man nodded. "I appreciate that, ma'am, and don't think I'm not grateful for what you've done for me and mine, but if I don't get out there, all the good land might be gone."

Ingeborg kept the rumors she had heard of the land quality to herself. More rocks than soil in some places, she'd heard, and less rainfall than here in the Red River Valley too. "Of course you have to do what you think best, but . . ." She spread jam on a piece of bread for Trygve while Kaaren made sure that Samuel got more of the meal in his mouth than on his head. She glanced up in time to catch the stare that Mr. Rasmussen sent to Grace and Sophie.

"They're talking, Mr. Rasmussen," Kaaren said gently. "Grace cannot hear, and we are all learning to use our hands to talk with Grace. We make letters with our fingers, called signs, and spell out the words."

"Well, I'll be. . . ." He looked back at Kaaren. "Did you make that up, the signs, I mean?"

"No, I was given a book."

Grace laughed at something Sophie signed to her.

"She really can't hear? Not a thing?"

"Nothing. She was born deaf."

"But . . . but she seems so bright, so happy." The look of disbelief he wore made Ingeborg want to roll her eyes. As if there were something wrong with Grace's mind just because she couldn't hear.

"Well, I better get back to the field. You want I should take the oxen out now?" he asked.

"Yes, please. And give what I said some thought, would you? I know my husband would be glad to have you working here through the winter. And maybe when Hjelmer, my brother-in-law, gets back, he could send out some feelers for land for you. He's the banker here in Blessing and our local representative to the Constitutional Congress."

Rasmussen pushed back his chair, belched, and stood. "Thank you for the good meal, and yes, I'll think about it."

When Elvira had taken the children who didn't go down for naps back out to finish scrubbing the cucumbers, Kaaren and Ingeborg sat back down at the table with a second cup of coffee.

"If he takes her west, she won't make it through the winter. Looks like the wind would blow right through her."

"Maybe he would go later, find a place, and then move out there in the spring." Kaaren dunked her cookie in her coffee. "In the meantime, we can get some meat on her bones. You think as pale as she is, she might be carrying?"

Ingeborg shook her head. "I sure hope not. She said she lost one just before they set out, and the baby before that died after living only a week. She doesn't look strong enough to carry another." Jealousy, sharp and hard, stabbed through her. Why was it that other women had baby after baby and she hadn't conceived since Astrid was born?

Lord, it's just not fair.

14

The Ranch
September 6

"Augusta, do you think you could eat something?"

The voice sounded as though it came from across a wide and deep valley, like those between the mountains of home. If only she knew what he said, for it *was* a man's voice. Something smelled delicious, so she sniffed again. She could see light through her eyelids, but opening her eyes seemed to take more strength than she had at the moment. But like an obedient baby bird, she opened her mouth at the touch of a spoon. Whatever it was, it tasted as good as it smelled.

After the fourth or fifth spoonful, she commanded her eyes to open, and this time they did more than flutter. She'd been right. The sun was shining in the window. Her gaze traveled around the room and stopped at the man leaning forward with another spoonful of the broth she'd by now identified as chicken. Sherry, that's what his eyes reminded her of, what little bit she'd had of it in her life. But dusting the bottles at one of the houses she'd worked in had let her know something of the world of drink. She opened her mouth without prompting.

Now, why in the world was he sitting here feeding her? Had she been *that* sick? Had he been caring for her all along? Vague memories surfaced of soothing voices, cool cloths, and some rank liquid that seemed to ease the coughs. She was sure she remembered a woman's voice too.

After another spoonful she shook her head. "No more." The motion made the room spin. She closed her eyes to stop the motion and fell asleep again before she could open them.

The woman's voice woke her again some time later. When Augusta opened her eyes, she could tell by the shadows that much of the day had passed. She tried to lift her hand, but the effort made her shake, so she just smiled back at the brown-faced woman by the bed and kept opening her mouth whenever the spoon presented itself. Or rather, was presented by a hand that smoothed back her hair and even washed her face with a warm wet cloth.

"Mange takk." The words came out raspy, like a door creaky from not being opened. She thought back to the lessons the man had been giving her in English. What was the right word for "mange takk"? The effort sent her back into oblivion.

Every time she awoke, either Kane or Morning Dove was right there spooning liquid into her and finally holding her up to drink from a cup. Amazing how such a thing one always took for granted, such a little thing as drinking from cup rather than spoon could be a victory. When Kane laid her back down, she missed the strength and warmth of his arm.

Such a strong and gentle man. *Perhaps*, she thought, drifting off to sleep again, *someday when God brings me a husband, he could be like this man here. Wouldn't that be nice?*

When she awoke fully again, the bedroom was empty but she could hear men talking in the other room. From the angle of the sun and the smells drifting in, she figured they were eating breakfast. She glanced around without moving her head much. Surely there was a chamber pot here somewhere. And she needed to use it. She carefully inched her way to the edge of the bed and looked over the side. Uh-huh, right there under the bed. But how would she manage standing and sitting when she didn't think she could even sit up?

"Heavenly Father, please help me."

As if sensitive to her slightest sound, the door opened and Morning Dove entered. "Good, you are awake. Today I think you eat." She set the tray she carried on the stand by the bed.

Augusta pointed to the pot and signaled her frenzy.

"Ah, I help you."

By the time she fell back in bed, Augusta felt as though her head might float up and bounce against the ceiling. She lay sweating and gasping and closed her eyes to bring the room to a halt.

"Mange takk." *At least I have a mind left, even if my body is failing me.* Never had an expression of gratitude been more heartfelt.

"Good. Now eat." Morning Dove propped her patient up with one arm and stuffed pillows behind her back with her other hand. Then she helped scoot Augusta up so she was sitting.

How long have I been sick? What happened

to me? Did I really awake to find Kane in my bed? The questions chased through her mind like kittens after mice, not catching answers any better than the kittens caught their prey.

Morning Dove set the tray across her lap, and Augusta stared down at the food before her. Did she really have the strength to lift that spoon herself? The spoon shook so badly that when she got it to her mouth, it was empty.

"Here." Morning Dove sat down in the chair and began feeding her.

"I am so sorry," Augusta said between spoonfuls, "to cause you all this trouble for a visitor." Morning Dove just nodded and kept on spooning. *When I get to Blessing I am going to have to find some nice gift to send these people for being so good to me.*

Her eyes drifted closed again after she drank the bitter tea that Morning Dove forced upon her. *How will I ever get strong enough to continue the journey if I keep going back to sleep like this?*

"How is she?" Kane met Morning Dove coming out of the sickroom.

"Much better. Eat, drink, now sleep again."

"That's best, I s'pose." He stopped at the sound of coughing.

Morning Dove shook her head at his look of concern. "She much better. You go work."

Kane gave the closed door another penetrating stare and turned to do as his housekeeper and friend said. "You'll call me if . . ."

"She is better." Morning Dove shook her head as if a child of hers didn't know when to mind.

"You know, I been thinking. . . ."

Lone Pine looked up from the bridle he was mending and waited. Finally he shook his head. "So?"

"You know, when Augusta talks, some of her words sound a lot like the German Herr Gedicks and his old mother speak. You suppose Norwegians and Germans can talk together?"

"Like Mandan and Sioux?"

"Yeah, like that. At least maybe get the gist of things." Kane knew he had a million things to do, but he couldn't seem to keep his mind on anything but the puzzles surrounding the woman sleeping at the house. If only he could make things easier for her, surely she'd be happier here sooner. Not that he didn't like teaching her English, but sometimes she looked so confused. As if she expected something of him, but he had no idea what.

He tried to look at his home through her eyes. All the buildings were good and solid and kept up. Even roses bloomed by the porch. The horses and cattle were in good health. Most likely she wasn't used to such great distances between farms and ranches, but neighbors within an hour's ride was a far cry from when he was a boy. If only he knew what she was used to. And her name — it just didn't sound quite right from what he remembered of her letter. Now, if only he could find the letter. He must have lost it on the way back from Ipswich. That's all he could figure.

"Think I'll ride on over to Gedicks' and ask him," Kane said to Lone Pine.

"Best wait till she gets on her feet again. She might like company more then."

"Ah, good point." If restless had a name, it must be Kane this day.

15

Blessing
September 7

"Ja, I have a room to let." Bridget forced a smile.

"For two nights, then?" The man looked as if he'd been traveling without sleep for half of his young life.

"Ja. Henry here will show you up. The towels are on the end of your bed. A hot bath is extra, but he will bring up a pitcher of hot water. Supper is at six." She pointed to the closed doors of the dining room. "In there."

Henry Aarsgard raised one snowy eyebrow in question and shook his head just enough to let her know that he didn't approve. When he returned to the parlor on the first floor, he shook his head again.

"I thought you were keeping that room for Augusta."

"I am — was. But she's not here, and

that nice young man needed a room. Augusta can sleep in my bed if she comes before he leaves." Bridget didn't add "if she comes at all," but the thought was implicit.

"You mustn't give up the hope, you know." His tone was gentle, like his spirit.

"I-I'm not. When my babies were baptized, I put them in the Lord's hands and promised I would leave them there. All these years, with my sons crossing the ocean and dying in this land, with Gustaf leaving me behind when he went to meet his Lord, even with Katy dying, I keep the hope, the faith." She stared at her hands crossed in her lap. "Maybe . . . maybe the faith is too weak and the hope dying. I do not think I can bear to lose one more of my children."

Henry knelt on the braided rag rug in front of her rocker and took her hands in his. "Ah, my Bridget, you have borne so much. Let me help you. See, I have strong shoulders. Sharing a burden makes it lighter, like two oxen pulling instead of one."

Bridget rubbed the backs of his thumbs with hers. "Henry I am too old to think of marrying again. That is for young people."

"No, no. Not at all. We who are older are

also wiser, and we know how important it is to love and have someone love us in return."

"But . . . but this is so soon. I have only known you since the summer."

"No. I been eating at the general store since before the first timbers went up on this boardinghouse. You heard me say more than once that Blessing needed a boardinghouse. Remember? And I always liked your pies the best."

Bridget reached out with one finger and traced the line from eye to chin on his seamed face. So different from her austere Gustaf, who had lost the gift of laughter when his sons left home. But before, when he was young, even though he tried to act stern, his children knew that he could be won over with merry laughter and loving patience. So did she. And since then, she'd had no one to fuss over like that. True, her grandchildren thought her the best, and they were the real reason she had come to this country, but still that was far different than having a man in her life, in her bed again. Did she really want to take this step?

Henry shifted and his knee creaked. "Ach, this getting old makes the joints complain an unhappy tune."

"Then get on up and sit on that chair."

Bridget pointed to a chair beside her. When he sat down, she looked at him again, this time her eyes and chin resolute. "I tell you this. I will not say yes, and I will not say no. Not until I have my Augusta beside me."

"But . . ."

"No. That is the way it must be." She leveraged herself to her feet with her hands on the arms of the rocking chair. "Now, I better get in there and help Goodie with the supper, or we will all go hungry."

Henry sighed and got to his feet too. "I think I smell chickens baking."

"You should. You butchered them this morning. I should ask Kaaren to bring in a couple of layers if she has any extra. My hens are barely keeping up with the eggs we need."

"Maybe you should just have her bring eggs."

"Ja, but then Lemuel won't have enough to do. He needs to keep busy, that boy, but Sam says he can use him at the smithy too. I tried to talk him into going to school, but his eyes rolled white then. I think when his ma comes back, things will be different."

"She has the two youngest ones with her, right?" Henry had been off on his job as a conductor on the railroad when Sam brought his family to Blessing, and immediately his wife and daughter, Lily Mae, left to run the cook shack for Lars and Haakan's threshing crew. They pulled the huge steam engine and separator from area to area, threshing grain for the farmers in return for either money or a portion of the grain in payment. The farther they were away from home, the more they appreciated getting cash instead of kind.

"Um-hum, but the two little ones are his brother's children." Bridget pushed open the door to the kitchen, her mind now on fixing supper. How many would they feed tonight? "Ilse, bring in eggs and buttermilk from the well house, would you, please? I think we need eggekake for dessert. Lemuel, start peeling the potatoes. Goodie, did you use all that dried bread for the stuffing? I was thinking we could use some for bread pudding."

Seeing that Bridget was back in action, Henry headed for the woodpile. He could tell the box was nearly empty. That rascal Lemuel was a good worker if someone kept their eye on him. But otherwise he tended to slack.

In exchange for room and board the few days he was in town, Henry helped out around the boardinghouse, making sure the wood was chopped and stacked, the house made ready for winter, and fixing anything that had broken while he was gone.

His main goal was to marry Bridget, and everyone in town knew it. The men made jokes about how long she would hold out, and the women teased her about her beau until her grandmother's cheeks blushed like those of a young girl in her first courting. If he'd had his way they'd have been married during the summer, but Bridget kept shaking her head. At least now she'd made a commitment to make a decision.

But when he brought the evening telegram to her just before dark, he knew that decision wouldn't be soon. Hjelmer had still to find anyone who could remember seeing his sister.

Bridget listened as he read the few brief words. Had Hjelmer written in Norwegian, she'd have read them herself, but while she spoke fairly good English, she hadn't learned to read it yet.

"Uff da." She sighed and shook her head. "Where can that girl have gone to? My Augusta would never have just run off without telling us."

"I think I will request a transfer to the

202

Minneapolis station for a time. That way I could maybe ask questions of people that Hjelmer might not know of. Conductors get moved around all the time, you know. Maybe he just hasn't found the right one yet."

Bridget picked up her knitting again. "Where would you stay?"

"On the trains. Just not take a day off like I do now. Wonder if Hjelmer is planning to come home sometime soon. We could talk more." Henry had been on a trip west when the news came about the missing daughter and had returned only after Hjelmer had already set out.

"I don't know." Bridget shook her head. "I just don't know." She turned back from the fear that lurked like a hungry wolf at the edges of her mind. What if Augusta were never found? "Do you think you could really help look for her?"

"I will go after my shift tomorrow. I been needing to pay my daughter a visit too. Get several birds with one stone this way." He went to stand in front of the screen door. The day had been cloudy, and now a chill wind whistled of coming fall. "Ja, I will do what I can."

"Mange takk." But as she watched him rocking back and forth in the doorway,

Bridget realized she didn't really like the idea of him being gone for who knew how long.

Uff da. Crazy old woman. You're going to have to make up your mind.

16

"All right, let's form the letter *R*." Kaaren held her fingers in the correct position.

Beside her, Pastor Solberg did the same, and then they walked around the schoolroom, helping childish hands do the same.

"No, this way." Four-year-old Sophie instructed Ellie, who was having difficulty getting her fingers to cooperate.

In the front of the room, Kaaren nodded and smiled. "All right, let's go back to the beginning, and we'll go through all the letters. *A* . . . *B* . . ." As she formed the letters, so did the students. "Now, remember, if you get stuck, ask for help."

"I wish I could learn this as fast as they do," Pastor Solberg said in an undertone.

Kaaren smiled and kept on signing. She added *S* and *T* and reviewed them all again. Fingers flew as the signs were made.

"Now, everyone sign your own name."

While several hesitated, with help they all managed.

"Now, watch and see if you can understand what I am saying." Kaaren signed good morning, rejoicing inside at the concentration on the faces before her.

"Good morning," Anji Baard called out, so excited she about leaped out of her seat.

"Please raise your hand first." The gentle reproof from Pastor Solberg made Anji's cheeks flame.

"Sorry."

"Teacher?" Toby Valders raised his hand.

"Yes?"

"Can you make a *V* again?"

Kaaren showed him the finger position, and he copied her, a grin splitting his face when he spelled his name.

"It is exciting to understand, isn't it?" Kaaren signed good morning again, slower this time and very precisely. "Now, let's do this together. G-o-o-d m-o-r-n-i-n-g. Again. Very good."

Clara Erickson raised her hand. "Can you sign in Norwegian too?"

Kaaren thought a moment. "I'm sure we can, but we would need new signs for the Norwegian letters that don't occur in English, like the *O* with a slash through it."

She turned to Pastor Solberg and raised an eyebrow. "Good question, eh?"

"Well, these signs were made up by a person, so why can't we make up our own?"

"Clara, let me think on that."

Thorliff raised his hand. "Why not make an *O* with a finger over it, like this?" He demonstrated.

"Why not?"

"Your big brother sure is smart," Deborah said, leaning over to Andrew on the bench across the aisle.

"I know," Andrew whispered back.

Kaaren heard them both. She smiled at them and then at Thorliff, who was concentrating on forming a word using the new symbol. He'd gone ahead of the class in learning the signing by borrowing Kaaren's book. He always had his lessons done far ahead of the others.

After class, Pastor Solberg finished setting his desk in order while Kaaren waited for the children who were riding home with her to gather their things. "You know, learning signing has been really good for Thorliff. Trying to keep ahead of him takes more than I've got at times. He's reading Latin now, and the other day he asked me if I would teach him Greek."

"And you said?" Kaaren's eyes twinkled.

"I said, 'Here's the book. Teaching you will be good review for me.' " Solberg shook his head. "So now he can speak Norwegian, English, Latin, and signing. Oh, and I gave him a book in German one day and he'd figured out half the story because of his Norwegian."

"Has he started on this year's Christmas program yet?"

"I think so." He ushered her ahead of him out the door. "I wish my advanced mathematics were stronger so I could be more help to him there. But he seems to pick things up well enough with the book. You know, we are going to have to either have a high school here soon or send the older ones off to board in Grafton."

"I hate to see them leave so young. I remember how hard it was for Penny when she went to Fargo for her senior year, working at the hotel and all. If you had another teacher to handle the little ones, could you teach the higher classes?"

They stood at the corner of the soddy and watched the game of tag going on. Thorliff had the horse hitched to the wagon, waiting for his aunt Kaaren.

"You see how crowded the room is now, and the bigger boys are out helping with harvest. I know Joseph says his boys are done schooling, but Agnes insists they should go on."

Kaaren took in a deep breath of the cool air. Clouds blocking the sun and a brisk breeze carried an autumn chill, reminding them that summer was on the wane. "And if I do this school for the deaf the way it looks like I should, that might add more children to the school."

"But not right away. They'd have to become proficient in signing first, right?"

Manda MacCallister drove the Solbergs' wagon around the building and brought it to a stop next to Kaaren's wagon.

"True." Kaaren studied the gleaming white church next door. "We could use the church for the older children."

"Or we could add on to the soddy." Solberg helped her up to the wagon seat while the children scrambled into the back. He waved good-bye and climbed up in his own wagon. "Thank you, Manda." He patted his pockets. "I've got a list for the store here somewhere. Maybe Mrs. Bjorklund will have some cheese for us to take home."

"There's a letter for you," Penny sang out when John Solberg and his two girls entered the store. "I just got a fresh wheel

209

of cheese, and . . ." She paused to wink at Deborah. "New peppermint sticks just arrived this morning."

Deborah looked up at her uncle, who nodded, so she whisked over to stand in front of the candy jars, trying to make up her mind.

Manda made her way to the boots, where Penny met her. Glancing down at the girl's shoes, she nodded. "I can see it is time for new ones. Those look to have patches on their patches. Are they too tight?"

"I keep growing right out of my clothes." Manda indicated the sleeves that no longer reached her wrists and the far-too-tight bodice. She nodded to Solberg, who was now deliberating with Deborah. "And they can't afford to keep me in clothes. Pa said I could keep some money when I sold a horse, so I better buy me some boots at least."

"Does your ma . . ." At the flashing eyes of the girl beside her, Penny reworded her sentence. "Does Mary Martha know your boots are too small?"

Manda shook her head. "I don't want to worry her none."

"Do you know how to sew?"

Another shake of the head. "Not really.

I'm most good with horses and other animals."

"I have an idea that Mary Martha would be mighty upset if she knew your feet were hurting."

"Maybe so, but I'm buying my own boots." Manda pointed to a pair. "You got any to fit me like that?"

"Black or brown?"

"Either. Don't make no difference."

"Well, if I don't have any that fit, we'll order them." Penny pointed to a stool, and Manda sat down.

"Take your boots off."

Manda flinched. "Do I gotta?"

Penny searched through the boots, looking for a pair about the size of Manda's foot. "If you want to try on boots, you do."

"Couldn't I come back later? We got to get on home."

Penny sighed. "I suppose, but this will only take a minute. What's wrong?"

"Well . . ." Manda studied the end of her boot, where her toe looked to be trying to escape.

Penny waited.

"I got holes in my socks." Manda huffed on the words.

"Oh. How about I give you a pair of new socks? Early birthday present."

"Ain't my birthday."

"I know. Manda MacCallister, sit yourself back down on that stool, get those boots off your feet, put on these new stockings, and try on this boot right now!" Penny plunked the boots down on the floor by Manda's knee.

"What's the problem back here?" Pastor Solberg asked from the other side of the shelves.

Manda shook her head and looked as though she wanted to fly out of the store.

Penny made a shushing motion with her hand and went around the other end to lead Pastor Solberg back up to the counter.

"What was that all about?" He lowered his voice at the look on Penny's face.

"Later." She smiled at Deborah and went around the counter to cut the cheese. "How much do you want?" She set the knife to cut a three-inch wedge.

"Bigger." He nodded at her next marking, giving her one of his questioning looks.

"Pa, did you give her the list?" Deborah tugged on his coat sleeve.

"Oh, thank you, my dear." He pulled the paper out of his pocket and handed it across the counter.

"Pa gets kinda forgetful at times, mostly when he's thinking about his sermon." Deborah gave Penny a woman-to-woman look that almost forced a smile past Penny's rolled-tight lips.

"Ah, I see." Penny kept her questions to herself, like when had Deborah started calling Pastor Solberg "Pa"? And why was Manda so afraid to say she needed new clothes? But most of all, where was Zeb? She hoped the letter would tell that. "Oh, I almost forgot, there's a letter here for you." She reached behind to the named boxes on the wall. "In fact, there are two things, one a package."

"Ah, my Greek text. Now I can help Thorliff with Greek lessons." Solberg took the package and letter and studied the handwriting on the envelope. There was no return address.

"Here, Deborah, one for you and one for Manda." Penny handed over two red-and-white-striped candy sticks.

"Thank you."

"You want a cup of coffee?" Penny asked Pastor Solberg, glancing toward where Manda hadn't appeared yet. "While I fill the rest of your order?"

Solberg glanced from Penny to the other section and rolled his tongue across his

213

teeth. "I guess that would taste mighty good about now. Why don't I just go help myself, let you get on with things?"

Penny's smile broadened. "Good idea. There's molasses cookies in the jar if you want. Deborah, you could get a cookie too."

As the two made their way back to the living quarters, Penny crossed to where Manda sat studying the new boots.

"Are they big enough?" Penny squatted down to push on the toe. "Stand up and walk around in them." She glanced up to catch a hint of moisture being dashed away from Manda's eyes. "What's wrong, Manda?"

"I ain't never had brand-new store-bought boots before in my whole life." She hiked her skirt up to look at the boots again. "Do they look all right?"

"They look just fine. You want to wear them home?"

"Can I?"

"Why not? They're your boots."

"How much are they?"

Penny named a price, and Manda let out air that had been trapped with her fear. "I got enough money too." She dug in her pocket and pulled out several bills and some change. "I've been saving."

Penny took the money from the girl's hand, wishing she could tell her to put it back in her pocket. But she knew better. Manda would be offended, and she didn't want that. Not if she was going to figure out a way to get her in dresses more befitting a blossoming young woman.

"Pastor Solberg and Deborah are having a cup of coffee and cookies if you'd like to join them."

"Nah, I'll wait in the wagon."

The bell tinkled over the door, and Penny turned to her new customer. She waved at Pastor Solberg as he called "Thanks for the coffee" and headed on out the door. If it hadn't been she needed to wait on the man who had just come in, maybe she'd have learned who the letter was from. She had a good mind it was from Zeb MacCallister.

"I got news for you," Pastor Solberg said to Manda when she had the team backed out and headed home. He tapped the letter in his hand. "This is from your pa. He's in Montana like we thought and looking for a homestead in that valley he liked so well. Says he'll be home before Christmas."

"To stay?" Deborah took her candy stick out of her mouth to ask.

"No, silly, not if he's got a homestead in

Montana." Manda flapped the reins over the team's back. "Giddyup now. I got work to do." The set of her jaw said she wanted no truck with anyone at the moment.

"Miz Rasmussen, there's some people here to see you." Thorliff stopped at the open door to Ingeborg's soddy, where the Rasmussen family were staying.

"Who is it?" The voice came from the dimness.

"Come see, please."

Mrs. Rasmussen did as Thorliff asked.

"We gathered up some things from all around to help you get started again." Dyrfinna Odell pointed to the wagonload of boxes, bags, and sundry furniture.

"F-for us?" Elvira Rasmussen stopped beside the wagon. "Wh-why? You don't know us."

"No, but we all know what it's like to be without anything." Dyrfinna patted the slender woman's arm. "Now, where would you like us to put these things?"

Ingeborg came from the cheese house. "Mr. Odell, Dyrfinna, how good to see you."

"L-look. They brought us all these things. How can we ever repay you?" She looked from one to the other as if afraid they might change their minds.

Ingeborg smiled at the question. "You can't. Just do for the next one that has needs. I'll call the boys, and they can help unload."

"Now, those two sacks are of wheat." Mr. Odell pointed to the two gunnysacks. "That's seed wheat for next year, for when you get to your homestead. The first year is mighty hard, and seed is hard to come by sometimes." He grabbed a sack by its two ears and swung it to the ground.

Elvira Rasmussen leaned over and spoke in her oldest child's ear. "You run and get your pa. He needs to help here."

The boy took off, racing across the field to where his father drove the team and plow around and around the field, laying under the wheat stubble so that the rich dirt looked even blacker next to the golden wheat.

Thorliff and Baptiste came from the woodpile and helped carry the things inside.

"Quilts, and look, a feather bed." Mrs. Rasmussen stroked the rolled-up bundle. "Why, how can people just give away these things? Surely they need them."

Like a swallow darting hither and there, she and her two youngest ones exclaimed over each addition as it came through the soddy door. When her husband arrived, she tried to take his hand to show him, but he shook his head.

"I got to help them." His voice turned hoarse, and he hawked and spat at the back wheel. Hefting a chair, he carried it into the soddy and set it next to a trestle table.

"That's it," Thorliff said, dusting his hands against his pant leg.

"Guess all we can do, then, is say thank you." The mister stuck out his hand to Mr. Odell. "How do we let the others know?"

"In church tomorrow. I'm sure Pastor will give you a moment either before or after the service."

"That I'll do."

So the next morning, it took two wagons to carry the Knutsons, the Bjorklunds, and the Rasmussens to church. As the new family met the rest of the folks of Blessing, Elvira Rasmussen had a hard time holding back the tears. Carl shook hands with all the men and tipped his hat to the wives.

"Don't you think we maybe could stay here instead of going on to the West?" Elvira looked around at all the people talking together after the service. "They been mighty good to us."

"I know, but land here is too expensive, and there's no homesteading left."

"We could work for someone else."

"If I told you once, I told you a thousand times, I ain't spending the rest of my life working for another. I got to have land of my own again."

Ingeborg wanted to go to Elvira, but she hung back. Leave it to a man to have the wanderlust like that. Dragging his family clear across North Dakota in the fall. Where would they wait out the winter? How she wished Haakan was home to try to talk some sense into the man.

17

The Ranch
September 8

Augusta hung on to the arms of the chair so she wouldn't slither right to the floor.

Morning Dove kept one eye on her patient while she stripped the bed and remade it with sheets fresh off the clothesline. "You stay there longer?" She motioned with her hands so Augusta might have an idea what she was saying.

Since the room had ceased spinning and she no longer felt in immediate danger of slipping off the chair, Augusta nodded. At least yes and no could be gotten across. She wished she had some idea how long she'd been sick. Strange to feel that days of her life were gone and she had no memory of them.

What memories she had made her squirm. She clamped her hands on the chair arms again. Had Kane been helping care for her in such intimate ways as she thought he did? Surely it had been his voice murmuring comfort to her as he changed the hot cloths for cool wet ones. At times they had both been there; at others it was this woman with the flashing eyes and warm smile. No doubt not thinking about it was the better choice.

"You hungry?" Morning Dove stood in front of her and mimicked eating.

Augusta's stomach rumbled as if it, too, had eyes and had seen the gestures. "Yes, please," she said with a nod, and the other woman left the room to begin making noises in the kitchen. She did remember standing in front of a huge fireplace and stripping off her clothes under a blanket, feeling the heat baking whichever side she presented to it. She could hear cattle bellering and horses whinnying. The rooster crowing woke her up earlier. She was on a farm. That was certain.

She skirted around the most important question. Why hadn't he taken her to Blessing? If this was on the way it most certainly was the roundabout way. She wasn't sure why she knew that, but it seemed she did. She looked down at the shapeless dress she was wearing. She'd traded her nightgown for this after washing her hands and face in the basin of hot water.

A few minutes later, a delicious aroma preceded Morning Dove into the room. A plate of ham and eggs and biscuits along with a cup of steaming coffee took up most of the wooden tray.

"Mange takk." Augusta inhaled the fragrances of real food, but when she tried to cut the ham, her hand shook so badly she laid the knife back down before she dropped it.

Morning Dove smiled and, taking the utensils, cut the ham and buttered the biscuits. She handed the knife and fork back to the woman in the chair.

"Mange takk," Augusta said again, then stopped and thought. "Th-thank you."

Morning Dove nodded. "You are welcome." Her smile showered approval on Augusta's efforts like a cloud-sprinkled rain in the spring.

"You are welcome." While the strange words came hesitantly, they came.

"Eat." Morning Dove pointed to the plate. "You need strength."

But after only a few bites, Augusta could hardly hold her head up. She'd never realized chewing took so much energy and it wasn't as if the ham were tough. On the contrary. But once the meat was chewed, even swallowing became an effort. She forced herself to finish the egg, and the fork clattered on the plate.

"Ah." Morning Dove entered the room almost at a run, which slowed when she saw her charge was all right. She whisked the tray off to the top of the oak commode and helped Augusta to her feet. The distance back to the bed looked as wide as one of the high mountain pastures the girls in Norway took the cows to every spring. Augusta had spent many summers herding cows until she was old enough to go out to work for a family in the city.

Once tucked back in bed, she was asleep before her nurse cleared the doorway.

"How is she?" Kane returned to the kitchen after peeking in the sickroom.

"She sat in a chair to eat breakfast," Morning Dove said. "Tired her out, and she been sleeping ever since. Rest make her well again."

"I know." He took his place at the table with the other men, all of whom were very careful to study their plates and not let him see the laughter dancing in their eyes. Kane said the grace, and the platter of fried pork chops, along with bowls of potatoes and gravy, made the rounds. The young Indian man by Lone Pine swallowed a chortle and had to be pounded on the back, he was coughing so.

"All right, let's get this out in the open." Kane laid his knife down by his plate. He caught a look that passed between the other two men. "What's on your mind?"

"N-nothin'." Red Wing coughed again and drank from his coffee mug with an air of innocence that wouldn't have fooled a blind man.

Kane stared at each of his men, willing them to answer. "Well." He put as much authority as possible in his voice.

All the men looked at Jake. With a beard red as a fox in full summer pelt, Jake took his time chewing the food in his mouth. He took a sip of coffee and cleaned between two teeth with the tip of his tongue. He didn't look at the others.

Kane did. The deviltry dancing in their eyes, which shuttered when they caught his stare, made him suspicious as a spooked range stallion. "I'm waiting."

Jake nodded. "Well, then, I guess we ought to . . ."

Since he left about a five-second pause between each word, Kane almost snapped his fingers to get him to pick up the pace.

But he knew that's what Jake and his co-horts wanted.

"To?"

"Wish you the best with this new wife of yours. We shore are lookin' forward to meetin' her."

A snort came from the other end of the table.

Jake gave a slight shake of his head and continued. "We jist been commentin' on how worried you be about the missus bein' sick and all. We ain't seen you that worried like since —"

"Mrs. Moyer has been very ill."

"Now, we know that, but you got to admit you been some flummoxed the last couple days."

"No." Kane shook his head. "Not at all."

With that, young Red Wing broke out into laughter. "No? Then why'd you leave the bridle in the oat bin?"

"I did —" Kane stopped. Had he really?

" 'Twas the filly's bridle. No one else used it." Jake cleared his throat of the chuckle that threatened to choke him. "Oh, and" — he turned to the grizzled cowboy at the end of the table — "what was that you saw, Hank?"

Only a red bandana around the neck gave the old man any color at all. The three or more days' growth on his face matched his lanky hair and eyebrows, and while the others still sported summer tans, his skin stayed gray due to the broad-brimmed hat he wore. "I found the lantern you been looking for."

"No." One syllable became nearly three. "Where?" But when they all broke into laughter again, Kane rolled his eyes and laid both hands on the table. "Well, if you jokesters can leave off pickin' on a newly married man, cut him some slack, maybe, you could finish your dinner before Morning Dove takes the plates away."

"No hurry." Morning Dove tried to hide her own smile.

"Please pass the pork chops."

"Soon as Mrs. Moyer is on her feet, we got something for the two of you, kinda like a wedding present," Jake mentioned as Morning Dove set the apple pie on the table. "Ooh-ee. Now, don't that look mighty fine." He reached for the pie plate only to get his knuckles smacked with the handle of her knife.

"Thank you." Kane took the plate with pie and set it in front of him. "I got a favor to ask. Any of you speak Norwegian?" At the shake of all their heads, he added, "German?" At the repeat, he sighed. "Sure would have made it easier."

"She don't speak English?"

Now it was Kane's turn to shake his head. "Only the words I taught her on the ride out."

"Ah."

The knowing tone made Kane shake his head again. "Eat your pie."

Augusta could hear the men in the other room, but she didn't want to bother them. They sounded as if they were having a good time. She turned her head and looked out the window. The sky wore a billowing blue dress, trimmed with clouds of lace. She eyed the chair where she'd sat for breakfast. Could she make it over there by herself? Looking out the window was preferable to staring at the ceiling any day.

She scooted upright, using both arms to brace herself, and sighed when she was actually sitting. Hard to believe that sitting up took so much strength. She checked the foot of the bed, thinking there might have been weights under the covers holding her in place.

"Silly." Swinging her feet over the side and sitting with nothing behind her to prop her up ate up another large chunk of her energy. The chair looked about as far away as the barn she could now see through the window.

A burst of laughter came again from the kitchen. They sure were having a good time. Was that the way it was around here all the time?

"The chair. We are going for the chair." Her throat felt as though she'd just gotten a face full of road dust. She hung on to the bedpost as she eased herself upright. The room stayed level at least, no swinging from side to side or around in a circle.

She took two steps, then turned and grabbed for the bed. The chair would have to come tomorrow or when Morning Dove could help her. Sitting on the edge of the bed would have to do for now.

"Ah, you're awake."

The male voice behind her made her grab for the covers. The quick spin sent the room into a matching dance, and she flopped back against the pillow. *My hair, my nightdress, my — oh, how embarrassing.* She tucked her feet under the quilt and pulled the top up to her chin.

"I didn't mean to frighten you. Morning Dove is bringing you some dinner, now that we know you are back in the land of the living."

His smile was enough to ignite a fire. If only she could understand him.

Morning Dove entered with her tray again, and Augusta's nose twitched, the food smelled so good. If only he would go away so she could be helped to the chair and eat. Instead, he sat on the end of the bed, crooking one knee up on the quilt.

"Would you please leave so I can have my dinner?"

He smiled at her and nodded.

"I said, would you please leave so I can get out of this bed. Now go!" She pointed a finger at the door, then made a brushing motion.

"Ah." He stood. "Sorry. I forget my manners at times." He turned to leave and stopped. "I forget that women are raised to be modest. Things will surely be different around here, eh, Morning Dove?"

"Yes." She set the tray on the dresser and came to stand beside Augusta. "Come now."

The trip wasn't nearly as far as Augusta had feared. When she sat down in the chair, she no longer felt as if she were running off the end like syrup, and most of the food got inside of her before her hand started clinking the fork against the dish. She even managed to hold the cup of coffee long enough and often enough to drink it dry.

But when Morning Dove returned from taking the tray to the kitchen, Augusta was more than ready to trek back to the bed. She slept clear through until dark.

The next day Morning Dove brushed and braided her hair so that when Kane came in after dinner she didn't feel like hiding her head under the covers.

"Hello." His smile hadn't lost any of its power overnight.

"Hello." Since he said this every time he saw her, it must be a greeting.

"Very good."

"Very good." Only hers sounded more like "goot."

"No, you needn't say that. I mean . . ."

She stared at him, puzzlement branded on all her features.

Father, give me wisdom. How do I do this? He pointed to her. "Augusta." Then to himself and waited.

"Kane Moyer." Her precise pronunciation made him smile.

"Very good." He held up a hand to keep her from repeating that back to him. He pointed to the bed and named it. Each thing he pointed out, she repeated after him, and when he pointed again later in review, she had most of them. *She's not only beautiful but learns fast.* When she pointed to the same things and said them in Norwegian, he stumbled over the words far more than she had the English. And when she pointed in review, he got only half.

Augusta shook her head and named them again in Norwegian, then followed with the English.

Kane only stumbled on one this time.

"Very goot."

He smiled back at her. "Yes, very good." *Sure wish I could go to Gedicks' tomorrow. We've got to have some help here.* Looking into her eyes was like falling into a clear stream, and he had no desire to get out.

Augusta held his gaze for a long moment, then looked away in confusion. *When he looks at me like that, I want to melt like butter in the pan. What in the world is happening to me? Must be because I'm weak from so much sickness.*

But after he left the room, Augusta had to admit that this warm feeling had nothing to do with being sick and everything to do with being too close to a very appealing man. What would her mother say if she saw her daughter sitting in her nightdress on the same bed with a man she hardly knew? Or with any man for that matter?

18

St. Paul
September 9

How many conductors did it take to run the trains anyway?

Hjelmer figured he had talked to about all of them twice. At least that's what it felt like. And most of them had shaken their heads, sorry to admit they hadn't seen his sister. Compared to talking with Dakota farmers about Farmers' Alliance business, at least it wasn't as hard to get the railroad men to talk.

But none of them said the words he wanted to hear.

"Hey, Hjelmer, how goes it?"

"Henry! What are you doing here? Thought you were on the western route for good." Hjelmer shook the man's hand and grasped his upper arm with his other hand. "You have no idea how good it is to see a familiar face."

"I take it your questioning ain't gone well." Next to Hjelmer, Henry looked as if he were standing in a hole.

"Everyone's tried to be helpful, but the fact is, no one remembers seeing Augusta on the first of September, nor the second either. And they said they would remember a woman traveling alone like that and not speaking the language." Hjelmer sighed. "I'm about out of time."

"Another meeting in Bismarck?"

Hjelmer nodded. "Yes, and I got things to do for that too. How are things in Blessing?"

" 'Bout the same. Your mother is having a real hard time with this."

How would you know? Hjelmer knew his mother kept about as stoic a face as any good Norwegian. If she had told Henry how she felt, she must care for the man more than her son realized.

"Come on. Let's get a cup of coffee, and you can tell me all that you've done. Then when you have to leave, I can keep looking."

Sometime later, their coffee cups dry after the third refill, Henry nodded. "So we have three men that aren't back in St. Paul yet. There were two other trains waiting by the St. Paul and Pacific, one that would have gone to Grand Forks and points west, the other south. What I can do is wait to talk with them, and if that don't help, then I can request the conductor job on either of those lines so's I can ask people along the way. When you get back, you could take the other line as a passenger. How does that sound?"

"Sounds like a lifesaver to me. I'll catch the late train to Grand Forks. I've talked with all the conductors on the St. Paul and Pacific and all of them are sure they didn't see her." He slapped Henry on the shoulder. "And you can bet your suspenders that my mor will love you forever if you find her missing daughter."

Henry's rosy cheeks turned slightly rosier. "Any way I can to find the shortest path into that woman's heart."

Hjelmer paused and studied the older man. "Ah, are you courting my mor?"

"Much as she'll let me."

"Um, shouldn't you be asking my permission, or some such?"

"Hjelmer, you might be the remaining man in the family but you aren't her father."

"No, but there's my older brother, Johann."

"You know what I mean." Henry pushed

his chair back from the table. "I'll be getting on with the asking. You got any other particulars you might tell me about Augusta? Ways that someone might recognize or remember her?"

"Not that are mentionable, nor helpful either. I racked my brain, as I know Mor did, but nothing other than her height and her lack of English."

"And her Bjorklund blue eyes?"

"Ja, that too. Good luck and God bless. If I haven't heard from you, I will be back here in a week or ten days. How can I get ahold of you?"

"Leave a message with the stationmaster. I'll check with him."

On the trip home Hjelmer drew the papers he should have been studying out of his valise and read them thoroughly. Far as he was concerned, with the final drafting of the constitution, his job was finished. And since the constitution was to be ratified by a popular vote in October, he didn't see any need to continue being involved in the politics of North Dakota. Besides, he'd promised Penny he would stay home more.

He stared out the window into the dark night, ignoring his reflection and letting his mind wander. Why was Penny in such an all-fired hurry to have a baby? Surely God knew best, and if He didn't see fit to send them children right now, that was fine with him. It wasn't as if she didn't have enough to do to keep her plenty busy. Between the church and the store and feeding train passengers and her sewing machine business, she was running faster than a spooked mare all the time anyway.

He shook his head and went back to his reading. With the enactment of statehood, it looked as if there would be changes in the banking rules, along with just about everything else. He planned to bring that up at the meeting. First Bank of Blessing didn't need a whole series of laws laid down by the eastern banking concerns. The people of Blessing had organized the bank for themselves, and so far they had managed not only to stay solvent but to earn interest for the savings depositors too. The money was mostly earned by investing in one another, like the loan for the boardinghouse, his machinery, and the Baards' new barn.

Even though he didn't really think Augusta had come as far as Grand Forks, he questioned the stationmaster and the ticket men there, all to no avail. When he swung off the early-morning train in Blessing, he was no closer to finding his sister than when he'd left. But he knew lots about where she wasn't and who hadn't seen her.

He opened the front door to the store carefully. "Hey, Mrs. Bjorklund, you got a cup of coffee for a weary traveler?"

"Hjelmer!" Penny spun away from dusting her spice shelves and darted across the well-stocked room to throw her arms around him.

"I think for a greeting like that, I should be gone more." He held her close and kissed the tip of her nose and then her laughing mouth.

"No, you don't." She thumped him on the arm and then stood on tiptoe to kiss him again, pulling instantly back when the bell tinkled not three feet behind them.

"You look good in red."

She glanced at her dress, started to say something, then her cheeks flamed even brighter. "Hjelmer Bjorklund, go pour your own coffee. I've got work to do." She straightened her apron. "How can I help you?" she greeted her customer.

"You can go on as you were," a laughing voice replied.

"Good idea," Hjelmer whispered. He

turned and smiled at the woman behind him. "Good morning, Tante Agnes." He touched the brim of his black fedora with the tip of his finger.

"Go on with you." Penny gave him a push toward their home off the store. "Good morning, Tante. What do you need today?"

"Thought I'd wait here while Joseph takes a wheel over to the smithy. You didn't have to send that handsome young man of yours off like that." Agnes Baard paused to look over the display of boys' boots that Penny had gotten in the day before, a smile dimpling her cheek.

"He just came home." Penny surreptitiously smoothed her hair back where Hjelmer's hug had pulled it loose from the bun she wore.

"Then you go on back and take care of him. I can just look around to my heart's content."

"The coffee is hot."

Agnes cocked her head and crinkled her eyes. "Well, now, that would taste mighty good, seeing as how we left home hours ago."

"What have you been doing?"

"Oh, took some things out to that new family, the Rasmussens. How they're going to be ready for winter is beyond me, 'specially if they go west like the mister wants. Going to take a miracle for sure."

"Or the women of Blessing Lutheran Church." Penny brushed aside the curtain that closed off the store from their living quarters.

"Well, I'd say that's a miracle in its own right."

"You would."

Agnes took the chair that Penny pointed her to and glanced around the kitchen-sitting room combined. "Ah, my girl, you have made this such a friendly home. No wonder those railroad men wanted to eat here."

"They seem to like it just fine over at Bridget's now. Haven't had anyone come here and complain I'm not serving anymore." Penny arranged molasses cookies on a plate and set that on the table. "If you want something more, dinner will be ready in an hour or so."

"No. This hits the spot." When the coffee cup was set before her, Agnes dunked her cookie in the steaming brew and nibbled off the spongy part.

"How is it at your house with all the children in school?" Penny set her and Hjelmer's cups down and took her chair.

"Too quiet. I find myself banging things just to make noise. You know, if we were to find some children like the White boys off the train, I sure would be pleased to take them in. I thought about that this morning out at Ingeborg's place." Agnes shook her head, and the light silvered some of the hairs at her temple. "But the best we can do there is provide for the whole family, if those folks aren't too prideful to accept our help. After all, we all been there one time or another."

"Are the children old enough for school?"

"One could be but is so shy." Agnes shook her head. "The other two are barely out of diapers, and the missus has another under the apron. She's so thin herself that the babe will come with problems, you mark my words."

Penny looked around her own cheerful kitchen and tried to imagine having nothing. Thanks to their generous friends, when she and Hjelmer married, they already had a good start on a household. And opened the store not much later. But then Hjelmer had already worked hard for his money.

Not to say Mr. Rasmussen hadn't. Losing everything you owned in a train wreck was a shock for certain. "I guess they must be grateful they were on another train."

Agnes nodded. "But it's hard to be grateful when you see all your work come to naught and have to seek help from people you don't even know. I think having Pastor Solberg to come to makes it easier for the askin', though."

"Tante Agnes, glad you could join us." Hjelmer came down the stairs, white shirts hanging over his arm.

"I suppose you need those for tomorrow?" Penny's eyes widened.

Hjelmer nodded. "Sorry. I'll bring in water."

"And the boiler?"

He sat down at the table, reaching for a cookie at the same time. "After my coffee."

"So tell us what you have found out." Agnes propped both elbows on the table and held her cup at sipping height with both hands.

"Nothing. If I didn't know better, I'd think Augusta fell off the face of the earth."

"Don't say it like that to your mor." Agnes's eyebrows flattened in a frown.

"I won't. I don't want to say anything to her. No news is good news, you know?"

"Humph, if that isn't a man." She turned

to her niece. "I got something for you, Penny. Thought it might come in handy here at the store." Agnes reached down in her bag and brought up some brown papers. She laid them on the table and opened one.

"An envelope?" Penny reached for one of the two-layer contrivances. She pressed the flattened sides, and the papers opened like a mouth. "There's no flap."

"No. I cut the paper, folded it in half, and pasted down the side and across the bottom. I figured you could put cookies or a piece of cake or a sandwich in them. You can fold down the top to close it. Easier than wrapping with brown paper and string like you do for cheese and such."

"What a clever idea." Penny opened another. "What should we call them?"

"Why, paper bags or sacks, I s'pose. I got the idea looking at a grain sack, only those are sewn up. Joseph says I got too much time on my hands when I have time to play with paper and paste, but I just thought it might be a good thing for you. You give me the paper, and I'll make more."

"That would be a good job for Andrew and Ellie. Those two scamps came by yesterday asking if there was anything they could do to earn a penny for candy."

"So what did you have them do?"

"Nothing. I gave them each a piece of candy."

"They could have picked up clinkers from the tracks. Save on your woodpile."

"They could have stacked wood too. Between Sam and Ephraim, there's quite a bit split." Hjelmer raised his cup, and Penny rose to refill it. He knew he should be getting on over to the boardinghouse, but the thought of his mother's sad face kept him in his seat.

"I know, but I love to watch them try to decide which kind to choose. That Andrew, he can talk a bird out of a tree, you know."

"So how many pieces did he get?" Agnes set her cup down.

"Two."

"Penny Bjorklund, you'll spoil that boy to death."

"I know, but . . ."

A knock sounded at the back door just as the store bell tinkled. Penny got to her feet. "You take that one and I'll go for the store." The curtain swirled behind her, leaving Hjelmer to answer the door and Agnes to chuckle over her niece's soft heart.

"Ah come ta get the tray ready," Sam

said after he and Hjelmer swapped the greetings of old friends. "Dat train be heah befo we know it." He sniffed in appreciation. "Miss Penny be one mighty fine cook." Since Sam came, he'd been taking cookies, cake, and sandwiches, along with coffe and milk, out onto the train to sell to passengers.

Hjelmer poured another cup of coffee and pointed to the fourth chair at the table. "Sit down. Those cookies on the table are just waiting for you."

"You know where my Joseph went?" Agnes asked.

"Right here." Joseph, going from lean to stringy as he aged, stepped through the store curtain. "Sam came through the back door, but I go around to the front. Figured I find you playing with that sewing machine."

"I wouldn't have to play with Penny's if I had one of my own." Agnes started to get up to pour the coffee, but Hjelmer waved her back to her seat and did it himself.

"Ah got no time for sittin'. Dat tray need fixin'." Sam sat on the edge of his chair.

"I'll start." Agnes got up and began slicing bread for sandwiches. Penny already had the cheese and meat ready to put on them.

"I can tell when I'm not wanted." Hjelmer headed for the door.

"Oh no. You can cut the cake and slide it in those bags." Agnes pointed to the cake pan with her knife.

"I need to talk with Mor."

"Not now. She's getting ready for the noon rush too." Agnes pointed at the cake again.

Sam chuckled as the blond young giant did the bidding of the string-bean woman with years-frosted hair. With all of them working, the tray filled rapidly, and using the new paper sacks, they were able to stack things more closely together.

"Now, don't that look nice," Penny said, coming back after her customer left. "Joseph, you two want to stay for dinner?"

"You know we never turn down a free meal." Joseph leaned back in his chair. "We timed this pretty good, huh, Ma?"

"Sure did. Now you can go fetch water for the boiler." Still holding her knife, Agnes pointed to the door this time.

"Ya got to listen up to a woman waving a knife," Joseph advised Hjelmer on his way out the door, leaving everyone laughing.

Some time later, when the train's boiler had been refilled and those who worked the line, along with the passengers, had their bellies full and the train had gone on down the track, Hjelmer moseyed on over to the boardinghouse, looking forward to talking with his mother about as much as he liked to sweat an iron rim on a wheel. If only he had some good news for her. If only he had Augusta in tow.

"You didn't find her, huh?" Bridget beat him to the words, elbow deep in bread dough.

"No, sorry." He went on to tell all he had done, hoping that would make her feel better.

It didn't.

"Henry might be able to accomplish more, him being a conductor and all. Maybe he can jiggle someone's memory." He reached forward and snagged a fingertip of dough, popping it into his mouth before she could scold him.

"Hjelmer Bjorklund, aren't you never going to grow up?"

"If never having dough again is the price, no thank you." Hjelmer leaned his haunches against the counter and crossed his arms over his chest. "You thinking of frying some of that? Would taste mighty fine with syrup."

"I might." Bridget pushed the heel of her

hand into the dough, turned half of it in with her other hand, and spun the fragrant mound at the same time.

Hjelmer watched her. The thump and push, roll and thump again of kneading dough had always intrigued him. Creating something so delicious out of such plain and simple ingredients. Of course that was his mor. Creating beauty in all she did, whether she realized it or not. He glanced around the kitchen. Several rosemaled plates lined a track around the ceiling, and he figured soon she'd have other things up there. Kerosene lamps, their chimneys glistening clean, lined a shelf above the dry sink, ready to be called into service for supper. The huge iron stove gleamed as though freshly blackened.

Did she never rest? He thought back to the times he'd heard her stifle a groan when she got up from her rocking chair or saw her knead the muscles in her lower back. She wouldn't do that if they didn't hurt.

He had tried to tell her that a boarding-house would be too much, but she and the church ladies nearly tore him limb from limb.

Now, if only he could find her daughter for her. *Where is she, God in heaven? Where?*

19

The Ranch
Mid-September

If they didn't let her get out of the house, she might go stark raving crazy.

Augusta ran her fingers through her hair, wishing she could wash it and sit outside to let it dry, the sun was that warm. After the frost two nights earlier, the weather had turned warm again, much like it did at home. She finished braiding the waist-length strands and wound the braid into a figure eight at her neck, securing the mass with hairpins from her carpetbag. The waistband on her skirt hung down around her hips. What once had been a full bust was no longer.

She stared at the face in the mirror. Hollows in her cheeks, bones like rocks under the skin of her neck — gaunt was the only word to describe her. How much time had passed, after all? She pinched the skin on her cheeks to get some color to return. Mor would call her a ghost, a spook. Never in her life had she been so sick. And to think she was stuck here with strangers taking care of her.

She could hear Morning Dove working in the kitchen. Augusta pinched her cheeks one more time and headed for the door. She would find something to do to help. Surely cooking and washing dishes were the same, no matter what language she spoke. Morning Dove would just have to get used to her helping until she could find a way to continue her trip to Blessing. Mor needed her!

But Augusta got sidetracked by the windows overlooking a creek lined with willows not far from the back of the house. Between the house and creek lay a garden, bordered by fruit trees on the east. A bench out by what looked to be the well house beckoned her. A long porch stretched the length of the building, similar to the one in front. Two willow-branch chairs sat against the wall, also extending a silent invitation.

She slipped out the door and leaned against the porch rail, savoring the air that smelled of fall. She waved to Morning Dove, who had left the kitchen and was now digging carrots and potatoes in the garden, dropping them in a basket at her feet. The fragrance of rich soil floated over to her, making her inhale deeply in appreciation.

Too much fresh brisk air in sore lungs made for a coughing fit that had her hanging on to the post for support. She waved Morning Dove away and finally was able to get her breath again. When she looked up, the Indian woman stood not five feet from her, hands on hips and a frown joining her black eyebrows. A sling on her back held her sleeping infant.

Augusta shook her head. "I am fine, or at least I will be. I am *not* going back in the house. Especially not back to my room." She felt like adding "so there" but decided a smile might be more appropriate.

It was.

Morning Dove's frown disappeared, replaced by a smile. "You." She pointed at Augusta. "Come out." She beckoned with one hand, then pointed to the garden.

"You?" Augusta pointed to herself.

Morning Dove shrugged. "Not really but . . ." She beckoned again. "Come."

"Come?" Augusta let go of the porch post and crossed the grass to stand beside Morning Dove, who nodded. Together they walked out to the freshly dug row. Morning Dove pointed to the vegetables, naming each.

"Potatoes, carrots, turnips, rutabagas, pumpkins," Augusta repeated after her. She picked each one up, brushing away the dirt and inhaling the earthy fragrance. Even the earth smelled and looked different than it did in Norway. She looked up to see a wedge of geese flying south, recognizing their familiar song. But never had she seen so many as she had here in this country. She looked down to find Morning Dove watching her, smiling and nodding at the same time.

"Geese," Morning Dove said.

"Geese," Augusta repeated.

They continued the naming of things as Augusta pulled the root crops that filled basket after basket. But it wasn't long before she could feel the strain, her face flushing in the heat and exertion. She wiped away the perspiration from her forehead with the back of a hand.

Morning Dove picked up one of the smaller baskets and headed for the house. "Come. You sit down."

Inside, Morning Dove pulled a chair out from the table. "Chair." She sat down and as she did said, "Sit." Then she repeated the action. "Sit in chair."

Augusta did as she was told, repeating the words "sit in chair" and receiving a smile for her efforts. How frustrating this was, not being able to talk with the woman. Surely there had to be a way she could learn the language faster so she could ask the myriad of questions gushing like a rain-swollen stream in her mind.

Why, oh why hadn't she spent the money to buy a language book? Hjelmer had told her to, Mor had told her to, and even Johann had done so. Stubborn, stubborn, stubborn. That was her, all right. Always thinking she knew best. Why hadn't she listened? All that time on the boat and train, surely she could at least have learned some rudiments by now.

Morning Dove brought over a pan of vegetables in water and a knife. She picked up a carrot and, using the edge of the knife, showed Augusta how to scrape the dirt and skin away, then handed both to Augusta and indicated the rest.

"Thank you." Augusta forced herself to use the English, even though "mange takk" sounded so much friendlier.

"Thank *you*."

When the vegetables were scraped and simmering on the stove, Morning Dove handed her a broom and indicated where to sweep. Again Augusta smiled and leaned into her task. Some things didn't need language.

By the time dinner was ready and Morning Dove rang the triangle that hung on the back porch, the two women had fallen into an easy camaraderie, sharing the tasks as Morning Dove gave words for Augusta to practice.

When the four men came in, Augusta wanted to disappear back in her room. Young Red Wing clapped his hand over his heart, and while she didn't know what he said, the action brought heat flaming up her neck.

"Now, boy, don't go embarrassing her thataway."

Augusta looked over at Kane, recognizing a thunderstorm approaching and wondering who was going to get rained on. Or struck by lightning. It didn't take long to find out. She wished she knew what he'd said to the young cowhand, but then maybe she really didn't want to know.

Everyone shuffled to their places at the table, the bantering gone with the blistering. For that was what it had been. Even though she didn't understand the words, the reactions made them clear. Augusta looked from the young man to Kane and back again. Surely that had not been necessary. Glaring at the older man, she set the plate of roast pork in front of the younger man and sent another glare Kane's way. Who did he think he was anyway?

And what did it matter that she'd been a bit embarrassed by the laughing glances of the younger hands? After all, while he might be their boss, he surely wasn't hers. She took her chair with a flounce and after grace passed the bowl of mashed potatoes to her left, carefully keeping her gaze from intersecting with that of the man at the head of the table. The fact that she was sitting at the foot didn't register.

Halfway through the meal, she felt a wave of weariness try to drown her. She put down her fork and straightened her shoulders, sucking in a deep breath at the same time. Her eyelids felt as though pound weights hung on them, and keeping them open became the battle of the hour.

As soon as the men left, she propped her chin on her hands and let her shoulders sink. The curtains at the windows faded into a blur. She didn't argue when Kane returned, swept her up in his strong arms, and carried her down the hall. His well-worn shirt felt soft against her cheek, and his heart thudded under her ear. She marveled at the strange desire to put her arm around his neck, but before she could act upon it, he deposited her in the middle of the bed in her room.

"Mange takk," she murmured, turning on her side and tucking her hands under her chin.

"You are welcome."

Was that his finger she felt trailing down the side of her cheek? She couldn't force her eyes open to check. She heard his boots click out a tattoo on the floor as he left the room.

How would she ever get to Blessing when the bit of work she'd done this morning wore her out like this?

Kane paused at the door and looked back at the slender woman lying in his bed. She'd tried to do too much on her first real day up, that was all. While his head knew that for a fact, his heart wanted to run back and check her again to make sure she was only sleeping.

She hadn't appreciated the dressing down he gave Red Wing, that was for certain sure. *Young pup, making eyes at my wife like that. Whatever came over him?*

But Kane knew. The only women his

men had seen lately were Indian squaws. Augusta's golden hair would attract attention anywhere in this vicinity. As soon as she was stronger, he promised himself that he would go visit Gedicks and see if his mother and Augusta could understand each other.

In the meantime, he had fences to build.

When they rode back into the yard as the sun was setting, Kane glanced up to see Augusta sitting in one of the rockers on the front porch. Flames from the dying sun set her blond hair afire. The urge to warm his fingers at those flames made him almost leave his horse tied to the hitching post and go to her. When he turned back from knotting the reins, the sun had set enough that now she sat in shadows, leaving him wondering if he'd really seen such beauty or merely been out in the sun too long.

Later that evening after supper had been cleared away, he motioned Augusta to join him at the chairs in front of the fireplace. She nodded and raised one finger in the air, then pointed to the bedroom. "I'll be right back." He seemed to get her meaning, so she hurried to her room.

He nodded, and settling into the leather cushions of a chair made of willow branches the size of his upper arms, stripped of bark and sanded, he picked up the guitar sitting to the side.

Augusta returned, knitting needles, wool, and a partially completed sweater in her hands. She stopped and watched as he cradled the guitar in his arms and set the instrument to singing with the magic of his fingertips. The tune tugged at her heart, and she sank into her chair with a sigh of delight.

He smiled over at her, his fingers continuing to pluck the melody in a speed she couldn't follow. She returned the smile, and her fingers took up her knitting where she had left off, turning the yarn into cables and ribbing that sang of the snowflakes and fjords of her homeland. When he finally set the guitar aside, she sighed in disappointment.

"You look so beautiful in the firelight like this. Of course you look beautiful all the time, but if I'd known what it would be like sitting here with you, I might have searched for a wife a long time ago. But then she wouldn't have been you."

Augusta smiled back at him and nodded at the warm tone in his voice, wishing for all she was worth to know what he was saying. Would now be a good time to ask

him when he would take her on to
Blessing? The thought of leaving him, this
place, made her eyes want to run.

20

Blessing
Third week of September

Now, he would make a fine-looking man for my Augusta.

Bridget caught another glimpse of the boarder when the kitchen door swung open to let Ilse return to serving the guests. Almost three weeks, and they'd not heard a word. When she let herself think about it, her heart felt near to cracking in two.

Father God, I am trusting you to care for my Augusta. Please, you've taken two of my sons and a daughter home to you already. Can't you find it in your heart to bring this one back to me? She stirred a pot of baking beans before putting them back in the oven, all the while continuing her internal conversation. *I know my children are better off with you, but this one, if she has come home to you, so be it, but if not, please keep her safe. You know, at least you could watch out for your son Hjelmer.* She gulped at her impertinence. *Father, forgive me for not being grateful for the years I had her with me. I am, truly I am. But it's the not knowing that's the hardest. If she is suffering somewhere* . . . She took over kneading the bread and sent Goodie out to check on the laundry steaming in the boiler over the fire pit.

Yes, I know. What could I do anyway? That's why I am reminding both you and me that I am putting her in your hands — again. And this time I will try my best to leave her there. The thump and push of kneading the bread started an ache in the middle of her lower back. Her thoughts turned to Hjelmer. *Please guide my son in his looking for his sister. I'm glad he has finished in Bismarck so he can continue looking. Am I showing my lack of faith for sending him out? Or am I being wise? You know, if you would just give me some sign.*

She sighed and straightened, twisting to the side to pull out an aching muscle. *I know I'm just a silly old woman. Maybe I should have listened to Hjelmer when he said a boardinghouse would be too much for me to do. Then Augusta would have been safe at home instead of who knows where. Are you punishing me? But I really thought this was your idea. Plenty of people have been blessed because they stayed here, and you know I pray for each of them, just like you said.*

"You all right?" Goodie stopped beside her. "Why don't you go sit down, and I'll bring you some breakfast."

Bridget gave the bread dough a final thump, then smoothing it into a ball, set it back in the deep wooden bowl Uncle Olaf had carved for her from an oak stump. She laid a clean towel over the bowl and set it on the top of the reservoir to rise.

"Why don't you sit down too? You've been charging around here like a wolf is on your tail." Bridget bit back a sigh as she leaned against the back of the chair, another creation of Olaf's. She often thought he'd do better making furniture full time than running the sack house. Once the grain was shipped, that's where he set up shop. He had his lathe humming all winter long, along with his saws and chisels. Between him and Sam, they could make about anything a body needed.

Goodie set a plate of ham and eggs in front of Bridget and returned to the stove to get the toast out of the rack she'd set over the coals in the firebox. Once they both had their meal before them, Bridget said grace, and they fell to.

"So, you have something you been wanting to tell me?" Bridget waved her knife at Goodie before cutting off another bite of ham.

Goodie looked up from buttering her toast. "How did you know?"

"Oh, you had that look about you, something like a cat who is sitting in a sunny window, licking the cream off his whiskers."

"Oh, land, and here I been trying to keep it a secret. But, you know, after losing the last two, one is almost afraid to hope." Goodie took a bite of her jam-spread toast.

"Ja, it seems God hasn't been blessing the women around here too much with babies. Ingeborg, Penny, Agnes, you, and even Pastor's wife."

"Hildegunn neither. She and Anner sure are thankful for those two boys."

"More so than Pastor Solberg." The two women shared a bit of laughter over the antics of Jerry and Toby Valders.

"Well, I better get them sheets rinsed and hanging on the line. Won't be too long before they're freeze drying rather than wind and sun drying. I tell you, I ain't looking forward to winter. Days are getting too short now as it is."

"Check on Lemuel and make sure he's

not leaving half the vegetables in the ground. I need that cellar plumb full if we're to feed all the boarders this winter. When are you due?"

"Oh, long about Eastertime, I think. Now wouldn't a son be a fine Easter present for Olaf? New life for him just like he brought new life to me and mine." Goodie got to her feet and picked up both their plates. "You just sit there a few minutes longer. It won't hurt nothin' for you to rest a bit."

"Bestemor! Pa's home!" Thorliff burst into the kitchen through the back door.

"Land sakes, boy, you about scared me half to death." Bridget laid a hand on her bosom.

"Sorry. Ma said to tell you we're having a welcome-home party tonight, and we want you to come for sure. Mrs. Wold, you too."

"Then who's going to make sure my boarders get fed?" Bridget waited, knowing Thorliff would come up with a good answer.

"They can eat early, or . . ." His blue eyes got even bluer, if that were possible. "They could come too. There's always plenty of food."

"We could bake a couple extra pies,"

Goodie said with a nod. "And Ilse could serve those who didn't want to go that far, although why anyone would turn down an invitation to a party is beyond me."

"I think we'll even clear out the barn for dancing." Thorliff's eyes sparkled. "I'll dance with you, Bestemor."

"Shame Henry's not here. We could use his fiddle if there's to be dancing."

I sure do wish I'd hear from Henry. Bridget amended her thought. *I wish I'd hear that Henry or Hjelmer, either one, had found Augusta. She loves to dance. How she would enjoy being here.*

"Baptiste and me are going hunting. Roast goose would taste good, don't you think?"

"It sure would. I'm surprised your ma hasn't been out hunting."

"She has, only we ate that catch already." Thorliff headed out the door. "See you tonight."

"Well, I better get to gettin'." Bridget started to stand, but Goodie laid a hand on her shoulder.

"Why don't you peel the apples, and soon as the sheets are hung, I'll make the crust."

That night half of Blessing gathered at

264

the Bjorklunds'. Kaaren and Ingeborg set up trestle tables, and as people arrived, they set their food out and gathered to visit. Wagons with the team tied to the wheels lined the lane and yard. The children played up in the hayloft or out in the field, where a game of Run-Sheep-Run soon got under way. The harvest moon rose golden, making the field and yard nearly as bright as day and lighting the group of men talking politics in the yard. The women bustled around setting out the food and calling everyone to come and eat.

After Pastor Solberg said grace and the men had filled their plates, Andrew, Ellie, and Deborah got in line together to get their food.

"I hope there's fried chicken left," Andrew said, trying to see around those ahead to the chicken platter.

"I saw a fancy cake over on the other table. That's what I want." Ellie brushed back a hank of hair that had come loose from her braids from sliding down the straw stack.

Andrew glanced over and saw Sam's two young relatives, Laban and Mary Jane, off to the side. "Come on over here. We got room for you." He beckoned and moved back to show the space. "Get your plates."

"They don't b'long with the rest of us."

Andrew spun around to see who said the ugly words. "It's not nice to say such things." His lower lip came out, and he hunched his shoulders.

"Andrew." Ellie glanced over her shoulder. "They're bigger than you."

"I don't care. My ma says black people are no different than white." He beckoned to the two children again.

"We'uns will wait."

"Yeah, if they know what's good for them."

Andrew handed his plate to Ellie. "Hold this." He started for the back of the line where the two Valders boys stood side by side.

Ellie ran for her mother but banged into Thorliff first. "Hey half-pint, where you going?"

"Andrew — Toby and Jerry . . ." She sent a frightened glance over her shoulder.

"Now what did they do?" He lowered his voice so the grown-ups wouldn't hear.

"I got to tell my ma."

"No, come with me."

Thorliff nodded to Baptiste and the two Baard boys, all four of whom were closer to man-size now than boyhood. Manda took Ellie's hand and gave it a squeeze.

Andrew and the two Valders boys stood toe to toe. "You take that back." Andrew's fists were clenched at his side, and his chin stuck out, the glare in his eyes enough to start a prairie fire.

"Nigger lover," hissed Toby. His brother sneered the same words.

"So?"

"Don't you know them niggers got nits?" Toby spat at Andrew's feet. "You'll catch 'em if'n you even stand by 'em."

Andrew took one step forward and let fly with a right that connected to Toby's nose. Blood spurted faster than anyone could blink.

Toby let out a shriek that could be heard clear to Bismarck and clapped his hands to his face. Blood leaked between his fingers.

"Good for you, Andrew." Thorliff grabbed his arm. "But that's enough." Manda and Baptiste flanked Thorliff on either side. Both of them winked at Andrew, but Manda studied the Valders boys through slitted eyes.

"M-a-a-a." Toby turned and screeched for his mother.

"What are you boys doing? Oh, my . . ." Hildegunn paused for one moment before descending on the now immobile group of children. "Tobias Valders, what happened?"

"H-he h-hit me." Toby pointed at the much smaller Andrew standing with his brother's hands on his shoulders.

"They said bad words." Ellie moved a step forward to stand by Andrew's side. She nodded to the two black children, who looked to be fading into the shadows. "About them. My ma said we was to never use such words." All the time she shook her head and stepped closer to Andrew, as if she could protect him from the wrath above.

Hildegunn turned to Jerry. "Is that what happened? You tell me the truth, now!"

Jerry started to shake his head, began to say something, then stopped, thought, and wilted. He nodded.

"And were you part of it?"

If he could have tunneled into the ground, it appeared he would have. Another nod. This time he studied the tops of his shoes as if all wisdom were written there.

"Andrew Bjorklund, what is going on here?" Ingeborg knelt in front of her young son and looked him directly in the eyes.

"Jerry and Toby said bad words about our friends, and Andrew socked him a big one right in the nose." Ellie told the tale so fast she ran her words together.

"Wait a minute." Ingeborg rose to her feet and planted one hand on Andrew's shoulder and one on Thorliff's. She looked her eldest straight, eye to eye. "Did you see or hear what went on?"

"Not really." Thorliff shook his head. "I think Andrew took care of it himself."

Hildegunn had a boy by each arm. "Wait until your father hears about this."

"But, Ma, I —"

"Don't you 'but Ma' me, young man. I want to know what you said." She shook them again. "And right now."

While the children all swapped looks under their eyelids, no one said a word.

"I'm waiting." Hildegunn drew herself up to her full height, seeming to grow like a pig's bladder puffed full of air.

Andrew edged closer to his mother.

Toby's nose quit bleeding.

Sounds from the others enjoying their supper and the visit seemed to float around them, unable to penetrate the circle.

Jerry scuffed his boot toe in the dirt. Toby wiped his bloody hand on his pants.

"I'm waiting."

Andrew looked up at his mother. "I

269

don't call people names like that."

Ellie shook her head. "Me neither."

"I won't never again," Toby muttered, elbowing his brother.

"Me neither."

"Then you can all shake hands and be friends again." Hildegunn glanced at Ingeborg, who nodded.

The boys shook hands, but anyone could tell there was no sign of friendship.

Thorliff turned around to see where the Negro brother and sister were, but they had disappeared.

"I don't like them," Ellie whispered as the two Valders boys followed their mother over to the pump to get cleaned up.

"And now we don't get to eat with Laban and Mary Jane, and I like them." Andrew sucked in a deep breath of air and let out a corresponding sigh. "Torly, why are they so mean?" He hadn't used the baby name for his older brother for a long time.

Ingeborg watched Hildegunn attend to her bloody son. "They just weren't raised like folks around here," she said, then put a finger under Andrew's chin and tipped his face up to look at her. "But that doesn't excuse what you did. Andrew, you have to learn to outthink people, not bash them."

"But, Mor, Toby and Jerry were mean to Laban and Mary Jane, and now they left and maybe won't come back, and . . . and . . . it's just not fair!" Andrew spit out the last word, his eyebrows making a straight white line across his wrinkled forehead. He sighed and shook his head. "They better . . ."

"Andrew." Ingeborg made her voice stern.

"What was all the ruckus about?" Haakan kept his voice low, but the hand he laid on Andrew's shoulder carried not only authority but a gentle squeeze of approbation.

Ellie told the story again, her voice gaining confidence as she recounted Andrew's exploits. "And . . . and it's not Andrew's fault, so please don't take him out to the woodpile." She took two steps closer to Andrew as if daring anyone to go through her to get to him.

Ingeborg pressed her lips together. "We will talk about this later. You children go ahead and eat your supper while there is still food left." She guided them toward the table.

Andrew took up his plate again. "Wouldn't ya know there's no fried chicken left." He looked around. While

Toby and Jerry weren't there, neither were Sam and his family.

Both Andrew and Thorliff danced with their grandmother and their mother too, but Andrew danced mostly with Ellie and Deborah, in between running up and down the ladder from the hayloft.

"You want to dance?" Baptiste stopped in front of Manda and held out his hand.

"With you?"

"Why not? You were willin' to fight alongside me." White teeth flashed in his tanned face.

"That's different. I don't dance." Manda scuffed her boot toe in the dirt.

"You do now." He grabbed her hand and whirled her into the intricate steps of the Pols. The fiddle sang, and the guitars kept the beat along with a washtub played with a broom handle and clothesline.

At the end of the dance, Baptiste led Manda back to her leaning place against the barn and squeezed her hand. "Thank you."

"I guess."

As he danced the next one with Ingeborg, she asked, "When's Metiz coming back? Have you heard?"

"No. But soon. She said before the snow flies."

"Good. I miss her. Penny said she would pay for any smoked geese you could provide the store. Bridget says the same with the boardinghouse."

"So I can hunt instead of school?"

Ingeborg laughed. "I don't think so. With your new gun, you can knock down a whole flock in one evening."

When the fiddles and guitars quieted, Haakan stood in front of the remaining friends. "Well, Lars and me and all the others sure do feel welcomed home. Thank you all for coming, and we'll see you in church in the morning."

"Mor," Andrew said when she tucked him into bed. "Do I have to ask for forgiveness for . . . for . . ."

"Hitting Toby in the nose? Yes."

Andrew sighed.

"Does he have to ask forgiveness for being mean to Mr. Sam's little kids?"

"I'm sure his mother is taking care of that, and the answer is yes."

"Does he have to say sorry to them?"

"I hope so."

"Do I have to say sorry to *him?*"

Ingeborg closed her eyes, then slowly nodded. "Yes, son, I believe you do."

Andrew groaned. "I *hate* saying sorry."

"Then don't do anything you have to feel sorry about." *Ah, such an easy thing to say and so hard to do.* Ingeborg's mind flew back to the baby she lost because the team spooked. *If only sorry made everything all right again. But it doesn't. Too often we just have to live with it.* She leaned over and kissed Andrew on the forehead. "You will be polite in church." It wasn't a question.

Andrew understood. He crossed his arms under the covers. "Yes, Mor."

Ingeborg made her way down the stairs, wondering what would happen next. Somehow she had a feeling this little fiasco wasn't over yet.

21

Hjelmer's Quest
Last half of September

"Did you see a woman about five foot nine with golden hair get off here?"

"When?" The stationmaster of Valley City, North Dakota, stared up from under his green visor. From the looks of the office, he did double duty as the telegraph agent.

"On September first, give a day or two either way. Her name is Miss Augusta Bjorklund. She's my sister, her eyes blue like mine."

The man behind the counter shook his head. "I would sure to have noticed her. No women by themselves been through here in ages."

"Thanks." Hjelmer turned away.

"Good luck."

"Thanks again. I think I need more like a miracle." Hjelmer didn't want to count the times he'd played out this scene. Sometimes the agent scratched his head before shaking it. One man squinted his eyes in deep thinking, but the final answer was still the same. No one had seen Augusta on this line. He had one more stop to go, and then it was back to St. Paul on the next train.

Perhaps when they connected again, he'd learn that Henry had better luck.

God, I think this has gone on long enough. I am sick and tired of traipsing around the countryside looking for a woman who seems to have vanished off the face of the earth. If I don't hear or learn something in the next two days, I'm going home.

He swung back aboard the train as the conductor cried, "All aboard."

He was sick of hearing that too. How could Henry put up with all the noise and the people and the rackety rocking of the train itself? He sank into a window seat and sighed. *Lord, I just want to go home.*

Back in St. Paul he checked with the stationmaster to find out when Henry would return from the run to Lake Superior. When the man said not until evening, Hjelmer decided to visit a couple of machinery places to see what the latest farm equipment was. One thing he'd noticed south of St. Paul was a tall framework with wooden paddles in a circle and one that looked like a rudder. He figured it had something to do with wind power and wanted to learn more.

He left the station and caught a trolley, watching the passing parade of horses pulling every type of conveyance known to man, from carts pulled by a single pony to drays with six up. The noise made his ears ring.

At the John Deere dealer, he wandered among plows and mowers, binders and threshers. He stopped at the massive steam tractor and shook his head. Hard to believe that people really thought that ten-foot-tall, two-ton monstrosity would ever replace horsepower in the fields. Although he had to admit the steam engine Haakan had did a great job powering both sawmill and thresher. But horses still had to pull it to get from place to place.

This tractor pulled itself.

"You want me to start it up so you can see for yourself?" one of the salesmen asked. "That's made by Case out of Racine, Wisconsin. John Deere hasn't made one yet."

Hjelmer shook his head. "No thanks. I've seen a demonstration already." He scratched his chin. "You sell many of those?"

"More each year. You don't have to feed them all winter, you know. And the power! Why, one tractor takes the place of ten horses, and it don't get tired by noon either. Long as you keep the steam up, this tractor keeps on rolling." He slapped the rounded metal that housed the man-tall, cleated-steel wheels. "You mark my words, farming with horses and oxen is on the way out. One day every farmer will have a tractor or two. Think how fast your fields would get plowed with one tractor pulling a four-bottom plow. You can buy either a straw burner or a coal burner."

"Ja, and when that boiler blows up, it kills everyone within fifty feet." Hjelmer had read of a steam engine that did just that. "And it takes two men to run it." He shook his head again. "Think I'll stay with horse-drawn for a while longer." He pointed over at a seed drill. "Tell me some about that piece. Looks like there's been lots of improvements since last year. Maybe it's time to start stocking those."

As they moved from machine to machine, Hjelmer took notes on a pad of paper he'd brought for just this purpose. "Oh, and what do you know about those tall rigs with paddles in a circle on top that

I've been seeing from the train? What are they used for?"

"They are windmills. They harness the wind to pump water from your well. You can keep your stock tanks full now without ever pumping again."

"Well, I'll be." Hjelmer looked around. "You carry them?"

"Nope. Wish we did, but you'll find a dealer about half a mile down the road. Different companies make their own model. Folks jumping on the bandwagon like crazy. Some of the funniest-lookin' rigs you ever want to see." The man shook his head. "But they work. Man, do they work."

"Well, thank you for your time. Think I'll go learn about windmills. Since the wind almost always blows in the Red River Valley, they might be a good thing to stock."

An hour later he had purchased four fans with vanes and ordered gearboxes, along with shafts that went down in the wells. He figured Haakan and Lars would produce the lumber to build the towers for now, but steel framework was the coming thing. He could hardly wait to get home and show Haakan the new contraptions and the diagrams for the towers. If he knew his farmers, there'd be windmills sprouting in the valley like sunflowers in the spring.

But first he had to find Augusta.

He caught the trolley back to the railroad station, hoping Henry had returned. He was there waiting for him.

"Hjelmer, I got good news for you." Henry wore a smile that near to cracked his face.

"Good thing. We're about due for good news."

"I think your sister got on one of the southern spur lines. McDonnell, the usual conductor on that line, has been off sick and just came back." Henry flashed Hjelmer a delighted grin. "He thinks he remembers your sister, though he ain't sure."

"So let's go talk to him."

"Well, that ain't so easy. He left half an hour ago and won't be back until tomorrow."

Hjelmer groaned. "Why didn't I come back here earlier?"

Blessing

"So when do you think Hjelmer will be home?" Agnes Baard continued to cut out the cookies with the new cookie cutter

Sam had made for them, this one in the shape of a diamond.

Penny opened the oven door and leaned down to check the doneness of the molasses cookies already baking. "I wish I knew."

The plaintive tone drew Agnes's attention from the rolled dough to her niece. "You still aren't with child?"

"No! And how I ever will be without Hjelmer home more than a day or two at a time is beyond me. Making babies does take two, you know." Penny closed the oven door with a bit more force than necessary. "I think he has a wandering foot, or rather, in his case, both feet. You watch, he'll come home all excited about some new piece of machinery that he just happened to learn about in St. Paul when he was *supposed* to be looking for his sister. You watch."

Agnes only made an agreeing sound and went back to her cookies. With the second pan full, she motioned Penny to open the oven door so she could slide it onto the bottom rack. "I think that first pan is done."

Penny half smiled. "I bet you wish you'd not said anything."

"Better to get it out with me than let it

fester and explode all over Hjelmer when he does come home."

"Do I do that?"

"I reckon so. We all do."

Penny lifted the round lid on the fire side of the stove and inserted two chunks of wood, then adjusted the damper again.

"I've heard tell that the more you worry about not having a baby, the less chance there will be to have one. Some folks just take longer than others. That's the way of it."

"You don't think God is punishing me, then?" Penny stared at the stove, her back to her aunt. If there'd been any other noise, Agnes wouldn't have heard the question, Penny's voice dropped so much.

"Pshaw. Whatever for?" Agnes gathered the bits of dough together and rolled out the last round.

"Oh, things like wanting the best store in the Red River Valley, being proud of my sewing machines, getting mad at Hjelmer — I can think of all kinds of things." She looked over her shoulder without turning around.

"Are you putting those things before Jesus?"

"I don't think so, but . . . ."

"I know. It's hard to tell at times."

The bell tinkled above the front store door, calling Penny back to work.

"Mmm, something sure smells good." Pastor Solberg sniffed again and smiled at Penny. "You've been baking."

"How can you tell?" Penny glanced down. She knew she'd changed her apron just before she walked through the doorway.

"Flour on your chin." He pointed to his own chin to show her where.

"Thanks. How was school today?"

Solberg rolled his eyes. "I might have to stuff a rag in Toby's mouth and tie Andrew to his seat."

"Oh-oh. Now what?"

"Just a carry-over from the party the other night. All the other children can accept our two new ones, but Toby and Jerry come from a whole different background."

"Have you talked with Sam and Eulah about this yet?"

"No one was at home. I thought to catch Sam here, but he's not in the smithy either. Is Eulah over helping at the boarding-house?"

Penny shook her head. "What do you think I am, the town keeper? Can't find someone, ask Penny?"

"Seems that way, doesn't it?"

"God dag, Pastor." Agnes came into the store, carrying a plate of still-warm molasses cookies. "Thought we'd get a third opinion on these. New recipe." She held out the plate.

John Solberg took one and after one bite said, "You better keep them under lock and key if you want any left by tomorrow. What's different?"

"Applesauce."

"Maybe we should have put sugar on top." Penny took a cookie too. "Of course what these really need is a cup of coffee."

"I wish. But I better get on my way. Maybe Sam is over helping Olaf." At Agnes's invitation, he took a couple more cookies and went out the door.

"Let's get some paper cut, and I'll make you some more of the bags. Maybe Ellie would like to come over and help me now that school is out."

"Sounds good." Penny stared toward the door. "Maybe Sam's two little ones could come too. Let me go find out. Tell anyone who comes in that I'll be right back."

"As if I can't wait on them myself?"

Penny headed out the back door and across the narrow field to the house on the other side of the sack house. She waved at a couple of the farmers with wagonloads of sacked grain waiting to be weighed, then knocked on the screen door. "Anybody home?"

"Hi, Mrs. Bjorklund." Ellie came to the door. "Come on in."

"Is Hans here?"

"Uh-huh." Ellie held open the door.

"How would the two of you like to come over and help us paste up paper bags? Maybe you could run over and ask Mrs. Lincoln about her two young ones also."

"Sure. Hans is doing his schoolwork, but he can do that later."

"Okay. Come as soon as you can." Penny stepped back off the porch and looked up at the trailing Vs of ducks and geese. She knew where Thorliff and Baptiste were for sure — out hunting. Maybe they'd bag enough geese that she could sell smoked goose again this year.

Ellie caught up with her before she got back to the store. "Pa needed Hans for a bit, so he'll come later. I can go over and ask Mrs. Lincoln, if'n you like."

Penny nodded, and Ellie ran off, jumping over a clump of grass and waving her hands in the breeze. The joy she saw made Penny almost do the same. Oh, to be six years old again. She looked around to make sure no one was looking and, with a running head start, leaped over the chopping block, her skirts and petticoat billowing around her knees as she landed. She spun in place and lifted her face to the westerly sun. Maybe she didn't need to be six after all, just act like it.

She smoothed her dark skirt back down and made her way up the path to the back door, managing to work a skip or two into her pace.

"Good day for vaulting," Anner Valders said when she returned to the store. The twinkle in his dark eyes betrayed the chuckle that daren't come forth.

Penny could feel the heat start up her neck. He'd seen her through the window in the bank room. "Ja, some days are good for most anything."

"Mr. Valders," Agnes called from the kitchen, "are you in need of a cup of coffee?"

"Yes, please." He nodded to Penny, the serious look he usually wore back in place.

"You know" — Penny entered the bank room through the arched doorway — "you need to smile more often, Mr. Valders. You've got nice eyes when they twinkle." Now the heat really rose, splashing over onto her cheekbones. *What in the world possessed me to say such a thing?*

He studied her as if he had to add up a column of figures without a pen. "You know, you are most likely right. Thank you for the compliment." When Agnes passed Penny with the cookie plate and a mug of coffee, Anner Valders looked up at her and actually smiled. "And thank you, Mrs. Baard. Fine day, is it not?"

The doorbell tinkled just in time to keep Penny's eyes from watering. *Must be due to the brisk air,* she thought as she turned back to the store. "I'm coming."

"Mail's here." The railroad conductor tossed a canvas bag on the counter. "What's that I smell? Molasses?"

"Mr. Haraldon, you could detect fresh cookies under a pile of hay. Wait right here, and I'll get you some." She had to remind herself that skipping wasn't quite fitting for the store's proprietress. It must be something in the air.

Later when she saw her name written on the front of an envelope with an Ohio postmark, she felt like skipping again but made do with a small hop. She could hear the children and Agnes laughing in the kitchen as they pasted up the sides of the brown paper bags. Folks had already gathered, as they did every afternoon, to wait for her to set out the mail, so she stuffed the letter in her apron pocket and went about her business.

What if this was from another one of her brothers or sisters? What if they were coming to visit? The letter seemed to burn a hole right through the cotton fabric.

22

The Ranch
Late September

"Come." Kane beckoned from the doorway.

Augusta tucked her knitting back in the basket she had found and got to her feet. She followed him out the front door and stopped on the porch. The roses growing on either side of the steps smelled sweet on the faint breeze. The frost the night before hadn't killed them as she had been afraid it would. Fall had dressed the elm and oak trees in shades from gold to russet with everything in between. A matching leaf skirt drifted over the ground beneath.

Kane stopped beside a horse that looked to have been painted with the same fiery red as the leaves. The horse rubbed its forehead against his shoulder as he motioned her to join him.

"Do you ride?" He pantomimed her mounting.

"For me?" Augusta clasped her hands to her breast. How she would love to ride free like the breeze, and this horse wasn't even a workhorse, not with those dainty feet.

"Come on." Kane motioned with his head this time and held out a stirrup.

Augusta glanced down at her skirt. Was it full enough that she could ride astride without showing parts of her legs that weren't supposed to be shown? She shook her head. "It is not proper."

He patted the horse's neck and motioned her to come again.

Augusta looked around. None of the other men were in view. The only other dress she had was a shapeless thing that Morning Dove had found for her. The skirt on it carried much less material than the wool one she was wearing. *I'll do it. Who cares about my ankles?* She smiled back at the man by the horse and strode down the walk. Placing her foot in the stirrup, she swung her leg and skirts over the saddle and found the other stirrup before rearranging her skirts. When she smiled down at him, her breath caught in her throat.

"You are so beautiful," he said, and while she didn't understand the words, the look in his eyes was unmistakable.

Warmth, caring, delight, a dollop of joy. She wanted to take hold of the hand that handed her the reins, to reach down and trace a finger over his chin. She felt as though she were drowning in his eyes.

The horse stamped a front foot.

"This is horse." He pointed to the horse and repeated the name. He almost said filly but realized he didn't want to try to explain that with the limited words at his use.

She echoed him and leaned forward to stroke the filly's mane to the right side. "Such a beautiful horse." Throwing her arms around the animal's neck didn't seem like the proper thing to do, but oh, how she longed to do just that.

"Th-thank you."

"You are indeed welcome."

Kane mounted his horse and led the way down the lane and out into the fields that led to the rolling hills. As they rode side by side, he pointed out a covey of sand grouse, a hawk screeching above them, a patch of late-blooming fall asters. When they came around the breast of a hill, she saw the deer drinking at the pond first and pointed it out without talking. After the deer bounded away, the yellow-headed blackbirds picked up their swamp chorus again, joined by both their redwing and tri-color cousins.

She leaned back against the cantle to ease the jog, and at her beam of delight, Kane broke into a lope. Her hair broke loose from its bindings and flowed behind her like a golden banner. Not since she was a child on the slopes of Norway's mountains had she ridden like this, but then she had ridden bareback. Thanks to the stirrups and the horn of the heavy roping saddle, she was regaining her balance and confidence with a speed beyond her imagination. She could ride. She really could, even if holding on to the horn at times seemed a wise precaution.

When Kane brought his horse to a stop, she laughed aloud in sheer delight.

Cows and half-grown calves put their tails in the air and ran from them, making her laugh again.

Kane's heart lurched at the sound of her joy. *Lord, I would do anything to make her laugh like that some more. Thank you for bringing this perfect horse for her and for bringing my Norwegian princess here to me. Was that love or at least caring I saw in her eyes? How long, Lord, do I wait before I make her my own?*

He watched her as she chuckled when a

calf hid behind its mother and then peeked out from around her haunches, the tail swatting the calf's face. Kane joined in with a chuckle of his own when Augusta's smile invited him to. She tossed her head, sending the golden waves rippling down her back. When she realized he was studying her, she tried to gather her hair back in some semblance of order, but at a brief shake of his head, she shrugged and let it go.

Augusta could feel his gaze burning into her flesh. She glanced at him, then down at her hands clasping the reins on the saddle horn. What did he want? Why was she getting warm all over? She wet her lips with the tip of her tongue. They felt crackly dry, like her throat.

Why doesn't he say something? She shook her head and felt the hair swishing against her back. Here she was, an unmarried woman, riding who knew where — well, he knew — with an unmarried man, her ankles showing, and her hair down her back. What would her mor say to this?

The picture didn't bear thinking of.

Thoughts of her mother banished the smile from her face and the song from her heart.

When would he take her to Blessing?

Surely she was healthy again, so that was no excuse. But he didn't seem in much of a hurry. At the thought of leaving this place, this man, a cloud turned gray and settled around her. But she'd given her word, had written to Mor that she was coming to help with the boardinghouse.

She started to ask, but he interrupted her.

"Come, we must go back." His face had gone from summer to winter without enjoying fall. What had she done?

She tried to smooth her skirt down with one hand. Until she had some hairpins or ribbons, there was nothing she could do about her hair. She turned her horse and followed behind all the way back to the ranch house. Convinced she had done something to offend him, she racked her brains all the way back. But what? What could she have done?

They rode up to the barn, and Kane dismounted, looping his reins over the hitching post. He turned back to her and, drawing the reins from her hands, did the same for her horse.

She glanced up to check, but the sun hadn't gone out. The sky was still blue, and the puffy white clouds gamboled like lambs across the hills. Was he angry? Sad?

What had happened?

She grasped the saddle horn and, leaning forward, swung her right leg back over the cantle and the horse's rump. But before she could find the ground, strong hands clasped her waist and steadied her descent. Her knees went soft like newly made pudding, and she sagged against him.

"I thought you might need help here." His breath tickled her ear.

Move, she ordered her legs. *Stay,* her mind whispered. The warmth coming from his chest and through her clothing constricted her breathing. His hands at her waist branded like fire. The urge to lean into his warmth rather than step away made her knees weaker. If she turned, would his face be hovering just above hers? His breath tickled the hairs on her neck.

Never before had she understood what people meant by the words "time stood still," but now she knew.

"Augusta." The very way he said her name sent shivers chasing up and down her spine. While she'd enjoyed the few kisses she'd shared with Elmer after their betrothal, nothing prepared her for the longing she was feeling now, the desire to turn and touch his face, to wait and see what he would do next.

"Kane?" Lone Pine came around the corner. "Ah." The one word carried a hint of laughter. "I go and come back later."

Augusta stepped out of the shelter of Kane's arms and only kept her hands from covering her face with great strength of will. She knew if she touched her cheeks, her fingertips might be singed. Her hair was all a-fly and her heart aflutter. What must he think of her?

She ran for the house like wolves were hot on her heels.

Kane glared at his foreman. "What is it?"

"Sorry." Lone Pine shrugged, his teasing look setting Kane's teeth on edge. "I didn't realize you . . . your woman . . . you . . ." He raised his hands in the air and dropped them, visibly trying to erase the glint of laughter from his eyes and mouth.

Kane crossed his arms over his chest and glared from under the brim of his hat. "Spit it out, man."

"Ah, brother, she's your wife, right?"

"Yes." Kane turned to unsaddle Augusta's horse.

"Then why all this . . . this . . ." He motioned confusion with his hands.

Kane paused in the act of pulling the leather cinch-strap free. *As if I need to explain myself to you, man.* But the two of them had shared far more than ranch work. They'd grown up together, more like the brother that Lone Pine called him. They'd taken turns saving each other's life. Lone Pine had rescued Kane from a bear once, and another time Kane had brought his brother back to life from a snakebite. Kane had thought seriously about taking a wife from the Mandan tribe like Lone Pine had, but something had stopped him. Now he knew what. God had in mind a golden princess for him and had kept him celibate until that day.

"Yes, brother, she is legally my wife, but I thought to give her time to know me and me her. That she would come to love it here, and . . ." *Love me. I don't just want a wife. I want her to love me as I love her. Then we will indeed be married, by ties far stronger than the vows we made and the paper we signed.* He pulled the saddle off the horse's back and swung it over the hitching rail.

The filly shook herself, her fiery mane and tail shooting sparks in the sun.

"She cares." Lone Pine hefted the saddle and pad and carried them back into the barn, slinging them over one of the pole braces nailed to the wall.

Kane felt like asking, "Are you sure? What makes you think so?" but he had no trouble recalling the feeling of her melting against him. So then, why did she run like that? He stared up toward the house, trying to guess what she might be doing. Fixing her hair, no doubt. How he'd wanted to run his fingers through the golden tresses. The scent of roses from her hair had teased his nostrils enough for him to want more.

He let the horses loose in the post-and-rail-enclosed small pasture and carried his saddle into the barn, looking around for Lone Pine. He came and went silent as a shadow. Shame he hadn't left without catching their attention earlier. Then he and Augusta might —

He chopped that thought off and went to check on the pigs. Once the weather turned cold enough, they had three to butcher. The remaining fifteen head he'd sell to the army. The major was always glad to purchase both hogs and steers for the mess tent.

He found Lone Pine working with the horses they were training for the army, all of which were now broken to saddle but some so green broke they snapped like twigs at the slightest provocation. The one he was trying to mount refused to stand still. Quick as a snake, Lone Pine had a loop around the horse's front leg and drew it up by tightening the rope around the saddle horn. Now when he tried to mount, the horse knew better than to hobble on three legs.

Lone Pine mounted and dismounted five or six times, then released the tension on the leg. With all four legs on the ground the horse stood still, his head down, sorrel shoulders darkened by sweat. He only shivered when Lone Pine mounted again and this time nudged him into a walk. Once around the corral and they stopped, starting all over again with mounting and dismounting, this time without a misstep.

"He'll make a good mount." Kane reached through the rails to stroke the horse's nose and nodded up at Lone Pine.

"Yup, he's a smart one. He don't fight the rope like that jughead over there." Lone Pine nodded at a horse tight tethered to a post in the center of the arena with one foot tied up, yet still he pulled against the rope that snugged him to the post. His nose and behind his ears were raw with the pulling, but he persisted.

"Might be good for nothing but horse-meat if he can't be broke." Kane knew that some of the wild horses never did give in. "Did you geld him?"

"No, but think we better. Might settle him down some."

"How old do you think he is?"

"Maybe four, five. Might have had some mares of his own, then another stallion took 'em. He bears the scars of a fight or two."

When the triangle rang for supper, they put away their saddles and headed for the bench that held steaming pitchers of water, soap, and towels. Kane looked down at his dusty pants and checked to see his shirt looked about the same.

"Think I'll go change after I wash up."

Lone Pine cocked an eyebrow but kept his own counsel, his stern look warning the others to do the same. Nary a snicker passed their lips as Kane made his way to the house, slapping the dust off his hat by slapping it against his thigh.

As soon as her heart quit thundering in her ears, Augusta crossed the room to the dresser that held a mirror, her brush and comb, and the small wooden box her father had carved that now held her hairpins. Taking the brush, she ambled back to the window and stood looking out as she brushed the tangles from her hair. One pin slipped forward to catch on her bosom. She watched the two men talking by the hitching rail and letting the horses out in the pasture.

All the time she called herself all kinds of names for her brazen way with Kane. While on one hand she heard, *Whatever's got into you?* on the other hand, she knew full well. She was attracted to him — that went without saying — but until she got to Blessing, she couldn't even consider him as a suitor. After all, she'd promised her mor to come and help out. "And she's the one who said that once you make a promise, you have to live up to it no matter the cost." Only the curtains heard her whisper, and while they and the breeze shared secrets, they'd never tell anyone else. She'd ask him tonight. "If only I could talk his language, it would be so much easier."

She finished her brushing, twisted her hair into a long coil and wound it around and around at the base of her head, then tucking the ends under, jabbed a couple of hairpins in to hold it in place. If it had been in a braid, it wouldn't have flown so freely. Before she rode next time, she'd do that.

If there will ever be a next time. She resolutely turned from that thought and headed for the kitchen to see if she could help Morning Dove. After all, no matter what the state of *her* mind, the men would be hungry.

She and Morning Dove fell into an easy rhythm, not needing to talk as they accomplished the tasks that needed doing. Periodically Augusta would hold up a utensil, and Morning Dove would tell her what it was. Asking the woman to tell her about Kane was, of course, beyond her comprehension, but the desire only grew rather than going away.

In spite of the aprons she so carefully wore when in the kitchen, her skirt needed washing, and while she could wear the other garment, more and more she wished for her trunk or some cotton to sew another dress, one that fit. And looked nice. And had a full enough skirt to ride comfortably.

To catch Kane's eye.

Blue would be good, a blue the color of sky — or her eyes. She opened the oven door to check how the pies were coming.

When the men came in for supper, she used every effort of control she owned to not look into Kane's eyes. She set the platter of fried chicken on the table, along with the mashed potatoes and gravy. Morning Dove brought the plate of sliced bread, still warm from the oven, a bowl of buttered carrots, and another of leftover baked beans.

As soon as the women slipped into their chairs, Kane bowed his head and asked the blessing on the meal. At the amen the men reached for the platter or bowl nearest them and dug in.

Augusta passed the dishes as they came her way, dished up her own food, and steadfastly kept her eyes on her plate or the person on either side, never once raising her gaze to the man at the other end of the table.

She could feel him watching her. The back of her neck grew warm, then the front, and up into her cheeks. If she'd had a fan, she'd have used it — gladly.

Later, as she and Morning Dove finished cleaning up and setting the sourdough to rise for pancakes in the morning, she heard the strains of his guitar from the other room. Removing her apron and hanging it on the nail by the stove, she brushed out her skirt and checked to make sure her hair was still snug in the coil.

Morning Dove waved good-night, her baby snugged on her back, as she went out the back door to the small house she and

Lone Pine lived in just west of the main house but before the bunkhouse.

Augusta thought of taking a kerosene lamp into her room and reading, but the pleading tune he played drew her into the firelight circle. She took her chair and picked up her knitting without looking directly at him; nevertheless, she could feel his gaze burnishing her skin. When she could resist looking no longer, he'd gone back to eyes closed, letting his fingers wander out whatever notes they wanted. He segued from song to song, light to dark and back again, wooing her with melodies that sang of heartbreak, joy, and majesty. Some of them she recognized, some not, but losing herself in the magic took no effort on her part. Her heart did as it willed.

She glanced up when the last note trickled away to find him looking at her with an intensity that made her squirm.

"I . . . I have to ask you something," she blurted before he said anything.

He shrugged.

"When are you taking me to Blessing, like you said?"

"Blessing?"

"Ja, when?"

"Blessing?"

She nodded.

The look he gave her was filled with such confusion, she clasped her hands in her lap until the knuckles turned white. He began to shake his head.

23

St. Paul
Late September

"Didn't her ticket say where she was going?"

"I . . . I suppose so." The florid complexion of McDonnell, the conductor, deepened even more so, if possible. "I-I'm trying to think what it said."

"It should have said Blessing, North Dakota."

The man screwed his face up, obviously trying to remember, then shook his head. "I just don't recall. If'n I'd seen that on her ticket, I would have put her off at the next stop 'cause she was on the wrong train."

"But you think you recall a woman matching our description?" Hjelmer felt like pounding out his frustration on the man, but the wall would do.

"I sure do. You can't miss eyes that match yours." He held up beefy hands.

"Not that I spent a whole lot of time looking into her eyes, mind you."

"No, of course not." Hjelmer took in a deep breath, hoping it would calm his leaping heart. Finally they had someone who remembered seeing Augusta. She really had made it as far as St. Paul. She wasn't lost someplace east.

"Do you recall where she got off?" Henry prodded his friend's memory.

"I think she went clear to the end of the line. Ipswich, it would be. I wasn't paying too much mind, you know, since I'd already done her ticket and she couldn't speak a word of English, at least not that she let on. My Norwegian is pretty sparse, you know." He looked from Henry to Hjelmer. "She just sat in the first double seat, looking out the window and knitting away. I don't know how women do that, knit and look at the scenery or something."

"Well, I better go buy me a ticket to Ipswich."

"You don't have to hurry. That one is scheduled to leave at ten-fifteen tomorrow. You already missed today's run." He tucked his watch back in his breast pocket. "There's some thought about making that an every-other-day schedule."

Hjelmer groaned. "That means I have to

spend another night here."

"Sorry." Henry stuck out his hand. "Thanks, McDonnell. We appreciate your help. You take care of yourself, hear?"

"Oh, that I do. Just wish I could be more specific."

"That's all right. We've at least got something to go on now."

Hjelmer did the same, and the two of them climbed the marble steps back up to the main hall, the never-ending noise assaulting them the closer they came.

"I'll see you soon, then," Henry said, extending his hand to Hjelmer.

"I surely do hope so, Augusta in tow. Tell Mor what all has been going on. This news will help pick up her spirits, I'm sure."

"I will. Seems like forever since I saw that woman." Henry rubbed his chin with two fingers. "You get her daughter there, and then maybe she'll give up and marry me. Leastways, my helping you can't hurt."

"I hope so. The better I've gotten to know you, the more convinced I am that you and she will be good for each other. And thank you, Henry for all your help. Without you, we might never have realized a conductor was missing. And just the right conductor too. He started to walk off, then turned back. "How about telling Penny that I'll be home soon?"

"Oh, I will. There'll be rejoicing in Blessing tonight."

I only hope it's not too soon, Hjelmer thought as he pushed open the bright brass-framed glass doors leading to the streets of St. Paul. He'd spend the hours at more machinery lots, have a nice dinner, and sleep in a hotel for a change, then be ready to catch the train to Ipswich, South Dakota — wherever in the world that was.

"Well, we meet again." Hjelmer nodded to McDonnell, now resplendent in his navy wool uniform and gold-billed hat.

"I got called in. The man on this run came down sick." He helped a young woman who appeared to be traveling alone up the steel step stool to the stairs. "There you go, ma'am. Take any seat."

When she answered in Norwegian, Hjelmer translated for the conductor and received a smile of gratitude. Hjelmer swung his valise into the rack above the seats and took a seat across the aisle from the young Norwegian woman. At least with a window seat he could see the country on the way to Ipswich and maybe see some other machinery in action, as he had the windmill.

He couldn't wait to get home and get to building the frame above his own well. Once he had that pumping, he knew he wouldn't be able to keep the parts in stock. Maybe he and Haakan could form some kind of partnership to build the towers and install the machinery itself.

"Mange takk for your assistance." Her voice caught him by surprise, he'd been so involved in dreams of gushing water without the labor of winding up the bucket.

"Velbekomme." He touched the brim of his felt hat with one finger. "What part of Norway are you from?"

"Oslo."

He nodded. "I went through there on the way to America. Busy place compared to the mountains of Valdres region where we lived. You have family here?"

She shook her head. "But I will. I am to be married as soon as I arrive. My fiancé sent my ticket."

"Ah." Hjelmer nodded. "I'm sure you will like it here. The work is hard, but the land, ah, it will grow anything, at least up where I live."

With an "All a-b-o-a-r-d" the train lurched forward, and the sound of hissing steam made conversation across the aisle difficult. Hjelmer looked out the window, blinking when the train cleared the subterranean station and broke into the sunlight. As the train picked up speed, warehouses and brick business buildings flew past, apartment houses took over, and then family dwellings with wash on the line and children playing in leaf-strewn backyards. When the houses spaced farther apart and became farms, Hjelmer settled back for the ride, knowing his destination was hours off.

"Tickets. Have your tickets ready." McDonnell's voice preceded him.

Hjelmer took his from the inner breast pocket of his suit coat and checked to see if the young woman understood what was needed. She did and smiled up at the burly conductor as he asked for hers.

"Going to Ipswich, eh?" He punched the requisite holes. "Just like that man over there."

At her look of bewilderment, Hjelmer translated again, bringing a smile and nod his way.

"You two ought to get to know each other," McDonnell said when he took Hjelmer's proffered ticket. "You can help her out some. Don't know what I'd do if'n I couldn't talk the language. First thing my grandmother and grandfather did was learn to speak English, them and their kids. Now most of us can't talk the old tongue a'tall." He shook his head. "Got to be American as ya can to get anywhere. Ain't easy nowhere, no matter what they say in them pamphlets they send out."

Hjelmer nodded. He'd spent a good part of the voyage learning English, that and poker. By the end of the time at sea, he'd become more fluent with the latter but knew enough English to survive. Passing by the card room at the hotel had been a temptation last night, but years before he'd sworn to never gamble again, and he kept to that.

"Mange takk again," the young woman said after the conductor made his swaying way up the aisle.

"You are indeed welcome. Is there no one traveling with you?" Hjelmer leaned back and relaxed. It looked as though he wouldn't get to watch the scenery as much as he wanted. But he daren't be rude. His mother had taught him far better than that.

"There was, but she remained in Chicago. I . . . I wish now I had learned some English before I left home. I . . . I just had no idea the land was so big." She shook her head. "I think everyone could emigrate from Norway and not even make a dent here."

"Most likely. I only know the way east and west. There is plenty of land to the south, too, and even more west from here. A friend of mine tells tales of mountains higher than those at home and valleys that take your breath away. He wants to head to Montana to homestead now."

"Montana?" She stumbled over the strange word.

"That's another territory on the western border of North Dakota."

"And we are going to South Dakota now?"

"Yes, but we're still in Minnesota and will be for several more hours." Hjelmer glanced out the window to see another windmill, this one different from the ones he'd purchased, since it had only three blades. The other seemed more efficient to him, even though the cost was slightly more. When he saw a steam tractor pulling not only a plow but a disc behind, he craned his neck to watch them as long as possible. The machinery salesman had been right. Farmers were using the monstrosities in the field. Most likely he should stock at least one.

But the cost was high, no doubt about

that. He'd better sell a lot of windmills first.

"I have a favor to ask."

Her voice again broke his thoughts, so he turned back, barely suppressing his disgruntlement.

"Would you please teach me a few phrases as we go? I hate to bother you, but I'm realizing how important this can be."

Hjelmer sighed and pointed to the seat opposite her.

"Oh, please. Yes, of course, please sit here." She motioned to the seat, relief evident in the relaxing of her shoulders. "At least this way I can tell Mr. Moyer hello when we meet."

Hjelmer changed seats and something in her tone made him pause. "Do you not know this man?"

She shook her head and stared down at her hands clamped around the handles of her bag. "I . . . I signed a paper with the Norwegian government to become a wife of someone from America. Mr. Elkanah Moyer wrote to the program seeking a wife. I have heard that there are many more men in this land than women, and so I answered Mr. Moyer's letter. I was supposed to come earlier, but my mor died, and I needed to be there to help out, so I came now instead. I sent Mr. Moyer a letter telling him of my situation."

Hjelmer knew this was not an unusual circumstance. Women were indeed wed quickly when they came to the frontier. So many died in childbirth and of other things that some men sent back east for wives or, like this one, to the homelands.

"So let us begin with the English lesson." He gave familiar phrases like greetings and other polite sayings and had her repeat them after him, then quizzed her on them a bit later. "Hello, my name is Asta Borsland." He had her fill in the blank.

This continued through various stops, and along with teaching her the language, he answered her avid questions of what life was like, about his family, and she laughed when he told her about things that went on in Blessing.

"That must be a very fine place to live." Her tone grew wistful. "From Mr. Moyer's letter, I know I will live on a ranch, far from close neighbors like you have." She squared her shoulders and reapplied the smile to her face. "But I will be very happy there. I know I will."

"Have you ever lived in the country?"

She shook her head. "No, but it can't be too different from the city."

Hjelmer nearly groaned. Oh, but did she have a lot to learn. "Do you know how to milk a cow?"

She shook her head.

"Plant a garden?"

She nodded. "Somewhat."

"Feed and butcher chickens?"

Her headshake included a shudder this time.

"Weave?"

"I can knit, and I'm a good cook and housekeeper. I've taken care of many children."

"That is good." He gave her several words for household things, and she repeated them back. "Have you ever made soap?"

Another no.

"Dressed out a pig or deer?"

She shook her head again.

Hjelmer sighed. That poor man. What kind of wife would she be for a rancher?

"But I learn fast, and I'm not afraid of hard work."

"I'm sure you will do just fine." And if she believed that, he was a far better salesman than he thought. She needed to be working in a boardinghouse or a fine house in St. Paul, of which he'd seen several in his travels. Someday perhaps he'd build such a house in Blessing, but not in the immediate future, that was for certain.

By the time they stopped in Aberdeen, his stomach was reminding him that dinnertime was noon, and that was past. A local hotel had set up a stand on the outside of the station, and he rose to go purchase a sandwich or some such. "Would you like something to eat?" He nodded to the stand outside.

"Oh yes. I'll . . ." Asta dug in her purse.

"I'll get it. Be right back." As he stepped down to the ground he thought of Sam at home bringing a tray onto the train to better serve the travelers. His Penny had the right idea all right. He studied the foods offered and chose two sandwiches, two cookies, and two red apples, then paid for them and took his time getting back to the train. A cup of coffee would be the perfect thing, but unlike home, no hot drinks were offered. Henry had told him that on the main lines now there were dining cars where one could sit down to a full meal or purchase food to take back to the seat. Coffee and milk were always included.

He swung back aboard, greeting McDonnell at the same time. When Asta insisted on paying him for her food, he pocketed the change and settled in to eat.

The bread was dry with no butter, the meat tough, and he found some mold on his cheese. No wonder seasoned travelers appreciated the food in Blessing. The stale cookie could have been improved with a good hot cup of coffee. He hoped there would be a hotel or some such in Ipswich. Perhaps his sister would be working there, trying to earn money for a ticket to Blessing if, as he suspected, she'd run out of money since they'd not sent her much beyond her ticket and enough food to last until she reached her destination.

He allowed himself a few moments to think on this perfect answer to his prayers to finding Augusta.

Midafternoon the train finally steamed into Ipswich.

"We'll be here an hour or so while we switch the engine and such, since this is the end of the line," McDonnell explained. "If'n I was looking for my sister, I'd ask the ticket agent. Ol' Abe here knows about everything that goes on."

"Ol' Abe?" Hjelmer raised an eyebrow.

"Abe Grossenburg. He's been here since Noah was a pup." McDonnell laughed at his own humor and swung off the stairs so he could set the stool in place and help the passengers down.

Hjelmer went first and set his carpetbag down, then turned to assist Miss Borsland. Far as he could see, there was no one at the station to meet her. She should have sent a telegram, that's what. What if her Mr. Elkanah Moyer didn't get the letter?

One glance at her face told him she was thinking the same thing.

Now what to do? He couldn't just leave her, with her not speaking the language. One more problem on the way to finding his sister. When he did find Augusta, he had a store of things to say. And none of them were especially nice.

24

Blessing
Late September

"Come on, Ellie, get Deborah. I'll get Laban and Mary Jane."

"Don't you go starting without us."

Andrew gave his best friend a look that clearly asked where she'd left her marbles. "I never do." He charged off around the schoolhouse, shouting for the other boys to come play Run-Sheep-Run. The older children were already lined up for Red Rover, but the smaller ones could never break through the line, so they usually played something else.

By the time he'd gathered up enough to play and headed back to the other side of the building, he heard a voice hiss. "You gonna get black spots playin' with those nigger babies."

Andrew ignored the voice, as his mother had ordered, and kept on going.

"Niggers too dumb to play, don't ya know?" The voice was a bit louder but still too low for the others to hear.

Andrew came to a dirt-digging halt. He spun around, searching for the owner of the voice he knew so well. "Toby Valders, you stop that!"

"Come on, Andrew, we're waiting," Ellie called.

Andrew started off again and this time did manage to ignore the singsong verse.

"What's wrong?" Ellie and the others gathered around him.

"Nothing." But Andrew looked over his shoulder with a glare that would drop a horse dead in its tracks.

"Come on, let's play, or recess will be all gone." Deborah grabbed one of his hands and Ellie the other.

Shouting and laughing they played until the bell rang, then all the children ran to line up from smallest to tallest.

Andrew glared at Toby, who strolled by him as if nothing had ever happened. When Andrew glanced up, he caught Pastor Solberg's questioning gaze and dropped his own. Somehow he would teach that . . . that — he couldn't think of a name vile enough. He'd teach that Toby a lesson he'd never forget.

"Hello, Pastor Solberg, children."

At her voice they all spun in their seats. "Mrs. Solberg, oh, come sit down." The children nearly bounced in their seats when Mary Martha Solberg entered the soddy.

"I thought maybe you could use some extra help today." She smiled at her husband.

"Can I ever." John closed the book he'd been about to assign lessons from and crossed the short space between them to take her hand. "Children, what shall we have her do? Help the Ericksons with their English?"

The three Erickson sisters nodded, smiles coming where they never had the year before. "Mrs. Solberg, we can talk English real good now," Clara, the youngest, said.

"Then maybe you don't need me."

"Oh no, that's not what I mean." Flustered, she slipped in a Norwegian word and blushed.

Mary Martha removed her scarf, and Pastor helped her take her coat off. "I was just teasing."

"You could help us with our reading," Ellie piped up.

"And we could sing," Anji Baard added.

"I think she should read us all a story." Pastor Solberg nodded. At the squeals of delight, he added, "That will be at the end of the day of course, and only if everyone does their best between now and then." Sighs and nods both came from his students. "All right, let's get going right now. Mrs. Solberg, you can take your English students over there." He pointed to the back corner. "Thorliff, will you please come and review sums with the first graders? And those fourth grade and up, please review for a history test that will be given in about half an hour."

As they all scattered to their assigned tasks, Pastor Solberg beckoned to Andrew. "Come with me."

Andrew looked to Thorliff, who shrugged and nodded at the same time. When he rose from his seat, the smaller Bjorklund looked as if he was headed for a whipping.

Pastor Solberg opened the door and stepped out into the sunshine with Andrew at his side. "Come, let's walk a bit." The silence stretched between them, making Andrew squirm as though he were sitting on a thistle bush. "Now, Andrew, I know something happened at recess, and I know, too, that you don't want to tell me about it. But

I have my suspicions, and you need to tell me the truth."

Andrew sniffed and clenched his fists.

"Someone said something that made you angry?"

Andrew nodded and sniffed again. He dug in his pocket for a handkerchief and blew his nose. Looking up, he wished he were flying with the geese — anywhere but right where he was.

"Now, I know you well enough to know that if someone called you a name, you'd just ignore it, but if someone calls someone else a name or says something bad about them, you get upset. Especially if it is someone you believe is weaker or more vulnerable."

Andrew looked up. "What is vul . . . vularable?"

"Vulnerable. That's someone who can be hurt easily." Pastor Solberg waited.

"Oh." Andrew's nose itched so badly he wanted to scratch it off. Neglecting his handkerchief this time, he used the cuff of his sleeve.

"Do you want to tell me what happened?"

"Uh-uh." Andrew studied the third button of his shirt as if it held the secrets of the world.

"I was afraid of that." Pastor Solberg pointed to a block of wood next to the chopping block. "Sit." Andrew sat, and the teacher took his place on the chopping block, leaning back slightly against the ax handle. "Now, I know that tattling is considered a sin right up there with murder, but if I don't know what is happening, I cannot teach those mistreating others to not do so."

All he could see was the top of Andrew's head, hair so gold it shone white. Solberg let the silence stretch again until the little boy had the fidgets so bad he would get splinters in his rear any moment. "Was it Jerry?"

Andrew moved not a muscle.

"Was it Toby?"

The nod was so brief that if Solberg hadn't been watching carefully he would have missed it.

"And was it about our Negro students?"

Another nod came, so minuscule Andrew's hair didn't even move.

Solberg nodded. "All right, Andrew, you can be relieved that you did not tattle, because you did not say a word, and while I will not do anything today so that they cannot accuse you, be assured that something will be done. And, Andrew . . ."

After a silence, Andrew looked up at his teacher.

"Please do not try to take this into your own hands. While your willingness to protect the weaker is admirable, sometimes you have to let the ones in authority do their job. I don't want to hear of any fistfights. Do you understand me?"

Andrew nodded, but he wore a stubborn look that told Pastor Solberg this boy would most likely get even somehow.

"Andrew, the Bible says that revenge is the Lord's. Our job is to love those around us, not take vengeance on them."

The boy's head snapped up. "You mean I got to love them?" The horror on his face made Solberg want to smile, but he disciplined himself to keep his lips straight.

"I know. God asks a lot of us, and most times His way is not the easy way." He laid a hand on Andrew's shoulder. "But violence begets violence, and we will not have that here." He stood. "Now, let's go back inside, unless you have any questions?"

This time the headshake was vigorous enough to set Andrew's hair to swinging.

"Good. Because if I learn of any retribution on your part, I will deal with you as severely as the offenders."

"Yes, sir." Andrew paused and looked up

at his teacher. "What is re . . . re—"

Retribution? That means taking the punishment into your own hands. Getting even."

"But . . ."

"But what?"

"Nothing, sir."

"Let's see that there is nothing."

"Yes, sir."

"Did ya get a whippin'?" Ellie whispered as Andrew took his seat again. When he shook his head, she breathed a sigh of relief. "Good."

Pastor Solberg watched, and he could see that Andrew had a hard time enjoying either the singing or the story at the end of the day. When school let out, Thorliff and Baptiste hitched up the wagon for the teacher and his family, much to Manda's disgust. After the schoolhouse was cleaned and in order again, they got in the wagon and Manda drove them home. Once there the girls headed outside for chores, and Mary Martha went to the kitchen to start the stove. John clasped his hands behind his back and thought what to say.

"I have a problem."

"I know. I can tell. Between you and Andrew, I wasn't sure who was more down at the mouth."

"Really?" He looked at her in surprise.

"Really. So tell me from the beginning, and we will see how we can work it out so that little boy doesn't have such a heavy burden to carry."

He followed her into the kitchen, and while she rattled the grate and added wood to the coals, he paced the floor, telling the story. At the conclusion, he stopped by the stove where the coffee water was now heating up. "Those two Valders boys are bringing so many bad things to these children that at times I wish they had never gotten off the train here."

"Ah, but how blessed they are that they did. They just have a lot of bad habits to unlearn, that's all."

"Seems the only thing they understand is the rod, and I hate to use it overmuch. I know if I tell Anner what is going on, he will apply the rod without a doubt."

"So you want another way." She measured the coffee she'd just ground into the pot and set the lid in place.

"Um. I wonder where their ideas about Negroes came from. New York isn't a southern city by any means, and that is where they grew up."

"Who knows what and who taught them, after living on the streets like they did . . ." Mary Martha shuddered. "Now, if they'd come from Atlanta or Charleston . . ."

"So what can I do?" John rubbed his chin, always a sign he was deep in thought.

"I'd say to pray first. God set this all in motion, so surely He has a solution."

John stopped his pacing. "You know, sometimes I wonder if God didn't make the wrong person pastor here." He came to stand behind her and wrapped his arms around her waist. "You, my dear, have the wisdom of the ages in that lovely head of yours."

Mary Martha leaned back against him. "I'd like to help at the school more often now that I seem to be over the morning sickness. Rushing outside to puke wouldn't make a good impression on your pupils."

His hands dropped lower and cradled her barely rounded belly. "So hard to believe a little life is growing in there. What a miracle."

"Yes, well, if I don't get going, the miracle will be that there will be food on our table for supper." She turned enough to kiss his cheek. "I'll let you go converse with the real Wisdom, but first please bring in an armload of wood."

Later that night when they were almost

asleep, John snapped his fingers. "I've got it."

"Good," Mary Martha murmured without opening her eyes. "Tell me in the morning."

"I might forget by morning." He turned on his side and cuddled her spoon fashion. "They say that hate comes from ignorance, so those two boys must gain knowledge. I will have them go through the Bible and look up every reference to people with colored skin and see what they learn."

"There aren't too many."

"I know, but it will be a start. Then I must find books that discuss this issue, and they can read those. In fact, I think the whole school should do this. Those two boys can start it off by giving a report from what they learned."

"They better learn to read better first."

"I know. Perhaps you would like to help them?" He kissed her hair.

"Good. Tell me again tomorrow." His chuckle made her smile, but she never said anything else because she fell sound asleep.

The next afternoon, while Mary Martha led the rest of the school in singing, Pastor Solberg took the two boys outside and sat them on a bench facing him. As he explained what he wanted them to do, their eyes grew round with horror.

"But . . . but that means I got to read the whole entire Bible." Toby flopped back against the sod wall. "I can't never do that, not in a million years."

"Me neither." Jerry kept shaking his head as if it hung loose on its axis.

"That's why you will do this together. I will make a list of the books of the Bible that have references you will need, so we can speed this up."

"Why are you picking on us?" Toby clamped his arms across his chest.

"Why do you think?"

"Just cause we don't like nigg— Negroes." Eyes slitted, he glared at Pastor Solberg.

Pastor Solberg pulled his coat tighter around him. The wind that kicked up leaves at his feet felt as if it blew straight down from the North Pole.

"Would you like me to add more?" His voice was soft, but the meaning unmistakable.

"Sh-sh-sh." Jerry nudged his brother. "Are you gonna tell our pa?"

"Only that you might need help with your research."

"I druther take a lickin'." Toby slumped back again.

"Not me. Pa said if we got another lickin' at school, he was gonna make sure we got a worse one t'home." He looked directly in Pastor Solberg's eyes. "But we ain't got a Bible, and the one t'home is in Norwegian. We don't have to learn to read it in that, do we?"

Pastor Solberg smiled. "No, son, you don't have to do that. I will make sure you have a Bible written in English. I'll have the book list ready for you tomorrow. Any questions?"

"No, sir." Jerry prodded his brother to mumble an answer.

The three of them got to their feet. "Oh, and boys, if I were you, I'd make sure to welcome our new pupils to our school, just as you were welcomed."

"Yes, sir." Though speaking through clenched teeth, the two did respond politely.

Solberg let them go ahead of him into the schoolhouse and smiled at their backs. A few months ago they wouldn't have known to say that. The Valders boys were making progress.

After reaching his desk, Pastor Solberg called the students to attention. "Since we are going to be studying slavery and the Civil War, I have a new book that Mrs. Solberg will be reading every afternoon." He held up a copy of *Uncle Tom's Cabin.* "This book has the reputation for starting the fight that nearly divided our great country in two. Have any of you read it?" Thorliff raised his hand. "Besides Thorliff, that is." When no other hand went up, he nodded. "Good. We all have a lot to learn."

"You think it will work?" Mary Martha asked on the ride home.

"I hope to heaven it will, or we will have a mighty tall stack of firewood split for the winter, not that Baptiste and Hamre aren't making a good start. Maybe I should make one of them a general in the Union Army and the other in the Confederate. Studying battles always catches a boy's interest." He turned to his wife and helped her out of the wagon at their front step. "You know, that's not a bad idea. Might spur them on to read more too." He took her hands and tucked one of them through the crook in his arm as he opened the front door. "See, you bring out the best in me."

"Oh, really?" Agnes Baard rose from the chair in front of the fire. The twinkle in her eyes told them she'd been watching out the window. "The coffee's hot, and I brung some cake and such. Thought you'd like to invite me to coffee, and I knew with both of you at the school, the baking should be took over by one of the other of us."

Mary Martha unwrapped her scarf and clasped the older woman's hands. "If you don't beat all. Now I reckon I can help at the school without feeling the least bit guilty."

"Good, and besides, I got me an idea for Kaaren's school that I thought you might like to hear about." Agnes picked up a pot-holder and grasped the handle of the steaming coffeepot. "Coffee?"

25

The Ranch
Late September

"You don't intend to take me to Blessing?"

Kane shook his head. "I really don't understand why you keep saying that word. You're asking me something, but I don't know what."

Augusta shook her head in frustration. *God, what is he saying? If only I could make him understand that I must go. Mor needs me, and I promised to come help her.* Augusta clasped her shaking hands to her breast. "But you said Blessing. I thought you meant . . ." At his look of confusion, Augusta felt like stamping her foot or using other language that he wouldn't understand but might help her feel better, even if they were words Mor had ordered her to never use. What had he meant when she asked if he was taking her to Blessing the day she arrived?

She thought back to her arrival on the train. Now that she thought about it, he had acted as if he expected her. How could he have? She rubbed her forehead with her fingertips. "Uff da!"

She looked at Kane, who was studying her with what — perplexity on his face? Was that pity she saw in his eyes? When she thought about it, he was most likely as confused as she.

Why, oh why didn't I learn the language like Hjelmer said? Why was I so stubborn, so sure I knew best?

But she knew the answer to that one. Because she had always been that way. So sure that she knew best. And it had been true. As the oldest daughter, she helped raise the younger children. That was the way of things. And many times she had kept Hjelmer from getting into trouble.

Ah, if only Hjelmer were here now to get me out of trouble. She almost laughed at her plea. Did God hear her? And would He be merciful?

Or was she stuck here in this wilderness?

She looked up at Kane again. How could she make him understand? *But do you really want to leave this fine man, his beautiful home and prosperous ranch?* The thought made her catch her breath. *Of course she wanted to leave — had to leave. After all, even with Lone Pine and Morning Dove here, she was an unmarried female living in an unmarried man's house. What would her mor say?*

How can I figure out what she wants? Kane shook his head. If he'd had any idea being married to someone who didn't understand the language would be this difficult, he might never have sent that letter.

Be honest, he ordered himself. *You'd do whatever it took to have this woman in your life.* But how do I help her? *Guess I better send Lone Pine over to Gedicks' and bring his mother back.* He sighed. *Can't anything go the way it is supposed to?* He thought a minute.

"Look, how about tomorrow we go to a neighbor's house to visit?" He racked his brain for the other word for German. *Deutsche, that's it.* "His mother speaks Deutsche, and maybe you can talk with her somewhat." He spoke slowly, knowing that she understood some words now.

"We go Deutsche house?" She strung together the words she did know.

Kane nodded. "Tomorrow."

"To-mor-row." While she repeated the word, the look on her face said understanding and saying the words weren't even close to the same thing.

"We'll ride the horses. That's faster than the wagon."

"Ride." Her eyes lit up, the blue so intense it smote his heart. "Ja, we ride — to Deutsche?"

"Tomorrow." He turned to the clock on the shelf by the fireplace and showed the hands going around twice. "Tomorrow."

"Ah, tomorrow." Again that flair of blue on understanding.

At least if she understood enough German and Mrs. Gedicks understood enough Norwegian, maybe they could begin to make sense of all of this. Kane watched her a moment longer. She seemed content with that.

"I've got plenty of work to do, so I better get on it." He raised his voice. "Morning Dove!"

The Indian woman appeared in the door, her moccasin-clad feet making nary a sound. "Yes?"

"You want to bake extra apple turnovers for us to take with us tomorrow? Bag up some apples too. I'm not sure they have any apple trees over at Gedicks' yet."

"Fine." Morning Dove beckoned to Augusta. "You come help?"

Augusta nodded. She glanced longingly

out the window on her way to the kitchen. How fine it would be to go riding again today, as she and Kane had done the day before. But she knew the word "help," and there were always things needing doing here just like in a home anywhere.

While in the kitchen peeling apples, she let her mind wander. Her mor must be frantic with worry by now. Or maybe they had given her up for dead. How would anyone find her clear out here? She must be a long way from Blessing. Was there any way she could send a message?

If only she could get back to the town where she'd disembarked from the train. If she had the money, she could take the train back to St. Paul and ask them there about Blessing. The more she thought about it, the more she tried to remember the way back. She could ride it far faster than they had come with the wagon.

But how to get money for the ticket?

The telegraph! She could let her family know where she was, and they would send money for a ticket. In the meantime, maybe she could work at the hotel for a place to sleep and eat.

The knife slipped and sliced into her finger. "Ow!" She dropped the apple and knife in the pan and clamped her fingers on the oozing red slash.

"Hurt bad?" Morning Dove looked up from rolling pie dough.

Augusta shook her head, held up the finger, and pantomimed wrapping it.

"I get." Morning Dove returned with a strip of well-worn sheet and, after wrapping it around the finger, tied a neat knot.

"Thank you." Augusta ignored the taunting voice within that called her several names, clumsy being one, and returned to peeling and slicing the apples. When she took a bite out of one slice, she closed her eyes to savor the crisp sweetness. Nothing tasted more like fall than fresh apples. The frost had only intensified the flavor.

She frowned at her bandaged finger. What a careless thing to do.

With both turnovers and pies in the oven, she and Morning Dove went back out to the garden to continue digging the root vegetables for the cellar. Potatoes, carrots, turnips, rutabagas, and parsnips. Each had a bin of its own and sand to cover the many layers. They would have plenty for the winter, and Morning Dove had already lined the shelves with crocks of pickled cucumbers, dried corn and beans, and canned beans too. Fruit, both canned and dried, and jams lined the other side.

The apples would be stored in the barrels on the west wall next to the mound of pumpkins and winter squash. Dried dill and other herbs and grasses hung in bunches from the rafters, along with braids of onions and some other things that Augusta didn't recognize. Each time she brought a wheelbarrow load down the ramp that covered the wooden steps, she stopped in amazement at the bounty stored in the earthen room.

The next morning she rushed through her daily ablutions to get ready to ride to the people Kane had spoken of. She packed their saddlebags after breakfast, donned her wool jacket that matched her newly brushed skirt, and stepped out onto the porch.

The sound of horses drew her gaze to the east where a group of blue-uniformed men were riding up to the ranch. Two wagons with waist-high racks brought up the rear. Morning Dove came up behind her.

"The army come for horses, pigs, and cattle."

Augusta got the drift. There would be no riding for her and Kane this day. After watching the man in the gray felt slouch hat greeting Kane and Lone Pine, she sighed and turned back to the house. The pies and turnovers would go to feed the soldiers, along with whatever they would make for dinner. She hung up her jacket, took out an apron, and wrapped it around her waist. Perhaps tomorrow they could go on the visit.

After all, what difference did one more day make?

26

Blessing
October 1

"There now, what do you think of that?"

Ingeborg stared at the thirty-by-forty-foot hole the men had dug three feet deep and were now setting in center posts to eventually help hold up the roof. The walls were to be made of eighteen-inch-wide sod blocks to help keep the cheese house cool in the summer yet prevent freezing in the winter.

"It looks huge."

"It should. Better'n half the size of the barn. We'll build a trough in the center, like the well house, to store the cream cans."

"And the back half or some part will be all shelves for ripening the wheels?" Ingeborg nodded as she studied the empty hole. "Ah, we might have to buy more milk cows to make enough cheese."

"We can get some milk from the other farmers around. Baard said they'd bring milk cans over every other day, and if Johnson isn't feeding all his extra to the pigs, he will too." Haakan dropped down to the floor. "Besides, you don't have to fill it all at once."

Ingeborg pushed a chunk of dirt into the hole with the toe of her boot. With the weather turning, they needed to hurry with the building, but Haakan loved to tease her.

"Thanks." He bent over to retrieve the clod and tossed it out. "You can come tamp this floor down if you like."

"Sure, me and all the babies. You want I should roll Samuel around on the floor? Trygve, now, he could hand you nails, and Astrid? She'd be up that post so fast you couldn't leap quick enough."

"I know, I know." Haakan raised his hands to ward off her barrage.

"Don't you know better than to tangle with our womenfolk?" Lars said, tamping down the dirt around the fifteen-foot post. They'd angled two-by-four braces down to the floor and pegged them in with stakes. A long beam that waited off to the side would be set on the posts to hold up the rafters.

Ingeborg turned at a cry from the door of the house. Trygve was awake, and soon Samuel would be too. Astrid had followed her outside, and she and Paws, Thorliff's dog, were playing in the grass beside the cellar door.

"Ma, the babies are awake." Astrid at four was just a few months older than Trygve, but she put him in the baby category along with Samuel. She waved a stick, and Paws crouched down on his forelegs, tail waving in the air, waiting for her to throw it.

"I know. Thank you, Astrid." Ingeborg turned back to her husband. "Thank you for such a fine building."

"It's not here yet."

"I know, but it will be soon. How many are coming tomorrow to help with the raising?"

"I've no idea, but the word has spread." Haakan looked over his shoulder at Lars' bidding. "You might bring out a cup of coffee in a while. We sure could use some."

Ingeborg nodded. "Ah yes, it must be more than an hour since the last one. How do you stand it?" She waggled her eyebrows at her laughing husband and headed for the house. Trygve could manage to get into trouble right under her nose, let alone without someone watching him. Last time he'd taken the spinning wheel half apart. In his case, silence rather than noise was a time to go checking on him. And he had disappeared from the doorway. She broke into a trot and took the stairs two at a time.

Bursting into the kitchen, she stopped short. "Trygve Knutson, you get down from there."

The little boy turned, flinched, and flailed as the box tower he'd built on top of the chair shoved against the cupboard tilted.

Ingeborg leaped in time to grab him as his child-designed ladder gave way. The boxes clattered to the floor. "Uff da, what am I going to do with you?"

"I was hungry, and you didn't come." Trygve gave her a look that said it was all her fault.

A yell from the bedroom let her know that the noise had awakened Samuel, and he always woke up hungry.

"Now see what you did?" She set Trygve on a chair at the table.

"Sammy's hungry."

"As if I didn't know it." She righted the other chair, set the boxes off to the side, and took down the cookie jar that the child had been aiming for. "Where is Astrid?"

Trygve shrugged. "Don't know."

"Astrid?" Ingeborg raised her voice to be heard above the now squalling Samuel.

"Here, Ma." This voice came from upstairs.

"What are you doing?"

"Playing dolls."

"Good girl." Ingeborg glanced up the steep stairs. "You want a cookie?"

"Milk too?" Astrid appeared at the head of the stairs, rag doll clutched in the crook of one arm.

"At the table."

While Astrid made her way down the stairs, Ingeborg headed for the bedroom to scoop up the red-faced toddler, who quieted the moment he was in her arms. Ingeborg laid him on the padded dresser top and swiftly changed his soaking diaper. "Was this what was making you yell so, or are you really hungry?"

Now that he had her attention, Samuel grinned and chuckled and reached for her face. She blew on his tummy, making him laugh again. A new flash of white brought Ingeborg to check his mouth. Sure enough, a new back tooth. No wonder he'd been fussy lately.

"One of these days you are going to wake up dry, and then no more diapers for you." She tickled his tummy again. "Such a big boy!"

"Ma?" Astrid stood in the doorway, her doll now grasped by one arm and trailing on the floor.

"What?" Ingeborg pulled a dry pair of knitted soakers over Samuel's chubby legs and lifted him to her hip.

"Trygve . . ."

"Oh, now what?" Ingeborg, toddler in arms, whirled through the door to find Trygve now on the table, reaching for the cookie plate.

"Trygve Knutson, get down!"

"But . . ."

"Now!"

One foot feeling for the chair, he backed up, and his foot slipped. Ingeborg grabbed him again, jostling Samuel, who set up a howl at the abrupt motion.

"Trygve's bad, huh?" The smug expression Ingeborg caught on her daughter's face made her want to laugh or scold. Astrid did like to lord it over her cousin at times. Ingeborg sat Trygve back down on his chair, pointed Astrid to another one, and settled Samuel in the high chair Olaf had made during the winter. It was so much easier than the box on the chair that Trygve was using. She tied a bib around his neck before pouring three cups of milk. She set them in front of the two at the table and let them each choose a cookie from the plate, all the while giving Samuel sips from his cup and a cookie to mangle as well as eat.

The jingle of harness and Paws' barking answered her unspoken question. Kaaren was home again — just in time.

"Now, isn't this a peaceful scene?" Kaaren swept in, followed by Grace and Sophie, who were being herded along by Andrew.

"You should have been here five minutes ago." Ingeborg poured three more cups of milk and refilled the cookie plate. Sometimes, like the few minutes earlier, she didn't regret not having more babies, but that was the odd moment, not the usual. There was something about a sweet-smelling baby that reminded her not only of her love, but the love of the Father. The Father who chose to withhold from her the joy of giving Haakan a son of his own. Sometimes the hurt made her weep, sometimes it flared in anger, but often now it seemed more like a passing dream than a driving need.

"So how did the signing go?"

"Ah, those children are so bright. They

are even learning from Grace and Sophie." Kaaren kissed Samuel, ignoring his plea to be picked up. "You girls get up at the table."

"Andrew, you want cookies and milk?" Ingeborg glanced around the kitchen. Usually he was the first one up to the table, and now he wasn't even in the room. "Where did Andrew go?"

"Upstairs." Astrid motioned over her shoulder.

Ingeborg and Kaaren shared questioning glances, and Kaaren shrugged. "He seemed all right at school."

Ingeborg settled the others at the table, poured Kaaren a cup of coffee, and set it on the table. "I'll be right back." She made her way up the stairs, wondering both if Andrew was coming down with something or if there'd been another conflict between him and the Valders boys at school.

She found her son lying flat on his stomach across the bed he shared with Thorliff. "Andrew, are you all right?" She sank down on the side of the bed, automatically laying a hand against his cheek to check for fever.

"Umm." Andrew twisted away from her hand.

"All right, son, what's going on?"

Ingeborg waited, knowing Andrew would talk in a minute or two. She felt his head again. No, there was no fever, and he didn't have a runny nose or blood anywhere.

"I hate Toby Valders."

"What happened now?"

"Pastor Solberg yelled at me."

"Oh, really?" Ingeborg stroked her son's hair back off his cheek. If Pastor Solberg yelled, which she seriously doubted, there must have been something terribly wrong.

"And it is Toby's fault. I hate him."

"So what did he do now?"

"He sat next to Grace."

Ingeborg could feel her brow furrow. "Was he mean to Grace?"

"No."

"Then what?"

"He might be mean to Grace."

"Ah." Ingeborg breathed a sigh of relief. Andrew, champion of the weak and helpless, got his feelings hurt when someone else stepped in. "So what did you do?"

"I told him to go sit somewhere else."

"And?"

"And Pastor Solberg yelled at me." Andrew turned a tear-stained face to his mother. "That's not fair."

"What did Pastor Solberg say?"

"He said" — Andrew stopped and sniffed — "that I had to be polite." Another sniff came. "That . . . that I should be grateful that Toby was helping." He dashed the back of his sleeve across his eyes.

"Was Toby or Jerry teasing Laban and Mary Jane?"

"No, they don't want to go chop wood anymore. They don't like looking up all the Bible verses neither." Andrew rolled to his side. "Did you know there are black people in the Bible?"

Ingeborg nodded. "God made people all different colors, but inside they are just the same as all the others."

"That's what Pastor Solberg said." Andrew thought a moment. "I can sign lots more than Toby and Jerry."

"That's because you have been learning it lots longer."

"I know. Ellie does good too." Andrew made the signs for his name. "Pastor Solberg said I had to be nice to Toby and Jerry 'cause that's what the Bible says." He looked up at his mother. "Did God make Toby and Jerry mean like that?"

Ingeborg shook her head. "God doesn't make anyone mean. We do that. You remember how we talked about where those boys came from? How they didn't have a ma and pa to make them mind and to take care of them?"

"I know." Andrew signed something that Ingeborg didn't recognize.

"What did you say?"

"Nothing."

"Andrew?"

"I said Toby Valders is a pig."

"Andrew Bjorklund!"

"Pastor Solberg said I have to pray for Toby and Jerry — every day, Ma, every day."

Ingeborg put her arm around her son and drew him to her side. "Ja, that sounds like something Pastor Solberg would say, and he's right, you know?"

"He read me a verse. It said to pray for your enemies and those who spit on you."

"Spit on you?" Ingeborg kept her smile from her face. "You mean spitefully use you?"

"I guess." He looked up at her, near-white hair brushing his eyebrows. "I don't want to pray for them, Ma, I really don't."

"How about if I help you, then? Tonight when you go to bed, we'll pray together, okay?"

"Okay." He stood in front of her. "But I

don't have to like them, do I?"

Ingeborg fluffed his hair. "How about we let God help you do that? We can pray that He makes you to love them."

Andrew stared at her, shaking his head. "Love them? How can I love them when I hate them?"

Ingeborg chuckled. "Good question, my son, but God can work miracles. You'll see, but we have to ask for His help." She stood and took Andrew by the hand. "Come on, milk and cookies might make things seem a bit better."

That night in bed, Ingeborg told Haakan what had gone on. "Pastor Solberg is really asking a lot of Andrew, don't you think?"

"Spit on us, huh?" Haakan chuckled again. "That son of ours. What a boy." He shook his head. "No, I think he is asking of Andrew just what he needs to do to grow strong through this. Pastor Solberg is a wise man and an excellent teacher and pastor. We are indeed fortunate to have him here in Blessing. When I think of that man Hildegunn wanted us to hire." He shuddered. "We'd have booted him out long ago, or the church would have died by now."

"Umm." Ingeborg tucked herself a bit closer to his side, if that were possible.

"God is good to us, huh?" But it wasn't a question, and Ingeborg knew it.

"Umm."

Haakan laid his arm around her side and cuddled her to his warmth. "Good night, my beloved."

"I like that." She pulled his hand up and kissed the back of it. "Thank you for my cheese house."

Morning came long before daylight. They all rushed around to get the chores done before the laborers began to arrive. Ingeborg slid the bread pans in the oven with one hand and stirred the oatmeal with the other. Those out in the barn milked as fast as the cows would allow, and Andrew had the chickens fed before they came off the roost.

Their breath steamed in the air, and hoarfrost whitened the ground.

"Just about time to start butchering too," Haakan said, thumping his pail on the kitchen counter. "I wanted to get this building up first. We can use it to hang carcasses that way."

"I don't want no blood in my cheese house." Ingeborg flipped the rack of bread

355

she had toasting over the open fire in the stove.

Haakan shook his head. "You sure get proprietary, don't you?"

"Plenty of room in the springhouse when the cheese ain't there." She set the pitcher of cream in the center of the table. "There now, come and eat, everyone."

As soon as Haakan said the grace, they passed the food around the table, with Ingeborg dishing up for Astrid on the higher youth chair beside her.

"I can help build, huh, Pa?" Astrid dug into her oatmeal with her spoon.

"No, you stay with the babies." Thorliff buttered his toast.

"I'm not a baby!" Astrid's lower lip came out, and her eyes flashed blue fire.

"Oops. Sorry." Thorliff looked to his mother, who shook her head. "I meant you need to help Ma and Tante Kaaren watch Samuel and Trygve."

"They are the babies."

"Don't tell Trygve that." Ingeborg smiled down the table at her husband, now the one shaking his head.

"Just make sure there's plenty of hot coffee. The way that sky looks, we could get rain or sleet by the time the day is over. Thorliff, you get the butts set up for the shake cutters. Lars and I are going to start cutting sod immediately. Won't have any pasture left, but it'll be back by spring. Strange to think we might be running out of sod on the Bjorklund acres. Never tried to sod a roof as big as this one."

"Are you sure that's a good idea?" Ingeborg spread jelly on the toast for Astrid.

"It'll keep the temperature more even, that's for sure. Like at the icehouse. Lars thinks we should build the roof at one level, box in the edges, and lay in sawdust six to eight inches deep, then roof with shakes."

"Which would be lighter?"

"Sawdust, but which is more effective?" He shook his head. "Wish I knew."

"How about doing half and half?" Thorliff reached for the jam.

"Might look rather strange."

"So? I saw a picture in a book from Norway where flowers bloomed on the end of the house closest to the hill behind it, and silvery shakes were on the front."

Haakan thought a minute. "But that was built right into a hill, right?"

"Umm." Thorliff nodded around his mouthful of oatmeal.

"Not too many hills here."

"No, but you dug down pretty deep."

Ingeborg grabbed Astrid's hand as she reached for the jam jar. "I'll get that for you."

"Something to think about. And talk about. You can bet there'll be plenty of opinions among the men here today. We'll see what other ideas there are. Remember, they laughed when we poured sawdust in the walls at Lars and Kaaren's house."

"And then did ours the next spring." Ingeborg shook her head. "What a mess that was."

Haakan pushed back his chair. "Come on Thorliff, Hamre, we got work to do."

By midmorning the sod walls were rising and so was the laughter, all fueled by the coffee kept simmering over the open fire. Tables were already set up in the machine shed in case the lowering clouds dumped their burden on the workers. The west wind shifted to the north every so often, keeping many of the children playing inside the house and barn.

Penny drove her wagon up to the house and brought in pies and cakes from both her kitchen and Bridget's at the boarding-house before letting Thorliff take the horse out to tie on a long line to a wagon wheel like all the other horses not being used to cut and haul sod.

"You won't believe what came in the mail," she said, setting another pie on the already laden kitchen table.

"No, what?" Kaaren tucked the light blanket around Samuel as she sat rocking him in the rocker by the stove.

"A letter from my brother Mark. He's the one next to me. She waved the letter and almost danced around the room. "He's coming with his family to visit. For Christmas." She waved the letter again. "Most likely they will stay through the winter if there is enough work for him here. He wants to go west to homestead. Can you believe it?"

"You've waited a long time." Mary Martha Solberg looked up from the baby sweater she was knitting.

"I know. To think last year I wasn't sure all of them were alive, and now I've heard from everybody." Penny shook her head. "I can't wait to tell Hjelmer, if he ever does come home again, that is." The laughter left her eyes. "Do you think he'll really find Augusta?"

"From the last telegram, I think he will." Agnes picked up Trygve, who'd been asking his mother to do just that and, taking his hands, played Roll-'em-and-Roll-'em with him.

Kaaren smiled her thanks and nodded. "I think he'll find her too. Hjelmer is one persistent man. If anyone can find her, he can. So where will you have room for this family coming to visit?"

"They'll all have to fit in our spare room, I guess. We'd talked about adding on, but there won't be time to do that between now and then."

"If we get the house built for Sam and Eulah, they could stay in the parsonage soddy." Ingeborg, with one finger on her lower lip, studied the table to see what they could be missing.

"Or over at our soddy." Kaaren set Samuel down from her lap and checked his diaper. He squirmed and tried to pull away.

"He's all boy, that one," Agnes said. "Oh look, the sun's out."

"Ma." Sophie came to the door. "Can we go play in the hay-mow?"

"If you watch out for Grace," Kaaren replied.

"M-a-a." Sophie shook her head. "You know I always watch for Grace."

"I know you do. No idea why I said that." She made shooing motions with her free hand. "Have fun."

The women smiled at each other as the

little girl went shrieking out the door.

The sounds of sawing and hammering ceased abruptly when the triangle rang for dinner. Pastor Solberg asked the blessing, and the lines that had formed at the food table began moving forward as the men filled their plates. Even the wind dropped, as if giving them respite.

When the children were all eating, the women filled their plates and took over the chairs left by men who had eaten quickly and taken their pipes to the benches by the house to have a smoke before returning to work.

Ingeborg walked over and peered in the open doorway. "It looks huge." She turned to smile at Haakan leaning against the sod wall. "How come it looks so much bigger now than before?"

"That's the way of building." He pointed to the trench just to the side of the center posts. "That was Olaf's idea. He's going to frame the water tank, and we'll pour cement into the forms. There'll be no leaking from that, I tell you."

She smiled again and returned to the tables, filling her own plate from the leftovers, of which there weren't a whole lot, as usual. Raising her face to the sun, she rotated her head from side to side and back to front, stretching the muscles and relieving a bit of an ache behind her eyes. She sat down on the stoop beside Penny so they could visit while they ate.

As the children finished cleaning their plates and chose a dessert, she watched them talking to Grace with their hands. Toby Valders managed to keep by her side, and even from here Ingeborg could see that Andrew wasn't too happy about it. But he stayed with Ellie and Deborah, racing them to the barn as soon as they finished.

The women sat chatting over their coffee cups, enjoying the sun while Manda and Anji watched the littlest ones, who would be going down for naps in the next few minutes.

Ingeborg watched as another layer of sod was set in place.

"Whoa there! Whoa!" The sound cut across the children's laughter.

"Catch him."

"Fool horse!" The shouts came from the pasture.

She heard the pounding of hooves and stood to see where the horse was running to and whose it was.

"Grace! Dear God in heaven, help us. Run, Grace! Run!" Ingeborg wasted no more time screaming! She ran for the child, who puttered at a gopher mound, blissfully unaware of the crazed horse, the singletree clanging behind him. The deaf child was playing right in his path.

27

Ipswich
October 1

"He's not here." Asta Borsland checked the station area again.

Hjelmer nodded. He'd surmised that already. "We'll go ask the station manager. Perhaps there is a message there for you."

They crossed the wooden platform, and he held the door for her to enter the one-room building. In a half-walled cubicle at one corner, a man sat at a desk, green eyeshade in place, fingers busily tapping out the Morse code of the telegraph. Benches lined the walls, and a potbellied stove stood regally in the center of the scuffed wood floor, ready to pour out the heat soon to be needed.

Hjelmer waited until the man finished sending his message and looked up. "Good day. We're looking for a rancher named Elkanah Moyer. He was to meet this young woman at the train. Might you have a message for Miss Asta Borsland?"

"Nope, no messages." The station manager flipped through a brief file of telegraph messages and checked another cubbyhole. "Sorry."

"But I sent him a letter." Asta leaned her hands on the counter. "Surely there is something."

"You might try the post office right across the street at the general store. Miz Monahan knows about everybody in these parts." The clicking began again, and the man returned to his work.

Hjelmer and Asta did as suggested, but the answer was the same. No message for Miss Borsland.

God in heaven, what do I do with her now? I can't find the woman I want, and here I end up having this one to take care of.

"Wait a moment," the postmistress said. "Did you say Elkanah Moyer?"

"Yes. I believe he has a ranch near here."

"Not near here, and he doesn't come into town often, but I believe something came for him the other day." She sorted through a stack of envelopes. "Aha. I thought so." Waving the letter, she returned to the window. "See."

Asta crumpled in on herself. "That's my

letter. I wrote it clear back in July. He never knew I was delayed." She turned stricken eyes on Hjelmer. "What do I do now?"

Hjelmer turned to the woman behind the counter again. "Do you know where his ranch is?"

"Not really, just the general direction." She smiled at a man waiting behind them. "Howdy Judge, be with you in a second."

"Any idea who might know where he lives?"

The woman shrugged again. "How about you, Judge, you know where Elkanah Moyer's ranch is?"

The white-haired gentleman shook his head. "That name surely does sound familiar, though." He extended his hand to Hjelmer. "I'm Judge Rhinehart, circuit rider for South Dakota. Ipswich is not only one of my stops, but it is my home. Why is it you are looking for him?"

Hjelmer introduced himself and his companion, then translated for the woman at his side. "Miss Borsland here came from Norway to marry Mr. Moyer on one of the arranged marriages. He purchased her ticket and all."

"Moyer, Elkanah Moyer." The judge snapped his fingers. "That's it. I married

366

him and a Norwegian woman, oh, about a month ago, the last time I was home for a while. She seemed a mite confused, but I put that up to the strange land and all."

When Hjelmer translated again, Asta gasped, her hand to her throat. "But . . . but . . . he was supposed to marry me. I . . . I have the contract right here." She fumbled in her bag and drew forth an official-looking document. "S-see."

"Can you tell me what the woman he married looked like?" Hjelmer was almost afraid to ask.

"Well, she was tall, her blond hair in a bun. Oh, I know, she had the bluest eyes." He glanced up at Hjelmer, who stood about six inches taller than he. "Like yours. Couldn't get over the color of her eyes. You related to her by any chance?"

"I might be. If she's my sister, that is. I've been searching for her for the last month. She was supposed to come to Blessing, North Dakota, but somehow got on the wrong train, and it looks like she got off here. Why in the world would she . . ." Hjelmer shook his head. "I don't want — no, I have to find her. You have any idea where this ranch might be?"

"Someplace west of here. Shame the land plats aren't here in town, or we could look 'em up. Tell you what. You could go to Pierre to the land office. They could tell you what sections he owns."

"Could I telegraph for that information?"

"Good idea. That you could. Would surely be faster. Ah, these modern miracles. Takes some getting used to." The judge stuck his hands in his vest pockets and rocked back on his feet. "Shame I got all my paper work done and sent in, or I'd have a copy of their marriage license here."

"What is he saying?" Asta tapped Hjelmer on the arm so he would translate, which he did with obvious hesitation.

"Married! I can't believe it." She took a handkerchief from her bag and wiped her nose. "Now what will I do? I have very little money left, I . . ." She looked wildly around the room like an animal caught in a trap and fearing for its life.

"Easy, now." Hjelmer turned back to the judge. "Is there a hotel or boardinghouse" — he nearly choked on the word — "where she can have a room until we sort this out?" How much he'd rather be at his mother's boardinghouse, even though she'd be haranguing him to find his sister. Even the arguing Congress would be better — and that was where he should be.

"Of course. Right across the street and down two buildings. Fine hotel, serves meals, full bar, cardroom. Can't ask for more." Judge Rhinehart offered his hand again. "I have an appointment, but if there is anything else I can do, please ask. I'll be here in Ipswich for another week or two. Holding court right there in the private dining room at the hotel."

"Thank you. I'll get Miss Borsland settled, then send that telegram. You've been most helpful and I — we appreciate it." He took Asta by the elbow and explained things to her as they went out the door.

But even after a nap and another recitation of the facts, Asta alternated winding her fingers together and dabbing at her eyes with a bit of cambric. Sitting at the supper table in the hotel, she asked again, "What am I going to do?"

Hjelmer heartily wished he were home hammering steel into a new shape. Right then he felt like hammering about anything. "I wouldn't make any hasty decisions until you speak with Mr. Moyer."

"But what if he really is married to your sister?"

And I have to be the one to tell my mor. Lady, you think you got troubles. But he kept his thoughts to himself and a concerned look on his face. "There are plenty of men in the Dakotas who need a wife. Have no fear, you'll be married soon."

The look on her face told him immediately that he had said the wrong thing. Why, oh, why had he been polite and invited her to supper?

Because your mor always taught you to look out for women. That is the polite and Christian thing to do.

As soon as was decently possible, he hustled her back up the stairs to her room and escaped to walk the town and ruminate on his own thoughts. He would drive out to the ranch, grab his sister, and drag her back with him to Blessing. *But what if she doesn't want to go?* The little voice in his mind could go jump in the Missouri for all he cared.

Here he had a perfectly wonderful wife at home, whom he loved being with. Her cooking far surpassed that of the cook in the hotel, and she would rub his shoulders when they were tight as knots. He consciously rotated his neck and let his shoulders slump. *God, please take care of Penny for me and, if possible, let her have a child, since that is the desire of her heart. You know I don't particularly care one way or another right now, but she does. And please comfort*

Mor when she receives this latest bit of bad news.

He strode on, not really seeing much of the town at all. Lights glowed from windows since dusk crept in around him, but the street was empty, making him even more aware of how lonely he felt. Whatever was he doing in Ipswich, South Dakota, when everything he held dear was miles to the north?

"Uff da!" He turned back to the hotel and made his way up to his room, bypassing the cardroom, where a group of men seemed to be having a fine time. If only he hadn't made that vow. He shook his head. He could probably even recoup the money he'd spent on this chase to find his sister if he sat at the card table for a time. Cards had always liked him.

He sighed again, pushed open the door to his room, and went to bed. Somehow in the morning he'd have to talk Miss Borsland into staying here in town while he went searching for the Moyer ranch.

But convincing Asta Borsland to stay in Ipswich was like trying to stop the Red River from flooding in the spring.

He should have just left without her.

After a breakfast filled more with arguing than food and armed with a telegram that gave the section numbers of the Moyer ranch, he and the stubborn Miss Asta Borsland set out in a rented team and wagon. The man at the livery assured them that ranchers along the way would be glad to give them a room at night. Visitors were few and far between, making strangers all the more welcome.

Two letters addressed to Elkanah Moyer accompanied them, one of them sent by Asta herself.

"I really think it would be better for you to stay in town until I return." Hjelmer tried to argue his point again. "After all, this is not seemly, me a married man and you an unmarried woman."

"Ah, what am I to do if he really *is* married?" At that she broke into tears again. The very thing that had undone him earlier. Soaking handkerchiefs seemed to be a special skill of hers.

Hjelmer never had been able to ignore a woman's tears.

28

Blessing
October 1

Ingeborg felt as though she were trapped in mud and couldn't run.

Grace held a handful of black dirt up and let it run through her fingers, unaware of the impending danger.

The horse pounded closer.

"Run, Grace! Oh, God, help!" Ingeborg could hear herself screaming as she ran. Someone else was running too.

A form flashed past her. Paws headed for the horse like a bullet shot from a thirty-ought-six. He leaped for the horse's nose and clamped on. The horse reared, flailing forefeet trying to dislodge the thing on his nose.

Ingeborg scooped up the little girl, clutching her to her breast. Heart thudding like a steam engine in full throttle, Ingeborg watched as Paws was flung across the yard by the terrified horse. Two men got hold of the bridle and brought the beast to a quivering halt.

"Thank you, God. Thank you, thank you." She panted the words, patting Grace who had begun to whimper. "It's all right, little one. You're fine now." She kissed Grace's cheek and handed her to her mother. "That was a scare, for certain sure."

"Mor, Paws!" Andrew darted to the dog's side and knelt in the dust. "Paws, good dog, you stopped the horse."

Thorliff skidded to a stop beside his brother. He knelt and felt Paws' chest. "He's still alive."

"He's not bleeding. Is he broken?" Andrew looked up with tear-filled eyes. "He's such a good dog. Please, God, let him be all right."

Ingeborg and Haakan reached the boys at the same time. Haakan opened the dog's mouth and peered at his gums. "Doesn't seem to be bleeding internally." He put an arm around Andrew and held him close while the boy struggled against the tears.

"Mor, he saved Grace's life." Thorliff stroked his dog's ears, turning his head so that he could wipe his cheek without seeming to.

"I know. Thank the Lord for that." Ingeborg stroked Andrew's hair. "Easy son." *Please, God, this little dog gave everything he had. Let him stay with us, please. You say you care about everything that we care about, and you can see how my boys are sorrowing.*

"Let's get a gunnysack and carry him over to the barn in the shade." Haakan nodded to Baptiste, who ran to the barn.

"If he's breathing, maybe he just got knocked out," one of the other men offered.

"Let's hope so." Haakan lifted the dog's eyelid. Paws flicked his hand with a weak tongue.

"Ma, did you see that?" Andrew's blue eyes sparkled through the tears.

"Thanks be to God." Kaaren, hugging Grace to her shoulder, said what everyone else was thinking. "Thank you, God, for a little dog who stopped a horse like that."

As she passed, all the women reached out and patted Grace. Sophie clung to her skirts, eyes still wide from the scene. The men went back to work on the cheese house, and the sound of hammers and saws again filled the air.

"Let's put him on a quilt by the stove instead. He could be cold from the shock."

Ingeborg looked to Haakan, who nodded his agreement.

Thorliff and Baptiste slipped the sack under Paws, then Haakan and Thorliff carried him, depositing him on the folded quilt by the stove in the kitchen. Andrew knelt beside him, and Paws tried to wag his tail, barely brushing the floor but moving nonetheless.

"Go get a dipper of water and trickle some into his mouth."

Thorliff did as told, and Paws licked his hands.

Ingeborg carefully felt the dog's ribs and along his back, watching for any sign of flinching. "I think he might have a broken rib." She felt the bone again and nodded. "I think so. That would make him hurt awhile, but like people he'll heal from it."

"I wish my grand-mère was here. She'd know what to do." Baptiste joined the boys in stroking the dog.

Ingeborg smiled at the boy's certain voice. Metiz had helped save other lives in the years they'd been friends, and Ingeborg missed her every day. It seemed she'd been gone for years and not just two months. She used to be gone all winter, but now that they'd built her a good solid house, she stayed through the year.

"I'll be glad when she gets back."

"Me too."

Ingeborg left the boys with the dog and went back outside to see what she could do to help. Grace came up and pulled at her skirt.

"Hi, little one." Ingeborg squatted down to be on eye level with her niece.

Grace's fingers flew in the signs for thank you.

"Slow down." Ingeborg made a slowing motion.

Grace grinned at her and nodded, then moved her fingers more slowly.

While Ingeborg had to concentrate, she got the drift. Now how to answer? Slowly her fingers formed y-o-u a-r-e w-e-l-c-o-m-e. While she knew Grace could do some lip reading, she felt honor bound to try to learn the signs like everyone else.

Grace flung her arms around her aunt's neck and kissed her cheek.

Ingeborg hugged her close, blinking several times. Such a terrible close call that had been. And it wasn't like no one had been watching her. In her mind's eye she could see again the little girl happily playing in the dirt. The others were running hither and yon, but Grace seemed to enjoy being alone at times.

Grace tugged on her hand, so Ingeborg followed her over to the rising walls of the cheese house. Grace peered in the section left open for a wide door. Since the floor was three feet down, one of the men was hammering together boards for stairs. Grace indicated the whole scene with a sweep of her arm and, grinning up at her aunt, clapped her hands.

Ingeborg smiled back, dropped a kiss on the little nose, and clapped her hands too. "Yes, my cheese house is wonderful."

"Sure 'nough will be big." Mr. Rasmussen grunted as he set another block of sod on the wall. He indicated the wall with a crooked finger. "I'm learning how to build a soddy. That is good, huh? That way I'll know how to get my own up. Did Mr. Bjorklund talk to you 'bout what I said yet?"

Ingeborg shook her head.

"I asked if my wife and young'uns could stay the winter here with you. I'll head west in the next couple of weeks and go scouting for land, then when I find some, I'll come back and work out the winter for Haakan. Soon as spring comes, we'll all head out. Take the train to Bismarck or Minot or so and get a horse and wagon for the rest."

Ingeborg nodded. "Seems a sound plan to me. I'll be glad for the extra hands here."

"Mor!" Andrew called from the back stoop. "Come quick."

"I'm coming." She smiled at Mr. Rasmussen and headed for the house. "What is it?"

"Paws is sitting up. Come see."

Ingeborg took the hand he extended and followed his tugging into the house. Paws indeed was sitting up, panting, but he lay back down with a slight whimper when she stroked his head. "Let's just let him sleep, all right?"

"But when we started to leave, that's when he sat up. I think he wants to follow us. You know how he likes it when so many people are here." Andrew sat down beside his friend.

"Maybe you should stay here with him for a while, then. You want me to get Deborah and Ellie so the three of you can play checkers?"

Andrew nodded. "Thanks, Ma."

After sending the girls inside, Ingeborg wandered over to the fire where the coffeepots hung steaming from iron tripods. Geese honked their way south overhead, making her wish for a chance to go hunting. She saw Baptiste look up and knew he felt the same. Once the cheese house was done, he would be free to hunt every afternoon after school. That's why he and Thorliff had been splitting so much wood to keep the smokehouse going.

She poured herself a cup of coffee and blew on the steaming mug.

"Come on over," Kaaren called. "We're discussing our school for the deaf. Agnes has a really good idea."

29

The Ranch
October 1

"I'd like you to meet my wife, Mrs. Moyer."
Kane nodded to the major standing beside
him. The men had just come in for supper
after the day spent rounding up the remaining cattle to be transported to the army
post.

"Pleased, I'm sure." The officer tipped
his hat. "Major John Grunswold at your
service. This is a recent occurrence?"

"Yes, about a month ago. The difficult
part is that she doesn't speak English, only
Norwegian. We are trying to teach her to
speak English." Kane smiled at Augusta,
who wore her stoic look. He knew she
wondered what they were saying.

Augusta watched them talk, wishing with
all her heart she knew what their words
meant. It seemed to be about her, the way
they kept glancing in her direction. *Oh,*

Lord, I am so weary of not understanding the people talking around me. Please give me some hint of what they are saying.

"I speak fair German. Learned it at my grandmother's knee. Perhaps I can help a bit. The languages are similar."

"Please sit down. Supper will be ready shortly." Kane indicated the chairs around the roaring fireplace. He seated Augusta in one and pointed to the nearest for the army officer and the other chairs for the two enlisted men who'd been standing by the door.

"Frau Moyer, sprechen sie Deutsche?"

Augusta gave him a strange look. "Jeg kan snakke Norsk, ein bischen Deutsche." She held thumb and forefinger half an inch apart to show "a little" and shook her head. "But my name is Miss Bjorklund, not Frau Moyer. You are mistaken." At his look of utter confusion, she repeated her comments more slowly.

"But Moyer here said you are married to him — have been for a month." He kept his German slow and precise.

Augusta's heart flew into high speed. "Nei!" She shook her head, her eyebrows flat together over eyes that snapped with indignation. "I was on my way from Valdres, Norway, to Blessing, North Dakota, to my mor's boardinghouse and must have got on the wrong train in St. Paul. Mr. Moyer said he would take me to Blessing." *Father in heaven, help me, please. Please let this not be happening.* She shot a look of consternation in Kane's direction.

He looked totally confused, like a child watching a game he'd never seen before and trying to understand it without instructions. He shrugged when he looked in her face. "I . . . I don't understand." He looked to the major. "Please, what is she saying?"

"She says she is not married to you, that you agreed to take her to Blessing."

"Blessing?"

"The town in North Dakota where her mother lives. She says she got on the wrong train, and when she got to Ipswich, you said you would take her to Blessing."

Kane groaned as the memory of their meeting flashed before his eyes. "But we *are* married. A justice of the peace performed the ceremony in Ipswich. Ask her about the paper she signed."

"But I thought that was for citizenship," Augusta answered the major, shaking her head again. By this time her head felt as if it were about to fall off from all the shaking. "I can't be married. I don't even know this man. I didn't have any more money, or I would have purchased a ticket back to St. Paul." She didn't think she could feel any more stupid if she tried.

Again the major translated what he understood, and now it was Kane's turn to shake his head.

Augusta was dumbfounded. She was married? Scenes flitted through her mind. The way he'd greeted her the morning she found him in her bed, the gentle way he helped care for her when she was sick. She could feel the heat climb her neck like a forest fire going up a tree. He'd seen her in her nightdress. If she'd been the type to faint, she knew right now would have been a most opportune time.

"Supper's ready," Morning Dove called from the kitchen.

"Excuse me, I . . . ah . . . I . . ." Augusta turned and fled to her room. After bathing her face in cool water from the pitcher, she smoothed back her hair, tucking a couple of errant strands back in the bun. No need to pinch her cheeks for color, that was for certain sure. She held the cool cloth to them again, then patted down her neck. If only she could hide under the covers and never come out again.

Kane — Mr. Moyer — thinks he is married

to me. What am I to do? Lord, what am I to do?

Would marriage to him be such a terrible thing? The thought made her stop her patting hand. *After all, you've thought how you might like a man like him.* The heat returned full force. She sank down on the edge of the bed and stared at her hands. She should be out there helping Morning Dove serve the meal.

Instead, she laid her hands along her temples as if to stem the thoughts chasing pell-mell through her mind. "I am married. I am legally the wife of Elkanah Moyer. Mrs. Elkanah Moyer," she said aloud. *Oh, Mor, I've made such a mess of things. What am I to do?* She looked around the room, recognizing the special things he had done in this room. "He had prepared for his bride. And he got me instead." Another thought crossed her mind, strong enough to bring her to her feet and make her stride out the door with enough force to carry her to the kitchen table.

"What happened to the woman you planned to marry?"

Major John Grunswold translated, and Kane shrugged.

"I don't know, but you were at the train station where she was supposed to be, and

I thought you were her."

She could tell he was getting a bit testy about the whole thing, not that she blamed him one bit.

The men stood behind their chairs while she chewed on her lip. When a man clearing his throat caught her attention, she felt the heat again. They were all waiting for her to sit. The whole creek outside wouldn't be enough to cool her face, or her whole self if she jumped right in. The thought carried great appeal.

"Excuse me, gentlemen, please be seated. I . . . I have something to check in the — er, the . . . the outside." Her feet barely touched the floor out through the pantry and to the back stoop. The cold air helped. Helped to cool her face, but nothing could help her mixed-up situation. This was more than a mix-up. This was a catastrophe.

Except he is a fine man, and this ranch is — was . . . Her thoughts were so jumbled she couldn't even finish this one. Instead, she opened the back door and, sucking in a final breath of cold air, returned to the kitchen, where all the others were now seated and passing around the bowls and platters of food. She slid into her place, keeping her gaze locked on her plate and the passing dishes. Since she didn't understand what they were talking about anyway, she let her mind gnaw on her own situation.

How could she stay here any longer? Yet how could she leave? Of course she could stay. She was married, after all. There was no impropriety. Except in her mind. The paper might say she was married, but she surely didn't feel like it. Or act like it.

Oh, for a fan.

When she sneaked a peek at Kane, he was studying her the way he studied the horses when he chose which ones to keep and which to sell. She went back to watching the gravy congeal on her plate.

"You aren't eating."

Kane's voice held what? A question? Reproach? Could it be caring? She looked up. He pointed to her plate. She shook her head and forked a bit of meat to her mouth. The more she chewed, the larger the bite seemed. Commanding her jaw to keep working, she drew circles in the gravy with her fork tines. And refused to look up again.

I have to leave. She knew that for certain by the time Morning Dove refilled the coffee cups. But how? And when?

"Augusta?" Kane motioned toward the

chairs in front of the fireplace after the enlisted men left them for their tents. "I have some things to show you."

Augusta glanced down the hall to her room, back to the sink where Morning Dove was preparing to wash dishes, and over to the fire. Kane stood beside her as if he would take her arm and drag her in there if she moved another way.

"He says he has things to show you." Major Grunswold stopped at her other side.

Flanked by the two men, Augusta thought she knew what being a prisoner led off to jail felt like.

Once she was seated, Kane left the room and returned in a few minutes with several papers in his hand. "This is our marriage certificate." He handed her the paper, and Grunswold translated for him. "And my letter to Norway asking for a mail-order bride."

Her hands shook as she accepted the second sheet. No wonder he'd been prepared for a wife.

"This is the letter from Norway accepting my offer. I somehow misplaced this on the trip home and found it again last week." Again Major Grunswold translated as Kane handed her the paper.

Augusta studied the signature. "But this is not my name. This says Miss Asta Borsland."

"But they sound amazingly alike," the major said, first in German, then in English. He looked up to Kane. "Fine kettle of fish we have here. What do you suppose happened to" — he studied the signature more closely — "to Miss Borsland?"

"I don't know." Kane shrugged and shook his head again. "But she wasn't on the train for which I sent her the ticket. Maybe she changed her mind." He gathered the papers together. "I truly thought this woman here was my intended bride when she got off the train. To be quite honest, I am perfectly happy with the arrangement the way it is. I have a wife now, and that was what I wanted."

Augusta looked to the major for translation. "But . . . but my mor . . . I mean, I . . ." She stopped. She'd come to recognize that squaring of the jaw that said Kane was digging in his heels. "Excuse me, gentlemen, I have much to think about." She rose and tipped her head briefly to each in turn. As she strode from the room, she could hear them begin to discuss things again. Most likely they were talking about her. So be it.

By the time the rooster crowed in the morning, she hadn't slept a wink. Round and round her mind spun the problem, dipping and swirling like swallows on the wing. No matter how hard she prayed, spending several hours of the long night on her knees at the side of her bed, or how fiercely she listened, God seemed far away and silent as only He could be. What was she to do?

She knew what she looked like without glancing in the mirror. Lack of sleep always gave her raccoon eyes. She brushed her hair and donned a clean apron over her dark wool skirt. With the cold breath of winter blowing around the hills on some mornings, her wool felt mighty good. But she didn't have the heavy petticoats and long woolen stockings she would need for winter. They were in her trunk — most likely in Blessing, where she should be. *I always come back to that.*

"Good morning." Morning Dove shot her glances from the corner of her dark eyes.

"Good morning," Augusta replied. But in her mind, it was anything but that.

The two women worked together in their usual way, preparing the meal of steak, potatoes, eggs, biscuits, and plenty of hot coffee. The ranch hands and the enlisted men came in first and then the major and Kane.

"Guten Morgen." The major nodded at Augusta and greeted Morning Dove in English.

"God dag." Augusta peeked at Kane, but he was looking the other way. Within moments she could feel his gaze on her. She didn't need to look.

After the blessing, the men fell to and the women ferried platters of food from the stove to the table. Afterward, Kane and the major repaired to the desk on the far wall of the sitting room, and the others went outside. When Augusta and Morning Dove sat down to eat, they could hear the men loading the squealing pigs in the high-sided wagons. The cattle and horses were waiting in the corrals.

"They go." Morning Dove motioned to the noise outside.

Go is what I should do, but how? Augusta nodded and cut another bite of steak.

"If there is anything I can do to help you," the major said when they returned to the kitchen.

"Mange takk." Augusta knew there was nothing he could do. She bobbed her head and managed a smile.

"Good-bye, then." Grunswold tipped his hat, and he and Kane left by the back door.

"We wash clothes." Morning Dove indicated her apron.

Augusta wished she had something else to wear so she could wash all of her garments, but other than asking to borrow something of Morning Dove's, that was an impossibility. She helped carry water to heat in the boilers and reservoir. One of the hands brought in extra wood, and soon the kitchen windows were dripping from the steam. They boiled the white things first, rinsed them in cooler water, then Augusta took them outside to hang on the line. The wind snapped the sheets in her face and bit any exposed skin. Though the sun shone, it had indeed lost its warmth.

Together they wrung out the men's pants and hung them before noon, when it was time to eat the beans that had been baking in the oven and the molasses bread Augusta had stirred up.

By the time all the clothes were washed and dried, her hands burned from both the soap and the cold wind. Back home she would have had goose grease to rub into her aching hands, but here no one had shot any of the geese that flew overhead by the thousands. What a pity. Fresh goose would taste mighty good.

That night after supper Kane motioned her to come sit by the fire. When they were both seated, he drew a paper from his pocket and held it out to her. She glanced down the two columns of words. "Deutsche?" She pointed at the left-hand column.

He nodded. "And English." He smiled at her, the first time they'd exchanged a direct look since the major announced his news. "So we can learn to talk." His hands fluttered between them.

She nodded. They would use the similarities between German and Norwegian to help her learn more English, a good plan. Talk she understood. Some of the German words she wasn't sure of, but she repeated those she did, and when he gave the English, she said that too. Then smiling, she pointed to a German word and gave the Norwegian.

"Ah." He nodded and repeated, stumbling badly over the Norwegian. Within minutes they were smiling over their efforts, then chuckling, and finally laughing out loud.

Augusta looked up from the paper and caught her breath. The look in his eyes — so warm, so deep she felt she could tumble into them and float like on the deepest of feather beds. His fingers touched hers at the edge of the paper, burning as if she'd stuck her hand in the fire.

She snatched her fingers back and, paper in hand, fled from the room. "Good night," she threw over her shoulder.

"We'll be gone for a day or two," Kane announced in the morning, "rounding up the remaining cattle and bringing them in from the farthest pastures." He looked directly at Augusta. He could tell she hadn't slept well again. Was the thought of being married to him so terrible to her? Last night before the fire, he was sure they were making progress, and here she looked as though she'd lost her best friend again.

Couldn't she at least be his friend or, more appropriately, let him be her friend? Though he knew in his deepest heart that they were destined to be far more than just friends.

While he'd thought in the beginning just having a wife would be enough, now that had changed. He wanted her to love him as he had grown to love her. After that, the real marriage could begin.

Maybe she would miss him while he was away.

After the men were all packed and saddled, Kane made a last trip to the front porch, where Augusta and Morning Dove stood ready to wave them off.

"We'll talk when I get back," he said, handing Augusta the paper with both English and German words on it. "Maybe you could learn these while I am gone?" He tapped the paper with one finger.

Augusta glanced from the paper to the earnest, nay, pleading look in his eyes. She nodded. "Ja, I will . . ." Her English came to a stuttering halt.

"Learn?" He nodded, encouraging her to go on.

She bobbed her head. "Learn. Ja, I will learn." Now it was her turn to tap the paper with a fingertip.

Oh, to take her in his arms and give her a real good-bye, the kind that would keep her thinking of him until he returned. Instead, he doffed his hat, kissed her on the cheek, and leaped down the stairs like a boy just released from school. He looked back to see a half smile and waved his hat, hoping to make her really smile.

Instead, he was left with the haunting

sadness he saw in her eyes. Those blue eyes that could sparkle like wavelets under the sun or cloud over to gray. This time, all he saw in spite of the smile was sadness.

He sighed as he mounted his horse. Was staying with him really causing her such grief?

Last night he'd been sure she cared at least a little. Now he wasn't sure. He wasn't sure of anything.

"Let's travel, boys." *So we can get home again before . . . before what?* He didn't know.

30

Blessing
October 2

"Hjelmer says he found someone who has seen Augusta."

"Where?" Bridget wanted to snatch the telegram from Thorliff's hand, but the words meant nothing to her, since she couldn't read English well at all.

"I don't know." Thorliff looked at his grandmother, shaking his head. "He says she's married."

"Oh, Lord in heaven, what has happened to my girl?" Bridget kneaded her apron between hands growing more gnarled all the time with the heavy work of the boarding-house. "Read the whole thing again. Surely it says where it is from."

Thorliff studied the telegram. "Ipswich, South Dakota. That's where the message originated. He says, 'Found someone who knows of Augusta stop She is married stop

More when I know stop.' " Thorliff handed Bridget the paper. "That's all."

Bridget sank down in a nearby chair. "Ja, well, if she is married, she surely won't be coming here, but why didn't she write and tell me?" Her heart clenched in sorrow. She rubbed her chest with one hand and pleated her apron with the other. What had happened? Would she ever see her remaining daughter again?

"Are you all right, Bestemor?" Thorliff laid a hand on her shoulder.

She looked up at this tall grandson of hers. He had his father's eyes and chin, and his hair was darkening as he grew older, just as Roald's had. If he continued to grow as he had been, he would have the stature of his father also. While Roald had a good head on his shoulders, this son of his teetered on the brink of brilliant, at least according to Pastor Solberg.

"Bestemor?" Thorliff leaned closer, looking deep into her eyes, concern evident in his every gesture.

"Ah, not to worry. Just getting lost in my thoughts there for a moment." Bridget patted his hand and heaved herself to her feet. "Don't let an old woman's wanderings worry you, son. The news was just a bit of a shock, that's all." She pushed open the swinging door to the kitchen, calling over her shoulders as she went, "Cookies are hot out of the oven, Thorliff. You want to take some home with you?"

The grin he gave her made her add, "Now, you make sure some of them get as far as Andrew and Astrid, you hear?" She pinched his rosy cheek and chuckled as she filled one of Metiz' low baskets, covered it with a clean white cloth, and handed him the handle. "You have Jack here, ja?"

"Yep, Pa says we're going to get a riding horse one of these days, maybe from Zeb, if he ever gets back, that is." Thorliff paused in the doorway. "Sure wish I was with him scouting Montana. Leastways that's what Manda said he's doing."

"Tell your mor about the telegram. She'll be wanting to know."

"And Tante Kaaren?"

"Yes. Was there a telegram for Penny?"

"Not that I know of." He filched another cookie from the cooling rack.

Bridget fished the missive from her pocket. "Drop this off for her, then, on your way by."

"So what . . . ?" Goodie raised one eyebrow.

Eulah stopped what she was doing and looked to Bridget.

Only the wood snapping in the stove broke the silence. Bridget sighed. "My Augusta is married."

"Wh-what?" Goodie dusted the flour off her hands. "Bridget Bjorklund, you just sit right down there till I fetch you a cup of coffee." She motioned to Eulah, who took three cups from the cupboard and set them on the table while Goodie brought the coffeepot. As soon as she poured, she took Bridget by the arm and guided her to the chair as if she'd suddenly become fragile and unable to do for herself.

Bridget sank and sighed at the same time. "That's what the telegram said. Hjelmer sent it from Ipswich, South Dakota — wherever in the world that is. He said he'd learned of Augusta there. I was so excited until Thorliff read the next line. She's married. More will come later." She propped her cup between both hands. "I don't know. I just don't know."

"Well, my land." Goodie looked to Eulah, shaking her head all the while. "Did you ever hear of such goings-on?"

Eulah shook her head, the tails of the kerchief she wore over her kinky black hair bobbing in the motion. "Might be somethin' bad happen to dat girl."

"What if she was kidnapped or something? Forced to marry? Land, what is this world coming to?"

Eulah squinted her eyes. "Dat Hjelmer, he go to fixin' dis. Dat man wrong his sister. He wrong dat man."

Bridget stared at the woman who spoke so assuredly. "How do you know that?"

"It's true, ain't it?"

"Ja, my Hjelmer, he is a fixer all right, but how did you know?"

"Years ago when he worked on the railroad wid mah Sam, he took care of dat ol' darkie. Made sure dey was food to eat and a place to sleep. Sam said he owed his life to Mr. Hjelmer. And now we's here in Blessing, we ain't never had it so good. All of us together, workin', playin', little'uns in da house, jest one big happy family. First time in years."

Bridget reached across the table and covered Eulah's hand with her own. "You said just the things I needed to hear. Mange takk from the bottom of my old Norwegian heart." She drained her coffee cup and got to her feet. "Well, we better get back to business here, or we'll have some mighty unhappy guests pounding on the tables out there. Anyone seen Ilse in the last hour or so? And Lemuel? Where is he? We're going to need some more wood split. That stack out back is getting mighty low."

"That's because Henry hasn't been around for weeks."

Seems more like months, Bridget thought but refrained from saying. Once Goodie got an idea what she was thinking, it would be all over Blessing before a dish towel could dry on a July day in a stiff breeze.

"Bridget?"

"Ja, Penny, I'm back here."

The door swung open as if blown in by a northerly. "I give up. That man is never coming home!"

"I'm sorry. He's trying so hard to find Augusta, and you know how much that means to me."

"I know, and I want him to find her too, but . . ." Penny hung her shawl over the back of a chair. "Brr, but it's getting cold outside. On top of that, big, I mean *big* crates arrived today. You should have seen Sam's eyes light up. You ever heard of windmills?" At the shake of the others' heads, Penny did the same. "That man can find more things to buy."

"And he'll make money with them too. He's got the Midas touch, that man." Goodie dusted off her hands. "I better see that those tables are ready. Eulah, you want to slice the bread?" Goodie left by the same door Penny entered.

Lemuel came through the back door with a gust of wind and dropped his arm-load of wood into the woodbox. "Mistah Olaf said we could have snow soon. I 'bout froze out there choppin' da wood."

"Chop fast, den. It warm you right up." Eulah waved her knife in the air. "Is Laban and Mary Jane home doin' der studyin'?"

Her boy nodded. "An sissy is out to Bjorklunds' helpin' wit da cheese. She said she not be home for suppah."

"You tell those young'uns and Sam to come here for supper." Bridget turned from forking the potatoes to see if they were done. "We got plenty."

"Thank'ee Miz Bridget." Eulah went back to slicing bread. "Lemuel, you run on and fetch dem. *After* you chop more wood."

"Penny, you stay too. No sense going home to a lonely supper."

"Mor, you'll go broke feeding half the town like this." But Penny put on an apron and pitched in with the supper prepara-tion. "When's Henry coming back?"

"How should I know? I ain't his keeper."

"Oh, s-o-r-r-y." Penny took a step back-ward. "I think you and me are in the same boat. Our men off somewhere else while we're here."

"He's not my man." Bridget's fork hit the counter with a clatter.

Penny and Eulah exchanged looks that said, *Oh me, something sure put a flea in her ear.*

"Maybe I better just go out and come in again, or maybe I better just go out." Penny stabbed the last pickle in the jar and quartered it into the serving dish.

"Oh, shush." But the smile on Bridget's face said she knew exactly what Penny was doing. *All this so I don't go worrying on about Augusta. Thank you, Lord, for my friends and family. Oh, you can call me blessed. And thank you my girl is alive.*

Since they only had three boarders in for supper, everyone ate around the tables in the dining room. When Eulah tried to say her family would eat in the kitchen, Bridget gave her a glare that said otherwise.

"I learned me a poem today," Laban said, his grin enough to light the room without the kerosene lamps.

"So what is it?" Penny sat next to the children, or they sat next to her. Whenever there were children in the vicinity, they gravitated to her side.

"He cain't say it all yet." His sister rolled her eyes and shook her head, setting her pigtails to flapping.

"I can too.

" 'Under the spreading chestnut tree,
The village smithy stands.
The smith a mighty man is he,
With large and sinewy hands.'

"Like mah Uncle Sam, huh, Miss Penny?"

Sam raised his hands. "Might be large to you, son, but . . ."

"An we ain't gots a chestnut tree heah neither. Ah asked Pastor Solberg, and he said no."

Penny tried to keep a straight face, but one look at the two earnest ones on either side of her and her chuckle escaped. It nabbed the others at their table and then flew on to the next and around the room until everyone joined in.

"Now, if that don't sound mighty friendly to a poor wayfaring railroad man." Henry pushed through the swinging door just as Bridget was about to pour coffee.

"Henry!" The coffeepot thumped down so hard it spouted brown lava, and she turned and almost fell into his arms right in the middle of the room.

"Now, if that ain't the best kind of greeting of all." Henry, cheeks matching hers for blazing red, gave her a hug that lifted her feet right off the floor.

"H-how did you get here? Henry, put me down."

He set her back down but kept a hand on her arm. "I planned on being here earlier, but the train was late." Belatedly he glanced up to see every pair of eyes in the room riveted on the two of them.

"Henry, you're blushing." Bridget's whisper worked something like Andrew's. Everyone within a mile could hear it plainly.

With that, his face flamed brighter than the sunset. "Come with me, woman." He grabbed her hand and hauled her through the swinging doors amid the cheers and laughter of all present. Once alone, he kissed her soundly.

Bridget started to sputter but gave it up and returned the kiss with fervor.

"You've missed me, then." He laid his cheek against the soft hair now looped down over her forehead.

"I didn't say that." She nestled closer, if that were possible.

"You didn't have to." Henry sighed.

"I've missed you far more than I ever thought I could. If it hadn't taken so long to locate that daughter of yours, I'd a been back much sooner."

"Oh." Bridget pulled back enough to look up into his face. She clapped her hands to her cheeks. "I forgot all about Augusta."

"Now." Henry nodded. "Now, that's the words I wanted to hear." He kept hold of her hand and pulled her over to sit down on his knee when he sat in the chair. With one arm around her waist, as if to keep her from escaping, he turned her chin so he could see her full face.

"I want you to know that Hjelmer has been doing the best he could, and I was too. I left him as he was about to get on the train to Ipswich. A conductor friend of mine remembered seeing Augusta on that train, but he'd been sick and not at work, so we couldn't talk with him earlier."

"Henry . . ."

"Now, just a minute, let me finish. When Hjelmer got on that train, he said he'd bring her back or die trying."

"Henry . . ."

"In a minute. I told him I knew his mother didn't expect that kind of commitment from her son but —"

"Henry." Bridget took his chin in her fingers. "Augusta is married."

"I told him —" He jerked loose. "What did you say?"

"Hjelmer sent me a telegram. He got to Ipswich only to find out Augusta was married. I don't know how he knows that, but knowing Hjelmer, there'll be a long, long story about all this. He still plans to find her." She shook her head. "I just don't understand, that's all. Why would she do this to me? To her family here?" She laid her head on his shoulder. "Ah, maybe I've lived too long. There is so much I don't understand anymore."

"Hush." He put a finger to her lips. "I have only one question now."

"What?" His shoulder felt so good under her cheek. She sniffed. And he smelled good too.

"Will you marry me?"

"Now?"

"Soon. I did what I could to help find Augusta, and now it looks like maybe she didn't want to be found."

"I don't think it's that. Not Augusta. She believes to the marrow of her bones that one lives up to one's word. And she promised to come help me with the boarding-house."

"I will help you."

"Yes, dear. But something strange is going on, you mark my words." She shrugged her shoulders and sighed. "Yes, Henry dear, I will marry you."

"When?"

31

The Ranch
October 4

"Think I'll go for a ride." Augusta took the last flatiron off the stove.

"Eh?" Morning Dove came through the back door with a basket of vegetables.

"Ride." Mimicking riding made them both laugh.

"Not far." The housekeeper motioned close.

"No, I won't." *God, please forgive the lie. I have to take this chance. If I ride hard, maybe I can make it to the train station in one day. After all* . . . She didn't continue with the "after all." When she'd finally made Kane understand that she wanted to go to Blessing, he'd been adamant that she stay here. She was his wife now, and he had no plans to take her to Blessing.

Just in case, Augusta rolled up a wool blanket and let it drop out the window of her room. She'd pick it up on the way out. If Morning Dove went back outside, she'd take some food from the kitchen. She didn't need much. It wasn't as if she were riding clear to St. Paul.

By tomorrow noon at the latest she would be there. If only Morning Dove would go back outside. Now she knew what waterdrops felt like on a hot skillet, all jumpy and full of steam. Only they didn't have to wait; they just exploded.

Morning Dove poured water in a pan and began to scrape the carrots.

"I can do that." Augusta motioned toward the dry sink.

"Good." Morning Dove handed over the knife.

Oh, please go back outside. Scraping away, Augusta looked out the window. Frost from the night before still sparkled on the undersides of the cabbages and now darkened sunflower stalks. But the sky was the kind of blue that called one outside. Augusta scraped faster. She cut off an end and popped it into her mouth. Even the carrots tasted sweeter after a frost. All the turnips were already stored in the root cellar, along with the rutabagas and potatoes.

"I go dig some more." Morning Dove

checked the baby on her back and picked up the basket.

"You want these to boil?" Augusta indicated the stove. Even though her English was still so haphazard, she and Morning Dove managed to understand each other. Shame she and Kane couldn't do as well.

Morning Dove nodded as she went back out the door.

Augusta dipped water from the reservoir into a kettle and set it on the hottest part of the stove. She cut the carrots in chunks and dumped them in the already steaming water, along with two pinches of salt from the salt cellar that sat on the upper warming shelf of the stove. With the lid in place, she tucked a couple of the carrots, a slab of meat from the leftover roast, and a half loaf of bread into a dish towel. Checking out the window to make sure Morning Dove was still busy, she flew to her room to get the wool jacket that matched her skirt. With a sigh of regret, she left her carpetbag tucked under the bed. Not that she had much in it, but it was one of her last links to home.

Perhaps someday Kane would send it to her.

You are married to him, you know. The little voice that she'd been trying to ignore all morning managed to break through her barriers.

"So he says," she muttered as she tucked a handkerchief up her sleeve. "But it sure enough wasn't because I said yes."

But you really do admire him, perhaps even have come to lo— She cut that thought off before it could go any further. Love was more than tingles up the arm and the flushing of the face. Love was trust and caring and sharing and much more.

So hasn't he been showing you those exact — She cut that thought off too. She stopped and glanced a final time in the mirror. "I have to get to Blessing. I told Mor I was coming, and she must be half dead with worry by now. They've probably already had a funeral for me, at least in their minds."

That thought made her feel even worse. *If only Kane had said he would take me there, as I thought he meant in the beginning.* "Uff da!" She spun away from her reflection and, gathering her few things, checked to make sure she was still alone in the house. There was not a sound.

Hurrying back to the kitchen, she set her parcel on the chair before the fireplace, then continued to slide the now boiling kettle of carrots to a cooler part of the stove. She stuck a couple of pieces of firewood in the stove, clattered the lid back in place, and with parcel in hand, out the front door she went, picking up her blanket as she passed.

The filly greeted her with a nicker and came trotting over as soon as she saw the carrot on Augusta's palm. Saddling and bridling her took only minutes, but the entire time the argument raged in her head.

Go. Stay. Stay. Go. No matter which, she'd make someone unhappy. Not that Kane would be too unhappy. At least she didn't think so.

Once mounted she waved to Morning Dove and jogged out down the lane she and Kane had ridden before. When Morning Dove called something to her, she waved again. "Ja, I will be careful," she called back. If only she could understand for sure what the woman had said. If only she could have said a real good-bye. After all, Morning Dove had been very good with and to her.

Augusta ignored the twinges of guilt, even after they grew to spear size. *Married.* She couldn't be married, for heaven's sake.

Once out of sight of the ranch, she kicked the filly into a lope. All she had to do now was follow the road back to the train station. About an hour out, time enough to begin to feel discomfort in her rear region, she came to a fork in the road. There were no signs anywhere. "So, girl, which way do we go?"

The filly snorted and blew. Dark patches on her neck reminded Augusta that she'd better slow down for a time and take it easy on her horse. "Which way, Lord? You have promised to guide the blind, and right now I might as well be blind."

When the bush off to the side of the road failed to burst into fire and tell her which way, she took the left fork because it seemed to go more north. Something she remembered from her trip from the railroad station made her think they had come south.

"Or was it west?" The filly's ears flicked at her words, but she kept up the gentle jog that could lull a person to sleep if they weren't careful.

All the hills looked the same. Rolling, not much higher than a two-story house, and with a decided lack of trees. Or farmhouses.

A deer bounded out from a thicket, and if she hadn't been alert, her horse would have bolted. As it was, Augusta brought the filly under control a ways down the road. Her heart pounded as though it wanted freedom from the confines of her chest.

While she'd already been thirsty, now her mouth felt drier than the sand that drifted on some of the hills. The breeze had kicked up when she wasn't looking, and she thought of using the blanket she had tied on behind the saddle for a cover.

Glancing behind her she realized why it had gotten colder. Towering thunderheads purpled the western horizon, reaching for the sun with flimsy fingers. She shivered and buttoned the top button of her jacket. Hadn't there been a creek that followed much of the road on their way out? At the pace she was going, surely she should have seen it by now.

"Why didn't I bring a jug of water? What was the matter with my head?"

You'd think we would have met at least one other traveler by now.

"Oh-oh. Something's up," Kane said to Lone Pine as he looked at the figure on horseback flying across the field toward them.

Morning Dove pulled her horse to a sliding stop in front of the two men. "She gone."

"Gone? What do you mean 'gone'?" Kane tipped the brim of his hat up so he could see her without getting a crick in his neck.

"She went riding and not come back."

Kane glanced up at the sky, now more black than gray. "Go find the others," he instructed Lone Pine. "Tell them to get back to the ranch as fast as they can."

Lone Pine nodded and swung aboard his horse. "You want them to bring in the cattle?"

"No." Kane grabbed the reins that had been ground-tying his horse. "What did she say?" he asked Morning Dove as he flipped one rein up from the other side, then gathered them both and stepped into his stirrup. He had his mount moving before he settled into the saddle.

"She said good-bye." Morning Dove reined her horse around and kept pace with Kane.

"Not see you later, or —"

Morning Dove shook her head. "Good-bye — in English. She been practicing her English all the time."

"I know." *Fool woman, where could she have gone?* Surely she knew better than to go beyond the ranch. After all, that's where they had ridden together and then she by herself. He'd shown her the boundaries. Not that anyone else would mind her riding on their land.

He felt a few drops on his hands and in his face. That's all they needed. Rain to wash away her tracks.

"Did she take anything along?"

"Bread and meat."

That in itself wasn't unusual. Unless, of course, they had already eaten dinner. But when he asked Morning Dove, she shook her head. So maybe she'd planned on a picnic. He pulled his hat lower to keep the rising wind from snatching it away.

Wonderful weather for anyone to be lost.

By the time they loped into the ranch, he'd called himself every name in the book and made up a few new ones. He'd found himself being real creative with names for his wife too. Perhaps she'd returned.

But when they got to the corral, he knew that was a vain hope. The filly wasn't in the corral, the barn, or out to pasture. While he waited for the others, he gathered up lanterns and filled them with kerosene, had Morning Dove fix food both for a fast supper and a meal on the trail, and tied a tarp around his blanket roll. By the time the men got there, he'd about worn a groove in the floor in front of the fireplace.

He took one man besides Lone Pine. While the wind pummeled them like a boxer attacking his foe, the rain held off, sending drops once in a while to keep them from getting too complacent.

At least there hadn't been a lot of traffic on the road, none in fact but a lone horse with what he hoped was a lonely rider. The question he couldn't answer was why? Had she been so unhappy that she had to run away?

But deep in his heart he thought he knew. She'd asked him to take her to Blessing, and he'd refused.

When they came to the fork, he held the lantern out so they could see better.

Lone Pine pointed to the left. "She go that way."

Kane shook his head. "Now, why would she do that? If she's going to Ipswich, it's that way." He nodded to the right arm of the Y.

"She lost for sure."

Kane shivered. The wind seemed to be trying to divest them of whatever protection they had. *Dear Lord, please take care of this headstrong woman you have given me. Please forgive me for not trying harder to understand what she wanted — not that I would have let her go anyway. But I could have taken her where she wanted to go.* He pulled his hat down farther to keep the wind from ripping it off.

Was she even wearing a hat — a *real* hat?

Augusta untied the latigos and carefully unwrapped her bundle. While she'd eaten part of her food earlier, now she wanted the blanket more than bread. Even more than the blanket, she wanted water.

Seeing some trees to the left, she turned her horse off the narrowing road, hoping and praying there would be a creek or spring. The last time she'd tried, the swamp water was so muddy she didn't dare drink from it. The horse, however, had no such compunctions and drank her fill. At least one of them was comfortable.

A tiny spring seeped into the ground about as fast as it trickled out between the two rocks. Augusta knelt on a rock beside it and cupped one hand beneath the trickle. With her other she clutched the reins. If her horse bolted now . . . She didn't even dare contemplate the thought. Slurp by slurp she slaked her thirst. When she finally creaked to her feet again — she wasn't sure which part of her anatomy hurt the worst — she leaned against the filly's shoulder for warmth. The horse dropped her head and began grazing on the clumps of grass watered by the spring.

Augusta wished she could do likewise. There was no sense in going farther this night, and the little glade offered some protection from the elements. She hadn't seen sign of any ranches or farms for hours, but then she hadn't explored down the long lanes that led off from the main road.

If only she'd gone right at the Y. If only she hadn't started out on such a foolhardy venture in the first place. She shivered and clutched the blanket closer. Surely she would find someone to point her in the right direction in the morning.

The wind roared around the hillside and snatched at her blanket.

"Father in heaven, if I've ever needed your protection, I surely do need it now." She thought about her words. As if He hadn't always been protecting her. But right now the warmth of His mighty hand would feel awful good.

She sat down with her back to a tree trunk and switched hands every now and then because the hand holding the reins turned blue rather quickly. "Do I let the horse graze, which means I leave this bit of comfort from the tree, or do I make her

421

suffer too?" The wind lashing the tree branches made hearing herself difficult even though she had the blanket over her face.

"Why didn't I think to bring a rope?" She shook her head. "Because I am one of the most hardheaded, stubborn, opinionated women I've ever had the displeasure of meeting." A picture of Kane reading to her in front of a roaring fireplace came to mind.

"Uff da!" Right now stronger words were more appropriate, but even so, she couldn't say them. "Uff da" did say it all.

A gust of rain rattled the bare branches overhead. Most likely it would start to pour soon, and then where would she be? "Right here, only soaking wet." She clutched the blanket closer to her throat to block an errant draft. "Father, how do you put up with me?" The horse pulled against the reins, asking for more slack.

"Just like me, huh? Always asking for more slack so I can go my own way? And you let me. And then I have to beg you to deliver me from the cold and the wind and the rain."

And I do, a quiet voice said.

"I know that, or I'd be so terrified right now. I'd . . . I'd . . ." She sighed. "This is going to be a long night." She rested her forehead on her knees.

She must have dozed, because she jerked when the horse pulled on the reins again. She moved over to another tree, which afforded the filly more grazing, and Augusta settled herself again in her warm cocoon. "Thank you for holding back the rain." She thought of other things to be thankful for and began listing them. Kane appeared at the top of the list. He *had* been good to her. *But married?*

She rested her cheek on her knees again. What would it be like to be really married to him?

"All right, Augusta Bjorklund, get back to finding things to be grateful for." Her list continued. She jerked again at the intrusion of her horse. If she wasn't careful, she'd be on foot come morning. If morning ever came again. She knotted the reins together at the very end and slipped her hand through the loop. Now if she fell asleep, the horse would wake her up.

Head down, she dozed under the blanket.

"Augusta! Augusta!" It was her father, Gustaf, calling. Ah, the dream was so real. "I've missed you so, Far." She could feel tears burn at the back of her eyes. And here she'd brought more pain to her mother. "Ah me."

"Augusta!"

The filly whinnied, jerking Augusta totally awake. When an answering whinny came from the direction of the road, Augusta leaped to her feet.

"Over here." Could they hear her over the wind? She screamed at the top of her voice. "Here!"

A radiance, a lamp lit against the darkness, preceded them as Kane and Lone Pine rode into her sanctuary.

Kane hit the ground running. He flung his arms around her and gathered her into the warmth of his chest. "You foolish, foolish girl. Whatever came over you?" His voice took turns at harsh and hugging. "Are you all right?"

Augusta burrowed into his warmth. Like God above, he had come for her, not leaving her to suffer her own stupidity, not waiting for her to come back, penitent and broken.

Kane had come for her.

While Kane alternately cussed and cuddled her, Lone Pine built a fire.

Augusta raised a tearstained face to seek answers in Kane's eyes. In the feeble light from the lantern and the barely flickering fire, his eyes were shadowed, his brows a straight line. She could see the slashes that had deepened in his cheeks. The bare light made them more so.

"I-I'm sorry." If only she knew the words in English. Would he understand?

"Augusta Moyer, you gave me the fright of my life." He gave her a bit of a shake for emphasis. "Whatever possessed you to —" He stopped at the look of bewilderment he saw before him and gathered her back to his chest instead. What couldn't be said with words could surely be shown with arms.

Augusta looked over his shoulder to see the moon, like a promise, peeking from the thinning bank of clouds. She sighed. Now how would she get to Blessing? Or send her mother a letter?

Once they'd had some food and hot coffee, Lone Pine put the fire out, and they mounted their horses again. But when he led the way past the spring and not back on the road, Augusta shook her head.

"No, we go that way. I know I'm not that confused."

"Ranch this way." Lone Pine indicated the swale between two hills.

Kane reached across between the horses and touched her arm. He pointed in the same direction as Lone Pine had. "Ranch this way."

She shrugged and shook her head again. She knew what they meant and surely they knew the land better than she, but still she was confused.

After riding for what seemed half the night, though she knew it had been only an hour or two, they trotted into the ranch yard. Morning Dove came to the door with a lantern and a spate of words that Augusta had no intention of trying to figure out. By taking the left hand of the fork, she must have ridden in almost a full circle. Grateful on one hand that they'd found her and disgusted with herself on the other, she dismounted, ignoring Kane's offer of assistance.

But when her knees turned to jelly, she gratefully slumped against his arms. Instead of letting her go when her legs got their strength again, he scooped her up in his arms and carried her into the house. After laying her on the bed, he gave her a stern look.

"Now, stay there." He added "please" as an afterthought. When she nodded, he smiled down at her. "I will take you to Blessing if you absolutely must go."

She understood "I will take you to

Blessing" and the rest didn't much matter.

"Mange takk — er — thank you."

She should be overjoyed. Instead she felt a terrible sense of letdown. Maybe by now he didn't want her to stay. She'd been far too much bother, and now he was willing to be rid of her. She forced a smile to lips that quivered. "Th-thank you."

"You sleep now, and we'll talk in the morning." He leaned over and kissed her cheek before leaving the room.

Augusta put her hand to her face. Perhaps he did care. She undressed, slid her nightdress over her head, and was asleep before she could blow out the candle.

She slept through the rooster crowing. She slept through the dog barking. But the sound of her brother's voice jerked her straight up in bed. Her feet hit the floor before her mind jolted into motion.

"Hjelmer! What is Hjelmer doing here? Surely there can be no other that sounds precisely like him. Maybe I was dreaming." All the time she muttered she was washing, dressing, and combing her hair. When a knock came on her door, she was just twisting her hair into a knot to pin at the base of her head.

"Augusta, are you all right?" How sweet the Norwegian sounded to her ears, her very own dear brother's voice.

"Ja, I am fine."

"Are you decent?"

"Ja, I am dressed. Give me a moment. How did you find me?"

"It's a long story. I'll tell you on the way to Ipswich." She flinched from stabbing her tender scalp with a hairpin.

"Ipswich? But I . . ." *He doesn't want me after all. Kane doesn't want me.* She choked back a sob. "I'll be with you in just a moment."

32

The Ranch
October 5

"But I am already married." Kane looked from Hjelmer to the woman beside him.

"Are you sure?" Hjelmer wore an expression of utter consternation.

Kane felt like walking out of the room. If these people had not been his guests, he would have. "If you mean, did we have a ceremony — yes. The justice of the peace married us in Ipswich when Augusta got off the train. I believed she was" — he nodded toward the woman standing slightly behind Hjelmer — "Miss Borsland, who had agreed to be my bride. I would not travel so far with an unmarried woman. It would not be proper." The slight curl of his lip said what he thought of Hjelmer for doing exactly that. He heard the crinkle of the letters being smashed by Hjelmer's hands as if they

429

were alive. What a shock to find two people on his front porch with the two letters in hand — one offering to buy some horses, the other . . . well, the other was what they were discussing.

For moments the toe of his boot took all of Kane's concentration. "And if you mean, has the marriage been . . . been . . ." He could feel his ears growing hot, knowing that their redness must signal his uncomfortable state. "I will just say that we did not share a room." *Nor a bed, and now it might be too late.* He refused to let himself think of that first night home when he'd awakened to find a screaming harridan on his hands. The thought still made him smile. Augusta in full battle mode was something to see.

Miss Borsland made a strangled sound and rolled her eyes.

Kane caught the motion and then glanced up to see Augusta standing in the doorway between the kitchen and living room. The questioning look on her face made him want to rush to her side.

Hjelmer saw her at about the same time. He crossed the room and took both her hands in his. "Ah, Gussie, I am so —" He stopped at her slight withdrawal. "All right, Augusta, sorry. I forgot. It is so long since I've seen you that I was beginning to doubt I ever would." He tucked her hand under his arm and brought her into the room. "What a mix-up this is. Here I've been over half of Minnesota and now South Dakota to find you. Mor never gave up hope that you were still alive."

"I . . . I feel so foolish. I just didn't understand the man at the station in St. Paul, and then when I got off the train, I thought . . ." She paused and sent a beseeching look to Kane, but he didn't meet her gaze. "I thought Kane was saying he would take me to Blessing."

"But why did you marry him?" Hjelmer's voice rose a bit as she shook her head.

"I thought it was for my American citizenship, that we were signing my citizenship papers."

Hjelmer groaned and tapped the heel of his hand on his forehead. "Augusta Bjorklund, I never . . ." He shook his head again. "Well, all that matters is that you are safe, and within the next two days you will *finally* arrive in Blessing."

"But what about me?" Asta sat forward on the chair she'd taken waiting for Augusta to join them.

"Excuse me." Hjelmer nodded to her.

"Augusta, this is Asta Borsland, the *real* mail-order bride destined to union with Mr. Moyer here."

"But I am already married." Kane enunciated clearly, having understood the gist of what was being said. He could feel his jaw tightening. Who had given this unwanted visitor the right to take over like this? He stared at Augusta, willing her to look at him.

Hjelmer interpreted Kane's words for Miss Borsland.

"I'm aware of that." Miss Borsland sheathed her words in hoarfrost. "As you can tell by my letter, I was unavoidably detained."

Hjelmer continued to interpret the words back and forth.

"But I didn't receive the letter."

"I'm aware of that, sir, but what are we to do about this confusion now? We had an agreement, as you well know." Asta locked her hands firmly in her lap.

All I care about is Augusta. You can go wherever you want. It makes no nevermind to me.

"Coffee is ready." Morning Dove appeared in the doorway and gestured toward the table.

"Thank you." Kane turned back to his

432

guests. "Please excuse my poor manners." If his words sounded as stilted as he felt, they must realize they were welcome about as much as a horde of locusts before harvest.

Conversation not only didn't come alive, but what was contributed lay on the table like a dying fish no longer even flopping about.

When Morning Dove offered to refill cups, she was met with headshakes all around.

Augusta couldn't finish her first cup. It had pooled like pond sludge in the bottom of her stomach. *So what do I do now? On one hand, I'm married. On the other hand, it's not been much of a marriage, not a real one at all. And the way Kane is about to break his coffee cup by glaring at it, I doubt there is much hope there.*

Kane felt like slamming his hand on the table until the cups and saucers bounced. *If only she would say what she wants. If only we could have a few minutes alone together . . . rather, a few years.* He amended his thoughts. *Many years, a lifetime. But she looks so sad. Why? Her brother has come, and now she will go to her mother, to that Blessing place she has been so insistent upon.* He studied her covertly, making sure she was not aware of his gaze. *But why is she so sad?*

"The only thing I can see that should be done is for me to take the two women back to Blessing with me," Hjelmer said in both languages so all could understand.

"But I have no money for a ticket," Asta said with a humph.

"I assumed that might be the case." Hjelmer glanced at Kane.

Kane clamped his hands together under the table and sealed his mouth. *If he thinks I'm paying for her ticket, he can think again. I already paid for one fare clear from Norway, and by the looks of things, I will end up alone — again.*

The silence stretched clear to Monday.

Hjelmer took in a deep breath. "That is settled, then. I will take Augusta home with me, and Miss Borsland can go on from St. Paul with us or stay there, as she wills." He looked sideways to his sister. "Since I know that you have few belongings here, you will be ready in about ten minutes or so, right?"

Kane, help me! Augusta pleaded inwardly. But he was staring at the tablecloth as if counting every fiber. Augusta felt like a puffball ground under the heel of a boot. "Ja, I will be ready." She spoke in Norwegian. Speaking in the little English she

434

knew would take far more than she had to give at the moment.

Perhaps this was for the best after all. But why had God brought her clear out here only to take her away again? *Silly, it wasn't God who brought you out here; it was your own stupidity.* She had to believe the inner voice was right. Once on her feet, she shot Kane another imploring look.

He refused to look up.

Augusta sucked in a deep breath and spun on her heel. If that was the way it was to be, so be it. Kane could . . . could — she couldn't think of anything vile enough.

Within the prescribed ten minutes, she had gathered her things and stuffed them in her carpetbag, said good-bye to Morning Dove and Lone Pine, and climbed up onto the wagon seat, leaving the back for Miss Borsland. Or she could walk behind the wagon, for all Augusta cared.

Kane was nowhere to be seen.

"We should at least tell him thank you." Hjelmer stared around at the barn and outbuildings.

"If you don't turn the horses around right now, I will." Talking was hard between teeth clenched so tight they ground together. Augusta's jaw hurt.

"Mr. Bjorklund, I can't possibly sit back

here without even a blanket."

Augusta leaped from the wagon seat, marched over to the barn, and tore a saddle blanket, so sweat-filled it stood alone, off a saddle. She threw it in the back of the wagon and climbed back up the wheel. "Now go."

Hjelmer went.

Several hours down the road with neither woman speaking and the creak of the wheels getting monotonous, he turned to Augusta.

"Mor will be so happy to see you, I cannot even begin to tell you." He waited. A crow made more talk than his sister did. He glanced in the back. Miss Borsland sat facing the rear, but the erect posture of her head told him in no uncertain terms that she wasn't sleeping. Her arms crossed like bars over her chest only added to that certainty.

"Wait until you see her boardinghouse."

Several miles passed between the clopping feet of the team.

"You won't even recognize Thorliff."

The crow announced their passing.

"Husband stealer." The Norwegian words were hissed from the back of the wagon.

Augusta sat like a Viking queen frozen in a pillar of ice.

33

Blessing
October 7

"They're here!" Thorliff burst through the door of the boardinghouse.

"Glory be to God." Bridget untied her apron and threw it over the hook by the door. It missed, but she didn't bother to pick it up. "Mange takk, kjære himmelske Far." She muttered the words over and over in Norwegian as she charged out the door. She didn't even apologize to the man she nearly ran over.

Thorliff ran beside her, laughing and calling her to hurry.

She and Augusta fell into each other's arms at the end of the station platform.

"I think they are happy." Thorliff grinned up at his no-longer-so-much-taller uncle.

"Thank God for that." Hjelmer sighed and rolled his eyes.

"Mr. Bjorklund." Even the sound of her voice made him flinch by now. While Augusta had spoken no more than the barest of necessary words, Miss Borsland had more than made up for his sister's silence. More than once he wished he'd bought her a ticket to Chicago or New York. He glared at his mother. It was all her fault. If she hadn't taught him to be polite, this young woman would not now be calling his name and making the hair stand up on the back of his neck, let alone the backs of his hands.

"What should I do with my bags?"

Hjelmer kept a glare from adhering to his face only by the utmost strength of character. "Thorliff, would you be so kind as to help Miss Borsland with her bags? Take them to the boardinghouse, if you will."

Thorliff looked up at his uncle again, a question mark arching his eyebrows. "Will she be staying?" He kept his voice low so only they could hear.

"That is up to your bestemor."

"Yes, sir." But clearly from the look on his face, Thorliff did not understand. But then, as he'd learned more than once, adults were frequently hard to understand.

"I'm going home to my wife."

"Yes, sir, but you better not look for her at the store. She's out at our house."

"And why, pray tell, is she out at your house?" Hjelmer could feel the heat start in his middle and work its way up. All this time away and his wife doesn't even have the decency to be here to meet him. *She's out gallivanting around the countryside while I chase all over half of America looking for my sister. All because my mother made me go.*

Hjelmer settled his fedora squarely on his head. "Thank you, Thorliff, now please go see to *Miss* Borsland." Pounding his feet on the dirt street, Hjelmer set off for the livery to saddle his horse.

Thorliff watched him go, shaking his head. He shrugged and turned to the young woman, also staring after the marching man.

"God dag. I am Thorliff Bjorklund, and I will help you with your bags." He tipped his porkpie hat with two fingers.

"Mange takk." She corrected herself. "Thank you. I am Miss Asta Borsland." She again looked off at Hjelmer, who was now sliding open the door to the barn.

"I will take you to my bestemor's boardinghouse." Thorliff spoke English now, but slowly, watching to see comprehension reach her eyes. At her nod, he picked up both her suitcases, then bobbed his head for her to follow him.

They passed Bridget and Augusta without a word.

Like a dam that breaks and floods until all the water behind it is emptied, Augusta couldn't stop crying. Her mother patted her shoulder, hugged her again, and murmured mother sounds, but still Augusta cried on. She drenched her mother's shoulder. She drenched both of their handkerchiefs. Even the front of her dark wool jacket wore the darker stains of tears.

Every time she started to dry up, she hiccuped and tried to stem the flood. To no avail.

"Come, Augusta, come with me, and I will pour you a good cup of coffee, and we will talk as long as you need."

Augusta let herself be led across the street to the boardinghouse, guided as if she were blind or feebleminded. Both of which were appropriately descriptive at the time.

Goodie took one look at the red-eyed young woman, whose hair had escaped the bun to hang around her face, and tsked her way to the stove to pull the coffeepot forward. She rattled the grate and added several chunks of wood to the firebox.

Eulah pushed the rocking chair nearer the stove and guided Augusta to sit in it. "Sit yoself heah an' rest while ah gets a wet cloth fo yo' eyes."

Cosseted and clucked over, Augusta sniffled and hiccuped. She wiped her eyes again, nodding her gratitude for a clean dish towel to replace the sodden handkerchiefs. Finally she leaned her head back against the chair and sniffed again. "I-I'm sorry, Mor. I don't know what came over me." Another hiccup forced a tear through the sieve of her eyelashes. "You know me. I *never* cry like this."

"Ja, that is true." Bridget handed her daughter a cup of steaming hot coffee. "Drink this and you will feel better. Then you can tell me the whole story from when you left home until now."

The telling took more than an hour. While Augusta talked and Bridget both listened and nodded, asking questions in all the right places, supper preparations went on around them. Goodie took Miss Borsland up to a room and informed her when the meal would be ready. Thorliff headed home on Jack the mule after helping Miss Borsland with her bags. Eulah kept the coffee coming.

When the river of tears trickled down to

a stream and then to a stop, Augusta sighed, her shoulders dropping and her head feeling as if it weighed forty pounds. Her neck could barely hold it up. She laid her head from side to side, then after dropping it forward to her chest, sighed again.

"So now what do I do?" Augusta asked her mor.

Bridget patted her daughter's hand. "I do not know. There must be a way to get out of the marriage, I would think. That is, if you want to?" Her snowy brows met in a question.

"I don't know what I want." *Liar.* The little voice had come with her, for certain, since she left the ranch. But it had been unusually silent.

Bridget braced her hands on her knees and pushed herself to her feet. "Ja, well, I know what you need, and that is for certain sure. You need a bed and maybe a long hot bath first. There will be supper after that or breakfast in the morning should you sleep all night. Everything looks better in the morning."

Augusta nodded. "Are you sure you have room for me?"

Bridget patted Augusta's cheek. "You forget, I *own* the place. I can put whoever I want in my rooms."

"But I don't want to take the place of a paying guest."

"Gussie, when I built this place, I built a room for you, for I knew you would come to help me." Bridget took the cup and saucer from her daughter. "Besides, your trunk is already there, and your things are in the drawers and on the hooks just waiting for you."

From her mother, the childhood name sounded safe and familiar, even though she hadn't allowed anyone else to use it for years. Her stomach rumbled, reminding her that it had been some time since she had food and the coffee needed an accompaniment. "Could I please have a slice of bread or something? I didn't feel much like eating on the train."

"Bless your heart, of course." Bridget started to retrieve a loaf of bread, but Eulah took the knife from her, and after slicing both bread and cheese, along with some leftover ham, she set the plate in Augusta's lap.

"Unless yo wants to come to de table?" she asked, motioning to the table.

Augusta smiled up into the dark eyes and shook her head. "Here is fine. The fire feels good, and I might never leave this chair."

Bridget returned with a glass of milk. "Here, this too will help. This is Eulah. She helps here, along with Lemuel, her son. Goodie Wold is turning the meat on the other stove."

"Glad to meet you finally." Goodie waved her fork in the air.

"And you will meet Ilse later. She lost her parents on the trip over, so she came out here with us. She takes care of the upstairs."

While she ate, they filled her in on the workings of the boardinghouse and the latest happenings in Blessing, at the same time going about their chores to get the meal ready. When Goodie pulled three apple pies from the oven, the cinnamon-perfumed air made Augusta almost smile.

"Oh, this feels so much like home." Augusta stood and took her plate and cup to the dishpan on the back of one of the stoves. "I think I'll pass on that bath for now. I'd drown falling asleep in the water."

"Come then, I'll take you to your room." Bridget pointed out the dining room and the parlor on their way up the stairs. She told who lived in which room, and at the end of the hall, she opened a room that was already dim from the dusk falling outside. She lighted the lamp with a spill from her own and set them both on the dresser.

"Mor, this is beautiful." Augusta admired the white curtains at the windows, the braided rag rug, the nine-patch quilt with all its brightly colored squares. "Are all the rooms this nice?"

"Most of them. I've had lots of help, and with that new Singer sewing machine, why I can't tell you how much easier it is to make the things I need." While she talked, she hung up her daughter's jacket and knelt to help remove her boots.

"Mor, I can undress myself." Augusta unbuttoned her skirt and let it drop, standing still in her petticoats and chemise.

"Here." Bridget pulled open a drawer in the plain oak dresser that Uncle Olaf had made and pulled out one of Augusta's nightdresses, made of pink-flowered flannel and trimmed around the neck and sleeves with white lace. She held it up and, when Augusta bent her head, dropped the rose-scented garment in place.

"Ah, my own things." She sniffed the sleeve. "And rose sachets even. Mor . . ." Tears filled her eyes again. "You will spoil me."

"Let me worry about that. You are my daughter come home, and I think we will throw a party."

Augusta sank down on the edge of the bed where Bridget had pulled back the quilt and sheet. "I'll never be able to thank you enough."

"Since when is there thanks enough in a family?" Bridget lifted the covers for her daughter to tuck her feet under. "Now you just sleep until you are rested. And if you need anything, you pull that rope over there. Ilse will come."

"Mange takk."

"Velbekomme."

Augusta was asleep before her mother closed the door.

"She knew I was coming home today," Hjelmer muttered as he saddled the horse. "You'd think she'd be here to at least meet my sister." He tightened the cinch and led the animal out into the westerly sun. He'd thought of checking in at the store but knew if Anner caught him, he'd want to discuss everything that had gone on since Hjelmer left. And Anner talked slow.

Instead he waved at Sam, busy at the smithy, shouted, "I'll be back soon," and kicked his horse into a ground-devouring lope. Here he had so much to tell Penny he was about to burst, and she wasn't even home.

He met her returning in the buckboard.

Even from a distance she recognized him and waved her wide-brimmed dark felt hat in greeting. He swung the horse in beside the wagon. *She is so beautiful. Why isn't she at home? What is so important out at Ingeborg's that she had to leave the day I was coming home?* While his thoughts churned, Penny pulled the team to a halt, wrapped the reins around the brake handle, and stood up, her arms wide in welcome.

"You better be careful. They could jerk, you know." His voice came out more gruffly than he'd planned.

Penny froze. Her chin raised a bit, one eyebrow cocked. She sat back down on the seat and gathered her reins. Hat beside her on the board bench, she clucked the horses forward.

Hjelmer knew he'd gone too far.

"I missed you at the store."

No response. She clucked the team into a fast trot.

"Well, I guess you don't care much about my trip, then." Watching her face, he knew he should keep his mouth closed, but the words kept coming.

"Did the crates for the windmills come?"

That eyebrow went higher.

"Well, did they?" If his mor heard him,

she'd wallop him for sounding like a spoiled child. *Why is she being so stubborn? You'd think she'd be glad to see me, much as I've been gone.*

Penny slowed the team to a walk. She kept her eyes straight forward, but since there was no sun, only clouds on the western horizon, the narrowed eyes weren't squinting against the light.

"They'd be large crates, hard to miss."

Penny turned her head, gave him the look she reserved for riffraff, and straightened her shoulders.

"Well, fine, if'n you can't be any more talkative than this, I'll see you at home." He kicked his horse back into a lope without looking over his shoulder. Her "men!" sounded somewhat like a swear word, at least if he heard it right.

"You find yo missus?" Sam asked when Hjelmer swung off his mount.

"Ja."

"Oh." Sam went back to pumping the bellows, bringing the iron bar in the coals to an incandescent white, separated from the black by a glowing red band. The smell of hot iron and burning coke filled the shanty.

Hjelmer stripped the saddle off his horse and led the animal into the stall, where he fussed with removing the bridle and buckling the halter in place.

From inside the barn he couldn't see or hear if Penny was close. If she wanted a fight — so be it.

Don't let the sun go down on your anger. Penny could hear her tante Agnes's voice as if she were sitting on the wagon seat right beside her.

She heard it again later as she set a plate of food before her husband, when she would rather have slammed it and gladly watched the gravy bounce into his lap.

And she heard it that night when she crawled into bed after banking the coals, filling the reservoir, putting the cat out, checking on the rising sourdough, and hanging his coat on the hook by the door. While he tried to sound as if he were asleep, she knew better. Besides, he never slept that close to the edge of the bed and on his side.

That was her style.

She sighed. This was no good. She had so much to tell him, and he was acting like — she knew it wasn't proper to think of one's husband as acting like a little boy, but that was what it seemed.

"Hjelmer."

A fake snore answered her.

"Hjelmer Bjorklund, quit acting so silly."

"*I'm* acting silly?" He rolled over on his back and crossed his arms over his chest, jerking the covers around in the process.

She sighed again. *Whatever did I do to deserve this?* "I'm sorry I wasn't here when you came home." She didn't add that they were butchering chickens so she would have some to sell in the store and so she would have one to roast for a special dinner for him tomorrow.

He grunted.

She waited.

He let out a sigh that missed being a huff by only a hair. "I had so much to tell you, and you weren't here."

She gritted her teeth and forcibly relaxed her jaw. "I know." Rolling over, she settled her arm across his chest and squeezed gently. "I've missed you." She could almost hear him thinking *funny way to show it,* but she ignored that and stroked his arm. She could feel him relax, and he settled deeper into the feather bed.

Why is it so hard for him to say "I'm sorry"? She waited.

He turned on his side facing her and cupped his hands around her cheeks. "Thank you." He kissed her, first her nose and then her lips. When he released her mouth, they both sighed.

"I was the rear end of Jack the mule, huh?" he whispered.

"Ja." She kissed the palm of his hand, her gentle chuckle bringing one from him. "So you finally found Augusta and dragged her home?"

"Ja, and she hardly said a word the whole way." He shook his head and tucked her under his arm next to his side. "I don't think there's a chance this side of heaven that I will ever understand a woman."

Penny chuckled and drew a circle on his bare chest. "You think it might be different in heaven?"

His low growl made her laugh. And when laughter leads to loving, all kinds of miracles can happen.

Her last thought before sleep claimed her was that Tante Agnes and God's Word were indeed right. If for no other reason, one slept better with the anger gone.

Augusta woke up crying. After drying her eyes and blowing her nose, she lay looking at the moon reflections through the curtains. The same moon shone on Kane. Was he seeing it too? Some time passed before she slept again, but when she woke at the first rooster crow, her pillow was soaked.

Wasn't she out of tears yet? She turned the pillow over and let her scratchy eyes drift shut again. She'd get up in a few minutes. Weariness far worse than that of hard physical labor dragged her down and down. If this was to be home, how could she get her heart to reside here?

34

Blessing
October 8

"Noon!" Augusta's feet were in hurry motion before they hit the floor.

"Sorry, Miss Bjorklund, I didn't mean to waken you, but your mor was getting worried and asked me to check on you." Ilse stood just inside the doorway twisting her hands.

"No, no. I had no intention of sleeping like this." Augusta glanced out the window to see people hurrying by holding hats on their heads with one hand, the other fighting the wind that tried to tear the coats from their backs.

"Can I get you anything? Hot water? Coffee?"

How good it was to hear Norwegian spoken, even though Augusta knew she should request English. Somehow she had to learn English, more than her rudimentary phrases, and fast. "Both would be wonderful, but I can't let you serve me like this."

"Why not? That is what I do." A look of pride came over her pale face. "I am in charge of the rooms and our guests. The others take care of the meals."

"All right, then. Hot water would be so good. Surely I can be of help downstairs if I hurry."

When the young woman left the room, Augusta swiftly made her bed and began brushing her hair in front of the mirror. *Mor must think me gone lazy like a cat in the sun since I came to America.*

A tap on the door brought Ilse back with a pitcher of hot water and one of cold.

"Mange takk, er, thank you."

Ilse took the hint. "You are welcome." Her smile brought color and life to her face. "Mrs. Bjorklund says to tell you the coffee is hot." She closed the door gently after backing out of the room.

Augusta turned back to the mirror and frowned at the sight of her own puffy face and eyes red from all the crying. Whatever had come over her? *Kane, that's what, or rather, who.* Even the thought of him brought the sting of tears to the back of her eyes. She dunked the washcloth in the

454

hot water she'd poured in the basin and held the steaming cloth to her eyes. "Uff da." *Will there be no end to it?* The cold cloth followed, dunked and wrung several times in the hopes of banishing the red.

One thing for certain sure, she did *not* want to talk about or think about Mr. Elkanah Moyer.

Once downstairs, her mother shooed her to a rocking chair out of the way of the bustling help and handed her a cup of coffee along with a plate of freshly sliced bread slathered with sour cream and chokecherry jelly.

"Now eat." Bridget stood in front of her daughter, waiting for her to take the first bite. When that happened, she nodded with a gentle smile. "Good. No wonder you were sad. You haven't eaten decent for days."

Augusta refrained from asking how Bridget knew that, but the bread and cream tasted heavenly. And her nose told her there was plenty of other good food for the asking. The cheerful bustle flowed on its prescribed course, as everyone knew what to do and went about their assigned tasks with laughter and teasing comments.

With coffee cup in hand, Augusta wandered to the dining room door and peeked into the other room. Four men sat at one table, and a man and woman shared a table over by the window. Her gaze continued on, then flicked back to the couple. *Asta Borsland! With that man. Whatever in the world? Who?* The questions nearly spilled out her mouth, but she clamped her lips shut on them until she caught her mother by the stove.

"How did that woman meet a man so fast?" She tried to keep from hissing but didn't quite make it.

"At supper last night. They hit it right off. 'Course I was kind of hoping you'd meet him, since he's so nice and all, but this could solve a problem or two." Bridget checked the chickens she already had roasting for dinner.

"But, Mor . . ." Augusta shook her head.

"I offered her work here for room and board until she can decide what she wants to do."

"And?" Augusta could feel her stomach churn. Not that Miss Borsland didn't have a good reason for being angry at her. After all, when it came right down to it, she *had* stolen the woman's intended husband.

Augusta hated putting it quite like that, but honest she was, no matter how painful.

"She said she'd be glad to. I told her she starts tomorrow. She can help Eulah with the washing." Bridget smiled up at her daughter. "I was hoping you would help me with the sewing. I need more quilts for the winter. Just wait until you hem sheets on that sewing machine."

"But I don't know how to use it."

"You will catch on in no time." Bridget handed her a pitcher of milk. "Here, set this on the table, will you?"

When the guests were served and all the help sat down to eat, Augusta joined them at the table.

"So," Goodie asked Bridget, "when will the wedding be? You got your daughter here now, so there can be no more excuses."

Bridget gave a bit of a headshake and glanced at Augusta, who was busy chewing.

Goodie flinched. "Sorry," she whispered.

But Augusta heard her. "All right, what is this about a wedding? I can tell you are trying to keep a secret."

One person looked to the next and the *look* passed on around the table, finally ending up with Bridget, who continued to eat as if nothing untoward were happening. But the twitching of a muscle at the right side of her mouth gave her away.

"Mor."

Bridget ducked her head as if to take another bite.

"Mor!" Augusta put a bit more force behind her words. Someone else snickered. Eulah got up to pour the coffee, her broad smile and wink making sure Augusta didn't give up.

"Henry asked me to marry him, and I said yes but not until you were found." The words sped from her lips.

Augusta pondered the muttered words and watched the red creep up her mother's neck. *Married?* Her mother was going to be married? The thought caught her like a punch in the middle. She stared at the woman with white hair and cheeks flaming bright enough to need dousing by snow. *But she is too old.* As soon as the thought came, she banished it. Why shouldn't her mother find happiness again? *Because she is married to my far.*

So? Not anymore. He died. Another memory flooded her mind and brought tears burning the back of her eyes. *I am not crying anymore!* She rolled her eyes, took a sip of coffee and a deep breath.

"So who is this man who is good enough to think of marrying my mor?"

The flash of smile from Goodie and the pat on the shoulder from Eulah told her that they approved of her response. The tension around the table relaxed as everyone, including Bridget, took a deep breath and let it out on a sigh.

"Mor?"

"You will meet Henry today when the train comes in. He is a conductor on the railroad and —" Bridget stopped and frowned at her daughter. "If he'd been on that line that day, you wouldn't have gotten out of that station on the wrong train, let me tell you."

And I wouldn't have met Kane. Augusta sighed and blinked a couple of extra times. After another deep breath, she forced a smile to lips that wanted to quiver. "So when is the wedding?"

"I think this Saturday. This is Henry's last run for the railroad. When he knew we had found you, he told them he was quitting." Bridget blushed clear to her hairline. "He wants to help me here."

Augusta ignored the pain that thinking of her mother with a man other than her father brought to her heart region. She knelt by her mother's chair. "I look forward to meeting this Henry. For if you love him, he must be a fine man."

"Ah, my Augusta, even with all those around me" — she indicated the others with a sweep of her hand — "and with you and Hjelmer . . ." She paused and cupped her daughter's face in gnarled hands that had not lost their gentleness. "I . . . I have lost much, but God has blessed me with more. Can I do less than take this gift and thank our Father for it — for Henry — for bringing you, whom I thought was gone too, back to me?" She thumbed away the moisture gathering at the edges of Augusta's eyes. "Rejoice with me, Gussie, and stand beside me at the church. Nothing would make me happier. Haakan is standing up for Henry."

Augusta nodded. "Ja, I will stand up for you."

"You're like a wildcat with a mangled foot, snapping at everyone." Lone Pine leveled a look at Kane that would have felled a lesser man.

Kane grunted and slammed the posthole digger deeper into the hole. The ringing of metal striking rock vibrated up his arm. With no longer suppressed fury, he flung the posthole digger to the side, then hefting a sturdy post, slammed it into the hole.

"Hold it." He kicked dirt back in the hole, tamping it with a heavy iron rod.

Lone Pine held the post straight, he, too, using his foot to scoop the fresh dirt back in the hole. "Mighty shallow."

"We'll brace it."

By the time they had another hundred feet of posts planted and the wire strung, the sun had oranged the sky, then flamed in red, purple, and magenta, all underpinned with gold. The cloud layers faded from fire back to mauve, lavender, and finally gray. The wind picked up, and one of the team whinnied at a sound neither of the men could hear.

"I imagine Morning Dove has supper ready." Lone Pine picked up the remaining roll of barbed wire and set it back in the wagon.

Kane didn't even bother to grunt this time, just threw in the tools and climbed to the seat. He had the horses in motion before Lone Pine got seated.

The jingle of harness and the *clip-clop* of trotting horse hooves lulled him into remembering. Something he'd sworn not to do. *Augusta, where are you? Are you happy in Blessing?* The sound of her laugh made him almost turn to see if she was riding in the back of the wagon. She hadn't laughed that much. Why was it so clear in his ear?

"You could go get her, you know." Lone Pine broke the silence.

Kane spun around, his jerk on the reins stopping the horses in midstride. "Who in thunder asked for your opinion?"

The team snorted and stamped. Guilt bit into him for the way he had just misused his animals, something he would have torn the hide off one of his hands for.

He clucked the horses forward again and tucked himself back into the shell that kept the pain in and others out. *She could have stayed. You are married to her. Go get her. If she doesn't want to be here, I don't want her to be. Liar.* Thoughts hammered through his mind like twin woodpeckers drilling a tree. But while the woodpeckers would be fed from their efforts, his yammering thoughts took him nowhere but around in a futile circle.

" 'Dearly beloved, we are gathered here in the sight of God and this company to unite this man and this woman in holy matrimony.' " Reverend John Solberg looked up from his service book to smile at the man and woman standing before him. " 'Marriage is a godly estate, ordained by God . . .' "

Augusta had a hard time keeping her mind on the ceremony. So different this was than the one she stood up for so long, no, so short a time ago. Such a travesty. She'd had no idea what she was agreeing to. Citizenship — hah! Where had her mind gone? She should have known better.

But Kane . . . Kane knew. She had fought the tears that woke her this Saturday morning, as they had every day and threatened to overwhelm her now. *You will not cry and ruin your mother's wedding. You will not!* She sniffed, and when she heard other sniffs from the gathered congregation, she knew they would think it only normal. Women always cried at weddings.

She forced her attention back to the service.

"Henry Aarsgard, do you take this woman to be your wedded wife?"

"I do."

That's what I said — I do. And Kane did too. Do you suppose he really meant it?

"And you, Bridget Bjorklund, do you take this man to be your wedded husband?"

The service continued, and by the end, Augusta wasn't sure if she'd heard any more or not. Her thoughts refused to stay in Blessing. They returned instead to a ranch in the sandhills of South Dakota, seeking the man who had kept her heart.

She made it through the big party afterward, meeting all the people she'd read of so often, helping to serve the food, and answering questions about those at home in Norway. No one asked about a ranch in South Dakota. No one asked about the man who was legally her husband.

And no one called her Mrs. Moyer.

35

Blessing
Late October

"I have a favor to ask." Augusta clamped her hands on a chairback.

"Of course. What is it?" Bridget turned from setting the platter of fried sausages on the table for all the boardinghouse workers.

"I *have* to learn to speak English, so will everyone please speak only English?" Augusta wished she could at least have asked in English.

"Ja, we can do that." Goodie spoke slowly with gestures and smiled when Augusta answered.

"Good." While she'd been picking up some of the language and asking questions, Augusta knew she needed to make a more concentrated effort. She also knew that speaking only in English would be good for her on the one hand and frustrating to everyone else on the other. "Thank you."

She glanced over to see the look of consternation on Asta's face. While Asta had proved to be a good worker, Augusta still stayed as far from her as possible. Besides, Asta's new man was taking up all her spare time when he was in town.

Concentrating on learning English kept Augusta's mind occupied at least some of the time.

Each morning for the next few weeks she told herself that she would feel better this day. Each night she scolded herself for hanging on to what was not to be.

One day Penny pulled her sister-in-law over to the long mirror she'd fastened to the wall in the sewing section of her general store and said, "Augusta Bjorklund, look at you. How long since you've eaten a decent meal?"

Augusta sighed. "I just don't feel hungry." She held the wool skirt she'd been sewing on Penny's machine up to her waist. She'd have to take deeper seams, that was all. To distract the other woman's attention, she patted the Singer sewing machine. "This is some machine, let me tell you."

"Forget that. Now we will talk about you." The bell above the door tinkled with an arriving customer. "Oh! Wouldn't you know it." Penny called out, "Be there in a minute," then turned back to Augusta. "You stay right here until I return, hear me?"

Augusta nodded, but as soon as Penny's back was turned, she gathered up her things and beat a hasty retreat out the back door. She didn't need any more advice from well-meaning friends. She thought back to the day before. Ingeborg had asked if she were sick, she looked so pale. Awful, bad dreams from the night before had caused the blue blotches under her eyes.

Kane had been calling to her. She was stuck in a swamp, sinking and screaming, but he couldn't hear her. She could still smell the swamp.

The Ranch

"Women are just too much trouble!"
Lone Pine looked at his boss and shook his head.

Kane stood looking out the sitting room window as rain pelted the ground, already splashing mud puddles, though the thirsty ground was sucking the moisture in as fast as possible.

"Coffee ready."

Lone Pine cocked an eyebrow at Kane and glanced at his wife.

"Not all women." They left the papers they'd been working on and headed for the table, the smell of fresh apple pie drawing them if the coffee hadn't.

"So you go get her." Morning Dove plunked a pie-filled plate in front of him.

"Now, why in thunderation would I do that?" Kane paused in the act of cutting a bite of pie.

"So we can get some work done around here. You jump from one thing to another, bark at the men like a rabid dog, and in general —"

"That's enough." Kane's eyebrows about met in the middle. "I ain't been that bad."

Lone Pine and Morning Dove exchanged the kind of look that snorted, *Oh yeah?*

"Well, just when you get used to having a woman around, she up and leaves."

"Did you ask her to stay?" Morning Dove studied him through dark eyes that alternated between compassion and frustration.

Kane took a swig of coffee to wash down the pie that seemed to clog his throat. Funny, usually Morning Dove made real good pie, but this time it seemed heavy.

Heavy, just like he felt.

He'd dreamed of Augusta the night before. She kept calling to him, but no matter how hard he searched, he couldn't find her.

Was she happy in that Blessing town with her family around her?

That evening he reached under the bed — he'd decided to sleep in the bedroom he'd made for her, since that bed was much more comfortable. A small square of cotton lay there, one of her handkerchiefs. He pulled it out and smoothed it flat on his knee.

"Oh, Lord, what do I do? She didn't seem happy here. Is she happy there? And if she is, I'm sure not. I thought you gave her to me for a wife, and sometimes it seemed she was coming to think good of me too. Soon as I understood, I should have taken her to Blessing, or at least promised to do so as soon as the cattle were rounded up." While he prayed, he continued to smooth the bit of cloth.

The dream came again that night.

Didn't they all realize Augusta was doing the best she could? After all, it wasn't as if she didn't do enough to earn her keep. Her mother had even remonstrated her for working too hard. As if any Norwegian ever thought another worked too hard. Or themselves either.

One night at supper a young man, tall enough to fit with the Bjorklunds, strolled into the boardinghouse. The wool in his coat was of finer quality than many, the fit more precise. With a recent haircut and his mustache trimmed perfectly he caught all the women's eyes.

But he looked only at Augusta.

"How can I help you?" she asked, being the one closest to the door and thus the greeter. She'd worked hard on phrases like that in English, so they were coming more easily. And people could now understand them.

He took off his hat and gave her a slow smile that made her breath catch in her throat. It was so much like Kane's smile that all she could think of was Kane.

"I need a room and supper please," the young man said.

"You are lucky. We just have one." She

glanced at his hands. "Do you have . . ." She had to think for a second. ". . . bags?"

"Out on my horse." He smiled again. "My name is John Heisted." He waited.

Augusta nodded. "I get Ilse to help you." She turned away not giving him her name, though she could tell he wanted her to. Norwegian would be so much easier. Unless, of course, he didn't understand it.

That night in bed, John Heisted's smile came back to her. And thusly Kane's smile. *God, what am I to do? You know all. You knew that I was being married to Kane without my knowledge. If you hadn't wanted that to happen, wouldn't you have stopped it?* She lay listening to the wind howl and whine about the eaves. An early winter was going to pounce any day now, at least that's what Uncle Olaf had said. Would God speak to her on the wind?

"So what do you want me to do now?" she said aloud.

What do you want to do? Was it a question of her mind, or was God asking?

"You know what I want to do." She thought again. "Do I know what I want to do?" Her whisper came so soft, the breath of it barely disturbed the air cooling from the chill windows.

She scrunched her eyes shut and her hands against her sides. "I want to see Kane. I want to ask him if he loves me." She waited, her eyes still closed. "I want to tell him that I love him, and I want to be his wife, now and for always."

A gentle sigh seemed to seep from the air around her and breathe peace over her mind and spirit.

The Ranch

"So how hard would it be to take the train to Blessing and look her up?" Kane spoke to the horse.

The filly shook her head and stuck her nose in the feedbox where he had dumped her oats.

"If she wanted to come back with me, fine, and if not, then I would just have to go on." Life without Augusta didn't bear thinking about. He brushed the horse until her coat shone. Like all the others, her winter coat was fast coming in. From the thick pelts on the animals, it looked to be a tough winter.

Which meant more time in the house. Alone.

That night he sat in front of the fire, and

for the first time since she left, he took out his guitar and played all the songs he could think of. How soon would it be before he could head for Ipswich?

Blessing

"You are going to do what?" Bridget's mouth dropped open.

"I am going back to the ranch and see if Kane feels about me the way I feel about him. Could you please loan me the money for the ticket?"

"Why don't you just write to him?" Bridget beat around the sides of the bowl with her wooden spoon and turned the cookie dough over again.

Augusta shook her head. "He doesn't get regular mail like we do here." Which reminded her that he hadn't written, and that was most likely the reason. "The ranch is too far from town."

"Why do you want to live in such a lonely place when you have everything you need right here? You got family, friends, a job."

Augusta shook her head. "But not Kane, and you . . ." Augusta glanced over at Henry who was bringing in an armload of wood and winked at his new wife as he passed by.

Bridget's cheeks pinked as she turned back to her daughter. She sighed. "I was afraid of this. My one remaining daughter, and she will be so far away I will never see her, nor my grandchildren, nor . . ." She shook her head, heaving a sigh burdened with sadness.

"Mor, with trains running, we can see each other once a year maybe." Augusta's smile wavered and then steadied. "I'm going, Mor."

"I can tell." Bridget stopped her stirring and took her daughter's hands. "God go with you, my daughter. Come with me upstairs, and I will help you pack. Goodie can finish these cookies."

"Augusta? Bridget?" Kaaren called from the door to the kitchen sometime later.

"Up here." Bridget went to the head of the stairs. "Come on up."

"What are you doing?" Kaaren stopped in the doorway. Two trunks stood open, and clothing, linens, and sundry household things were scattered all over.

"Packing. Augusta is planning on going to her young man."

"Ah." Kaaren sat down on the edge of

the bed. "When are you thinking of leaving?"

"Tomorrow, I think." Augusta held up a petticoat, discovered a rip in the seam, and set it on a pile of mending. "Why you come to town?"

"I have good news, and I had to tell someone while I wait for school to be out." Kaaren withdrew a letter from her reticule. Taking the paper out, she looked up. "You want to hear this?"

"Ja — yes." Augusta rolled her eyes. She had to think what to say all the time.

" 'Dear Mrs. Knutson, thank you for your quick response to our letter. As you suggested, we will bring our daughter to you for teaching at the beginning of the new year.' "

"Oh, how wonderful." Bridget got up from sitting in the chair by the bed, her knees creaking as she rose. "Uff da. Such noise."

Augusta looked from one to the other as they both laughed. When Bridget explained in Norwegian, Augusta laughed too. *There will be no one at the ranch to translate the hard things for me.* The thought made her roll her lips. She would just have to make do, that's all.

"So we will indeed have a school for the

deaf. Agnes has been suggesting that I put a notice in the Fargo paper and the Grand Forks', maybe Grafton, too, to let people know about our signing program. I think I will do so."

"Maybe a new school building with rooms for your pupils will be the next building for these men of ours."

"Perhaps. I talked with Asta about coming to help me. She said she would, but I have me a feeling she'll be married and gone by then." She looked at Bridget. "Ilse said she would like to come and help. I know that would leave you without enough help here, so I said we'd think about it."

"Ilse would be good at that, especially with children. She misses the children here. So do I, but . . ."

Augusta studied her mother. Wasn't this getting to be too much for her, in spite of how much Henry and the others helped? How could she leave her?

How could she not?

Augusta took the train two mornings later.

As the clacking wheels drew her nearer, her mind kept pace. *What if he doesn't want me? How will I find the ranch? God, you know. I am in your hands.*

The wheels clacked her words. *God, you know, God, you know, God, you know.*

She knew she was on the right train this time leaving St. Paul. This time she knew she was going south. South — to South Dakota. To Ipswich, not Blessing. And would there be a blessing?

"Ipswich. Next stop, Ipswich." The conductor swayed down the aisle, nodding to make sure she heard him.

Her heart took up residence directly below her throat. Swallowing no longer worked. *God, you know, at least I hope you know.*

The train slowed. The whistle blew.

Please, God.

The train stopped, steam billowing up clear to the windows.

Augusta stood, gathered her things, and whispering one more prayer, headed for the exit.

"Thank you." She took the conductor's hand as he helped her down the stairs and stepped to the wide board platform. Smiling up at the blue-uniformed man, she clasped her bag more tightly and looked over to the livery. Would they rent her a horse and wagon when she wasn't sure how she would get it back?

Of course, she could be bringing it right back. She glanced down to the baggage car to see them unloading her two trunks. Nothing for it but to head for the livery stable.

But first she would send the telegram she'd promised, so Mor wouldn't worry. She made her way into the station and waited in front of the desk. *How do I say "telegram"?*

"I . . . I want to . . . write . . ." She motioned and pointed to one of the papers.

"Oh, sure, ma'am." He pushed a pencil and paper to her.

Augusta took out the sample she and Goodie had written and passed it to the gentleman.

"Oh, good." He read it over and named the price.

Carefully she counted out her change, smiled at him again, and walked back outside, knowing that the livery was next on her list. She glanced over at the train when the conductor called, "All aboard." A man with broad shoulders, a dark broad-brimmed felt hat, and the walk of Kane mounted the steps.

Surely she was seeing things. The conductor set the step stool up in the doorway and swung aboard.

She had to find out. Steam rose. The whistle blew.

The man sat down by the window without his hat. Was it Kane?

Augusta ran across the wooden platform to see better.

The train wheels screeched a protest at starting another trip.

It was Kane!

"Kane!" She screamed his name.

The train rolled forward.

"Kane Moyer!" The whistle about drowned her out, so she screamed his name again.

The conductor leaned out the doorway. "You want someone?"

"The man you — that man!" She pointed at his window and, putting all the breath she'd ever used to call cows in the high meadows of Norway, called his name again.

Kane looked out the window. "Augusta!" He leaped to his feet and headed for the doorway.

The train was picking up speed, but he grabbed the bar and swung down.

"Your things, sir." The conductor tossed him his hat and his carpetbag.

"Thank you!" Kane caught them, clamped his hat on his head, and leaving his bag, crossed the platform in two strides.

"I almost missed you." He took her hands in his. "How come you are here? Ah, Augusta." He wrapped his arms around her.

Augusta hugged him back. This was much easier than trying to think of the right words to answer him. His heart thudded beneath her ear. She leaned back and looked up at him.

"Where you go?"

"To find you."

"Ah. I come here for you."

"Good." He tipped her chin up with one finger and discovered that her lips were even sweeter than he'd dreamed.

"Will you marry me?" he whispered in her ear. "I love you, Augusta Moyer."

"We are marry," she whispered back.

"I know, but I want to make sure you know what you are doing this time."

She hesitated, trying to understand what he'd said. "We go to Blessing?" Her eyes twinkled.

"Ja, 'tis a blessing you are here." He grinned back at her and kissed the tip of her nose.

And while they missed the celebration of statehood, they didn't much care. They were too busy exploring the blessings of married life.